The Duke of Morrison Street
A Leopold Larson Mystery

Published by Salish Ponds Press, LLC
editor@salishpondspress.com
ISBN-13 978-0-9824564-0-8
ISBN-10 0-9824564-0-9
www.salishpondspress.com
LCCN 2009908350

The Duke of Morrison Street

A Leopold Larson Mystery

By
Orrin Onken

SALISH PONDS PRESS LLC
FAIRVIEW, OREGON

To Margo

Chapter 1

I spent every Sunday afternoon for fifteen years doing the New York Times crossword puzzle on the bar at Hal's Place. Hal's was a dive that served liquor to inner city alcoholics. Hal's knew its place in the world. No pool tables, no little wienies from a jar, no video poker. Just cheap strong drinks. Hal's Place was a service to the community. Drunks, drug addicts, hookers, and small time criminals could meet at Hal's, make a deal, find a mate for the night, and drink. People smoked cigarettes and told each other lies. People shot dope in the bathrooms. Hal, a somber gray Santa Claus of a man, presided over it all from his stool by the register. They said he had a forty-five caliber pistol and a baseball bat under the counter. I never saw either one, but I believed they were there.

Winter had come full force to Portland and the rain had begun in earnest. Everything was wet. The incessant drizzle fed a moss that climbed up the walls of buildings and turned the sidewalks pale green. It hung in tendrils from telephone wires and would grow up a man's leg if he stood in one place too long. The wet cold made my fifty-year-old joints ache.

I pushed my empty glass forward to let Hal know I wanted another shot of soda water. He slid off his stool and waddled down the bar. I watched his hands as he filled my glass. His tattoos had turned the color of bruises.

"Leo," he said, "I told a guy you would be here today."

"Who?"

"A guy I know. A biker. He needs a lawyer."

"I can't keep people out of jail, Hal. I'm a probate lawyer. I do wills and shit like that."

"I know what kind of law you do," Hal said, "You think everybody I know is a criminal?"

"That's exactly what I think," I said. He snorted and shuffled off to his stool.

On that rainy Sunday I had been off the booze for a little over three years. Certain irregularities involving client funds had cost me a five year suspension from the practice of law. I drank my way through the suspension driving forklift, then checked myself into rehab. To get the license back I had to complete rehab, cut out the booze, and go to meetings of Alcoholics Anonymous. It was the price of being allowed to practice again. Nothing in the deal said I had to quit doing crosswords at Hal's.

Back in the law business, I waded into the world of wills, trusts and discontented heirs. The idea came from a Mormon mortician I met in rehab. When I met him, he'd been kicked out of his profession, kicked out of his marriage and kicked out of his church. In between watching *Days of Wine and Roses* and going to counseling sessions, the two of us schemed ways to make money when we got out. He figured to do low-budget cremations and send the family legal work my way for a modest kickback. I didn't know much about probate at the time, but lawyering ain't rocket science. Doing law for dead people sounded like a quiet practice. No criminals with a nasty tendency to hold a grudge if you didn't win their cases. No fighting over who had to take care of somebody's snotty kids.

I never heard from the Mormon again after getting

out of treatment, but with rehab behind me and license in hand the probate thing still seemed like a good idea. When sober I could make a living doing most any kind of law. The day the Oregon State Bar handed me my ticket back, all I wanted was a safe little office gig doing something that would leave me a few bucks at the end of the month.

"What's this friend of yours want?" I asked.

"Something to do with his old lady," Hal said. "Her father died and she thinks she's entitled."

"They got any money?"

"Can't say for sure, but I don't think this guy would be asking about a lawyer if he couldn't pay." That was a good sign. Most people looking for a lawyer in a place like Hal's were on the scam for freebies. No matter how uneducated, every drunk knows enough Latin to say *pro bono*.

"This guy got a name?" I asked.

"Churley. Churley Dowd."

"Never heard of him," I said.

I kept coming back to law because, when it comes right down to it, the work is easy. I knew from earning a living during my suspensions that painters, fork lift drivers, taxi drivers, and just about everybody works harder than lawyers, but lawyers get paid more. Lawyers don't make money like, movie stars, professional athletes, or dentists, but everything considered, lawyers get paid well enough. Maybe we live in a litigious culture. Maybe lawyers grease the wheels of justice. I couldn't care less. I am a lazy man, and practicing law is the only way I know how to make a living sitting in a chair.

The first time I saw Churley Dowd he was soaked. He came through the door of Hal's and stood inside letting the rain drip off his leathers onto the floor. The Oregon rains are not kind to motorcycle riders. Churley was a small thin man who even in boots had to stand straight to reach five foot two. He was normal, not a midget or a dwarf, just small.

He took off his wet jacket and laid it on a table by the door. The emblem on the back said "Rebellion Dogs" and had a graphic of a pit bull. The motto at the bottom was "Clean and Sober." He looked at Hal, and Hal nodded toward me.

"Coke please," he said, and took a seat on the stool next to me. Hal popped the tab on a Coke can and set it in front of him. Looking at me, the biker asked, "Are you the lawyer?"

"I'm a lawyer," I said, "Leo Larson."

"Churley Dowd." He stuck out his hand. "I'm pleased to meet you, Leo."

I gave his hand a shake. It was wet from the rain. "Yeah. Same here," I said.

"What kind of law do you practice?"

"Little of this, little of that. Wills and trusts mostly. What do you need?" Churley took a drink of his Coke. He had the stained hands of someone who works with motors.

"Anything else? Criminal defense? Personal injury?"

"Nope. Just probate. I represent the dead, the nearly dead, and their greedy relatives."

What I told him wasn't strictly true. After law school, when I had a lot more energy, I did criminal defense and learned that I didn't like criminals. My criminal clients were all whiners with some complaint against the world that they just couldn't get over. With the exception of drug dealers, I hated all my criminal clients. I didn't like the drug dealers much better, but the drug dealers didn't whine, didn't claim they were innocent, and didn't ask for credit. They put cash on the desk and asked only that I do my best. The rest of my criminal clients wanted miracles on a payment plan. After a couple years I was doing all drug dealers, a business that might have worked if I hadn't started taking a lot of fees out in product. My association with drug dealers led to my first suspension and my first trip to rehab.

"Do you help people get inheritances?" Churley asked.

"Yeah, I do," I said.

"How long have you been doing that kind of law?"

"Churley, if there is any cross-examining to be done here, I'd like to be the one doing it."

After dumping criminal law, criminals, and criminality in general, I did what every shingle-hanging lawyer does: personal injury. Doing personal injury law has the same combination of tedium and excitement as playing slot machines. You watch different combinations of the same mind numbing pattern hoping for the fates to grant you that one perfect alignment of facts, law, and insurance coverage that will make you rich. You spend your days listening to stories about how some sad bastard will have to spend twenty years in chiropractic care because there was a broken bottle of ketchup in the middle of the aisle at Safeway. You pay the office rent taking thirty percent of a lot of nickel-and-dime whiplash cases while waiting for the big one. Like addicts dreaming about the big heroin score, personal injury lawyers dream of that one verdict which will pay off the debts and buy a vacation house at the beach. For me and a lot of other lawyers that case never arrived.

I hung in with personal injury for seven years, hating every minute. Then came the problems with the trust account which led to the aforementioned five year suspension and another trip to rehab. Five years was the most they were allowed to dish out. The next time it would be disbarment.

"I'm sorry," Churley said. "I am not trying to be rude. My wife needs a lawyer who knows about inheritances and Hal said you did that kind of thing. I respect Hal and don't mind taking his advice. On the other hand, seeing a lawyer in a place like this does not instill me with confidence." Although oblivious to the ridiculousness of his appearance, the diminutive biker was not as dumb or roughly hewn as I had expected.

"I suppose not," I said.

Churley took another drag on his Coke and eyed my drink. "You a friend of Bill's?" he asked. The question was an insider's way of asking whether I was a member of Alcoholics Anonymous. I hated the question.

"Yeah. I'm a friend of Bill's," I said.

"Me too."

"I figured that. I saw the jacket."

"How long have you been clean?" he asked.

"Three years."

"That's good," he said. "My wife's name is Daisy. Her father died in January of this year. She is pretty sure she should inherit something, but doesn't know how to go about things."

I put one of my business cards on the table. "Have her call me to set up an appointment."

"She didn't take my name when we got married.

Her name is Twill. Daisy Twill."

"I'll remember."

I figured nothing would come of it. People you meet in bars don't call. I watched Churley Dowd put on his wet leathers and head back into the rain. I knew his wife. I hadn't really met her, but I'd spent some time in the same room with her, and once you've been in the same room with Daisy Twill you never forget her.

I rented my office in the Villanova Building in February of 2002, the same month my reinstated license took effect. My landlord was a divorce lawyer who leased the extra offices in his building to lawyers, accountants, and insurance salesmen. The directory by the front door listed me as "Leopold Larson, Attorney at Law."

The Villanova Building was a stone's throw from auto row in a commercial neighborhood known for car lots, gypsies, hookers and cheap rents. My office window looked out on the back lot of Mel's Patriotic Used Cars where there was no credit check for vets. The squat gray Villanova Building housed eight small offices arranged on either side of an unheated hallway. The building always had a vacancy, and the sign visible from the street had a permanent neon announcement of space for rent. The owner of this white collar tenement and occupier of two of the offices was Torkum Masoogian

Torkum Masoogian stood five foot eight and tipped the scales at over three hundred and fifty pounds. Balding, with a gray comb-over that levitated about an inch above his shiny bald head, he ran "Torkum Masoogian and Associates." The phrase "and Associates" in a law firm name usually means the named member is an egomaniacal asshole who imagines himself a firm, but in reality employs a series of timid, beaten lawyers willing to accept a regular salary in return for doing the actual work in the office and putting up with the owner's abuse. Or at least that's how it worked with Torkum. The sad part was that in a different time and in a different building I'd been the associate of Torkum Masoogian and Associates. So when it came time to hang out my shingle and try the probate thing, it was as natural as rain in Portland for me to look him up.

Torkum made most of his money from being a landlord, but he also ran a moderately successful divorce shop. His shtick was a regular ad in the newspaper announcing, "Divorce Attorney For Women Only." The implication of the ad was that Torkum had some special skill or special sympathy for women in divorce. The truth was that he was a misogynist who'd found women less adept than men at uncovering his incompetence.

Of all the crappy lawyers I'd met over the years, Torkum was the worst. If he ever got the law right in one of his cases it was because his associate had done the work. But when he got a whiff of money, Torkum was tenacious. He clamped on to his cases and never let go. Other lawyers backed off, gave up, abandoned their clients and left the profession—anything—just to get out of a case with Torkum on the other side. He was the kind of man who made other people think *life is too short for this.*

When I walked into Torkum's building in 2002 to ask about a place to rent, he was typing in the reception area. He had wedged his flabby butt onto a wheeled steno chair like Bob Dylan's mattress on a bottle of wine. He always maintained a secretarial station at the front of his office and used it a lot, but hadn't had a paid secretary since Peggi Iverson, ten years earlier.

"Four hundred dollars a month. First and last up front," he said.

"Nice to see you too, Torkum, after all this time." I stepped up to the counter that separated the small waiting room from the secretarial space.

"I heard you got your ticket back. What are you going to do this time?"

"Probate. Guardianships and conservatorships. Old people law," I said. He stood and waddled across the reception area. The steno chair stayed put proving that it had not been up his ass. Torkum took keys from a drawer and tossed them to me.

"Office 106," he said. "That will be eight hundred bucks." I counted out eight one hundred dollar bills onto the counter, took the keys, and walked down the hall to the office of Leopold Larson. I was in the law business again.

The nice thing about the law is that it doesn't require much start up capital. You pony up for bar dues and you are a phone, word processor, and case of copy paper away from being a professional. I'd managed my forays into and out of the profession with two valuable tools. The first was a long term lease on a ten-by-twenty storage space at Donnelli's Mini-storage where I kept everything from the staple removers to my yellowing college degrees. The second was Peggi Iverson.

Peggi Iverson was the finest legal secretary, receptionist, paralegal, and all purpose assistant in Portland. I met Peggi when we were both working under the miserable fat thumb of Torkum Masoogian. We both quit Torkum's office on the same day. I quit because he was a miserable fat fuck. She quit, I think, because he tried to stick his hand down her pants. And thus, we ended up together. Peggi had no training, no education, and no social skills. What she did possess, however, was that steel-cold loyalty, born and bred in trailer parks and rent-by-the-week motels, that motivates certain women to stay with lazy drunken men in the face of all adversity and logic. At home in the backstreets of the Heartland Mobile Estates she had given birth to two children by two different fathers. These two criminals in training were the love of her non-working life. When I had work, she was the only other person I would ever allow in my office. Law is a business where, for good reason, members of the staff loathe their bosses. Much evil comes from that. Peggi Iverson kept the evil away from me.

As far as I could tell, Peggi's stout pear-shaped body was completely covered with freckles. In idle moments I had pondered the question of whether her wide butt, the bulwark of her pear shape, was as freckled as her face. Having seen her angry response to Torkum's sexual advances I was careful to stay away from any physical exploration that would have answered the freckle-butt question. That did not mean, however, I wasn't interested. On several occasions over the years she had inadvertently leaned over in a way that allowed me to see a fully freckled breast. She had no more breast than you would find on an obese man, but what she had was covered in freckles.

Peggi lived in a mobile home at the end of Lonely Street. Lonely Street wasn't an official Portland street, but rather the name of the single road that ran down the middle of the Heartland Mobile Estates, so named because the previous owner had been a bi-polar Elvis fan before he killed himself. Down at the end of Lonely Street, Peggi raised her two children and gossiped across the fence with the kind of men who wear mullets and know how to fix Camaros.

After renting the office from Torkum, I called Peggi. In the past I'd done a little free work for the folks on Lonely Street and had a few favors I could call in. When Peggi put out the word the pickups rolled and in no time the desks, computers, pictures, and other lawyer's tools disappeared from the wet caverns of Donnelli's Mini-storage into office number 106 in the Villanova Building. Peggi, who had been directing traffic at the airport in my absence from the profession, put away her reflective yellow vest and took out her good white blouses. Several years earlier she'd made herself a name tag that said, "Peggi Iverson, Legal Assistant." She took the tag from her jewelry box, affixed it to a pressed blouse, and once again had more than just a job. At the Heartland Mobile Estates, being able to earn a living sitting in a chair was testimony that you had intelligence above that of the common mob.

While Peggi worked on her phone persona talking to the dial tone—"Office of Leopold Larson, may I help you?" "Leopold Larson's office, may I be of assistance." "Leopold Larson, Attorney at Law."—I set about becoming a probate lawyer. When I first fired up the computer at the Villanova building all I knew about probate was what I'd learned while reading *Bleak House* during rehab. To me probate meant rainy London streets, courts of Chancery, and interminably long hearings about the distribution of es-

tates—hearings which eventually resulted in the lawyers getting all the money. Portland had many a rainy
street. Courts still sat in equity, that peculiar arm of
law which does without juries and the other annoy-
ances of citizen participation. The probate court in
downtown Portland was close enough to Chancery for
me, and I didn't object to mind-numbing cases about
other people's money as long as I got a reasonable
chunk of it in the end.

My home life was simple. Three years into my last
suspension my third wife got fed up and ran off with
my car mechanic. I called up Don Yerke, the titular
boss of Lawyers Helping Lawyers, a support group for
lawyers recovering from alcoholism. Despite the fact
that I was drinking at the time he steered me to a
second floor flat in a lime green Victorian down by the
Willamette River. The riverfront on the east side of
Portland was the warehouse district, but fifty years
earlier it had been a thriving residential community.
Quite a few crumbling Victorian walk-ups still survived in the nooks and crannies after light industry
and warehousing had pushed out the families. The
place Yerke got me was sandwiched between a mattress factory and a print shop. Out my front bay window I could watch the loading dock of Haven Appliance, a wholesaler of appliance parts, or the comings
and goings at Avian House, some sort of fraternal organization that seemed to have run out of members. I
liked the apartment mostly for the sounds. I could
hear the freeway traffic from my bedroom window.
The big trucks arriving early in the morning rattled
my windows. I like the sound of cities.

The only other place in my life was Murdock's.
Murdock's was the AA group closest to my apartment.

It was Hal's Place without the alcohol. After graduating rehab, I had to find an AA meeting where I could get those slips signed to prove to the Bar that I was staying sober. There were a lot of clean respectable places I could have gone to do that. Murdock's was not one of them.

Murdock's held its meetings in a run down rented storefront about half a mile from my apartment. The group got its name from John Murdock, a man who decades earlier had started the group among the homeless drunks and addicts who slept in the doorways of Portland's skid road.

Murdock's wasn't listed in the official directory of Portland's AA meetings. Real AA in Portland didn't want to admit that the place existed and the people at Murdock's liked it that way. One Saturday in the days after rehab, but before the Bar had given me my license back, I was taking a morning constitutional through the warehouse district and encountered the AA symbol on the door with the words, "This is the door you have been looking for." People were going in so I followed and took a seat in the back. Having been sentenced to AA several different times over the years, I had seen a lot of it. What happened at Murdock's was different.

The AA I had been used to in the church basements and community centers was a cheery AA with a lot of hand holding, hugging, and loving people until they could learn to love themselves. The people at Murdock's weren't like that. The people at Murdock's were mean.

At Murdock's, the book *Alcoholics Anonymous* was the meat and potatoes of every meeting. The chairman read aloud from the book and when he got the urge, would call on someone to speak. The speakers never used "My name is Whatever and I am an alcoholic" for an introduction, and if the speaker bothered to identify him or herself at all there was no chorus of "Hi Whatever" from the audience. People did not applaud. People didn't hug or hold hands. It was a place where you could sit in a crowded room and still be alone.

I went to Murdock's my required three times a week to listen and get my slips signed. By that damp autumn of 2005 I had been going there enough to recognize the regulars and not get glared at when I came in late and took a seat in the back. Most of the people at Murdock's were society's rejects: ex-criminals, ex-cops, and all manner of people who identified themselves by what they used to be. Mental illness was as welcome as alcoholism. The members of Murdock's didn't claim their program could cure depression or schizophrenia, but believed that the mentally ill were better off sober than drunk.

So when Churley Dowd told me his wife's name, I smiled. The time I had spent with Daisy Twill had been in AA meetings at Murdock's.

Chapter 2

"I don't see how you manage to stay in business." I was at my office and Torkum Masoogian had his fat arm draped over the counter waiting for me to write the rent check. Peggi was typing at her desk.

"I do a good job for a few clients and let them tell their friends," I said. "You should try it sometime."

"Yeah," he said, "like that would work." He stared at the ceiling waiting for his money. "How is the probate stuff anyway? Representing dead people?"

"It's more litigious than I expected," I said. "I thought I'd stay out of court this time around, but I think I'm downtown as much as I ever was."

"You're a Pollyanna, Leo. Probate is divorce work without the pussy."

"Be careful Masoogian," Peggi warned.

"Jesus Christ, Iverson, get over it already." Torkum waddled away with his rent check.

Masoogian wasn't right about much, but he was almost right about my practice. I made my best money off dysfunctional families, and my best paying cases were based upon raw sibling rivalry. I represented children who wanted the family money and were willing to fight about it. What was different in probate wasn't the fighting but the fact that everybody in my cases was old. Young people don't inherit much. With life expectancy the way it is, children who inherit from their parents are already at retirement age. I was a middle man in the transfer of wealth from the World War II generation to the baby boomers, sixty-year-olds getting money from eighty-year-olds.

A lot of my cases were easy. I filled out forms, shuffled papers, and made sure the money got from dead mom to living kids. Charging a hundred and seventy-five an hour I could make a few thousand dollars on a middle class dead guy. It pissed me off that the real estate agent who sold the family home usually made more than I did, but I made enough to pay Peggi and take home a few bucks for myself.

Peggi thrived. She took to wearing high heels that pushed her height to a full five feet. She gave up on the name tag, studied the probate manuals I'd gotten from the Bar, and began wearing makeup.

One thorn in my side was Bonnie Kutala. Bonnie worked for the Oregon State Bar Office of Morals and Ethics and had dedicated her life to protecting the citizens of Oregon from lawyers like me.

"It's Ms. Kutala," Peggi said. I rolled my eyes and picked up the phone in my office.

"Bonnie, how are you?"

"Leo, I don't have your AA slips." A condition of my probation required that I send signed slips proving that I had been going to Alcoholics Anonymous meetings.

"I've got them here in the desk, Bonnie. I forgot to send them."

"Leo," she said, "I am still very concerned that you are practicing without supervision."

"I don't have supervision, Bonnie, because no firm will hire me. No firm will hire me because you keep dragging me into disciplinary hearings."

"There are things you could do other than practice law. Some people just aren't cut out for it."

"How long have we been having this conversation, Bonnie? You try to get me disbarred. I get off with a suspension and probation. Can't we call a truce?"

"Leo. It is my job to protect the public, and I take that job seriously."

"What public?" I pleaded. "I have never had a single complaint filed by a client."

"You have taken client money, you have neglected cases, and you have ignored court orders. Need I continue with the list?" She was right. I had done all those things, but out of some quirky twist in the fabric of the universe, I had never had a client complain. Other lawyers complained, a couple of judges complained, and one time my own bank turned me in, but never a client.

"But not a single client complaint," I repeated. "I think you're jealous because you've never had a client." Bonnie had prosecuted people her whole life. For a while it had been with a local prosecutor's office. Then she worked for the Attorney General, but for most of her legal career she had chased misbehaving lawyers.

"I have a client, Leo. My client is the people of the State of Oregon."

"Well couldn't you advise your client to quit picking on me and go bother someone else?"

"The O.M.E.," what she called the Office of Morals and Ethics, "does not pick on people. It enforces the Rules of Professional Responsibility."

"I'll send you the AA slips in today's mail," I said.

"Thank you."

"And about those rules, the professional responsibility ones, I promise you I am going to read them one of these days."

"Promises, promises," she said.

"Are you feeling okay, Bonnie?" I asked, "You

sound almost cordial today."

"I'm fine," she said. "You know, Leo, I do like you. I am actually trying to help you. I see you doing the same things, getting into the same kind of trouble, over and over. I don't think private practice is for you."

"Will you give me a job in your office?"

"I don't think that would work, Leo."

"Will you let me take you out for a nice romantic dinner?"

"I don't think that will work either."

"Then I guess I'm stuck here. No job. No date."

"Next time you cross the line I will have you disbarred."

"Goodbye Bonnie." I hung up.

Bonnie was one of a pack of females who had found the perfect outlet for their anger at the world by working for a guy named Dick Crabtree, director of the Office of Morals and Ethics. At any given time Dick kept a harem of eight to ten of them, each sworn to weeding out the bad apples practicing law in Oregon.

I had learned that once you are a bad apple in the eyes of the Office of Morals and Ethics, you can never get back to being a good one. When I did criminal law the cynical observation shared among defense lawyers was that "they are all guilty." Despite the talk, nobody in the legal system really believes in reform. For Bonnie, prosecuting unethical lawyers was no different than prosecuting common criminals. Everybody was guilty and once you were guilty you stayed guilty forever. Like a school teacher who, after twenty years in the classroom, begins to act like a child, or a cop who adopts the mannerisms of criminals, Bonnie had started to behave just like the bad apples. For me that was good. I knew what to expect from her.

I once tried to convince Bonnie that I had corrected all my office procedures and would never get in trouble again. We were sitting out in the hall waiting for one of my disciplinary hearings to begin. I had lost seven hundred dollars of client money.

"It's not about office procedures," she said to me, "it's about character." Bonnie was a tightly wrapped woman who used undergarment bondage to disguise her feminine attributes. Her head emerged square from her broad shoulders, and she kept her large breasts strapped firmly against her ribs. Most people walk a line, one foot in front of the other. Bonnie walked with her feet apart, like an advancing sumo wrestler. She walked square and sat square. She looked me square in the eye when she spoke.

"What happened with the money was an accident," I explained.

"I know it was," she said.

"To be guilty of stealing client funds, I have to have intended to do it. Accidents don't count."

"I know the law, Leo. You are saying you didn't do it."

"I've been saying that all along."

"It's a technicality."

"The fact that I didn't do it is a technicality?"

"You did something else," she said. "It's about character. You don't have the character to practice law. If you didn't do what I charged you with this time, then it's for one of the things that I never found out about. You could make a list of those things and give it to me, but you don't have the character to do it."

"That's crazy."

"That's the way it is."

"How do you know I don't have character?"

"I know."

Over the years, Bonnie never wavered and never gave up. She could disappear for months at a time, but Bonnie and the Office of Morals and Ethics were always waiting for me. I took to asking her out on a date every time we talked. She rejected my overtures with the same disgust that she exhibited toward my practice.

Peggi and I managed to make a go of the probate thing in spite of what Bonnie thought. The population of Oregon was aging. Death was everywhere, and probate has been employing lawyers since Roman times. People needed trusts for their psychotic or drug-addicted relatives and guardianships for grandma who won't wear clothes in public any more.

We began to meet our other neighbors. Wounded Knee Collections opened across the hall, a two-man operation collecting debts owed to Indian casinos. Next to them was Arlene Remington, Child Custody Mediation Services. An immigration lawyer named Rashim Tatamarina moved in down the hall.

I left my flat in the green Victorian every morning at seven-thirty, got to work about eight, took lunch at noon, and locked it up at five. When there wasn't enough business to fill those hours I studied probate manuals or napped. Peggi studied too and was coming close to becoming a real legal assistant. Outside on Eighty-second Avenue the gypsies went from one dealer to another looking for cars to paint and resell. The hookers leaned on the lamp posts waiting for Johns and the Mexicans peddled tacos. I was close enough to all that to keep the rent down and far enough away that my clients didn't have to notice it unless they wanted to.

"Your ten o'clock is here," announced Peggi from the doorway of my office.

"Who is it?" I asked.

"Ms. Daisy Twill."

I came out into Peggi's reception area for the introduction. Daisy Twill, pacing in the front office, stood nearly six feet tall. She had large hard breasts, thick muscular limbs, and an attitude that suggested she could and would use her physical strength to get her way. She had shoehorned her body into a short black skirt, white blouse, and brown leather jacket. It was the outfit that a hooker might imagine as office attire. From seeing her in a tank top at Murdock's I knew that underneath the blouse and jacket her arms and upper torso were covered with rose and thorn tattoos. I introduced myself and invited her into my office.

Daisy lived in a society made too small for her. She was a bull around whom the world had built a china shop and when not in her element she lived in fear that she would break something. In my office she wedged herself into a client chair and hunched her shoulders trying to make herself small.

As soon as we were both seated Daisy began talking to her hands. "My father died last January. He had property and I think I should inherit something. Nothing has happened. I need a lawyer."

"Is there an open probate?" I asked.

"What's that?"

"Court proceedings. Have you received any documents with numbers down the left side?"

"No. I think my brother is keeping the papers from

me."

"Your brother?"

"He's a lawyer."

"What's his name?"

"David Twill. He works downtown at a law firmed called 'Evanson Tribe . . .'" She couldn't remember the rest.

"Evanson Tribe Elber and Williamson?"

"Yeah, that place," she said. Evanson Tribe Elber and Williamson was the most expensive law firm in town. The firm occupied the top three floors of Big Pink, Portland's tallest building. Evanson represented banks, stock brokerages, professional athletes, and millionaires.

"What does he do there?" I asked.

"I don't know," she said, "Something to do with stocks and bonds. He and I don't get along. He's a dickhead."

"Skip dickhead then. Tell me about your father."

"My father was in an old-folks home. His sister and him both lived there. She still does. One day last January, Anita calls me and says he's dead." Daisy raised her gaze to meet mine. She had light blue eyes that opened wider than most people's making her look like she was in a perpetual state of astonishment.

"Anita?"

"His sister. She's in the same old folks home."

"What is the name of the home?"

"Everland Village. That's E-V-E-R-L—"

"I know how it is spelled," I said. She looked back down at her hands. What she called an old-folks home was an expensive assisted living center on the east side of Portland. If her dad kicked the bucket at Everland Village, he could well have had a little something to pass on to his loving tattooed daughter.

"A couple of months before he died he gave me this." She pulled a folded sheet of blue lined school notebook paper from her purse and handed it to me. The writing inside was the shaky cursive writing of an old man. It said, "Daisy. I am proud of what you have done with your life. I am sorry we were apart for so long. When I die, you and the kids will be taken care of. Elmo."

"His name was Elmo?"

"Yeah," she said. "I never called him dad."

"Were you estranged?"

"What's estranged?"

"Did you not get along?"

"I ran away from home when I was fifteen. David ran away too. He's younger than me. I went to the streets and got into drugs and stuff. He went to college and become a lawyer. My father was an alcoholic. He never got sober. I did. Me and my kids made peace with him at the end and I'd go see Anita and him sometimes. Then he ends up dead."

"How did he die?"

"Fell in his room or something. He hit is head, they said, but it don't make much sense. He was fallin' down his whole life from drinking. He hit his head a lot of times but it never killed him before that. Aunt Anita found him. There weren't no funeral. Anita and David just had the body burnt up and that was it."

"What did he do for a living before he moved to Everland?"

"Nothin' that I know. He said he was in real estate, but I never knew him to work at it. Before he moved to Everland he just drank in the bars on Morrison Street."

"Living at Everland is not cheap," I said. "How did he pay for that?"

"He had a monthly check to live on. It was from money he had somewhere, and at the end, when he said that the kids and I would be taken care of, he wasn't lying. I knew when he was lying, which was most of the time, but this time he wasn't lying. There is money and my brother has it."

"Where did the monthly check come from?"

"I don't know where it came from, but he always had it. I think he had money stashed away."

"Your husband, Churley Dowd, sent you here, didn't he?"

"I told him I needed a lawyer and he said to call you. He said he talked to you at Hal's and you seemed okay. But I seen you before. I seen you at Murdock's."

"I've seen you there too."

"I like Murdock's. I like it you go there too. Maybe we'll see each other at meetings sometimes."

"We probably will."

I signed Daisy to a fee agreement, promised her I would look into her inheritance, and she disappeared into the rain on Eighty-second Avenue. When she was gone Peggi came in.

"She's scared of us," Peggi observed. "Did you sign her?"

"I did."

"What do we have to do?"

I leaned back in my fake Aeron office chair. "We have to find her daddy's money."

Chapter 3

The next morning I stopped in to see Olga at probate court.

Of the three branches of government the judiciary is the furthest removed from the purse strings and the Multnomah County Courthouse showed it. While the other arms of local government had, over the years, migrated from the old style municipal buildings to modern steel and glass structures that allowed the occupants to believe that they competed on par with big business, the judges continued their work in one of those column and gargoyle gray buildings built for a different era. City hall and the police got new buildings, but the courts never got anything other than busier. Everything unnecessary to the raw administration of justice disappeared in the name of moving more and more cases through smaller and grimier courtrooms.

Now and then events at the Multnomah County Court House made the news. Big cases went to trial. Famous people went to jail. However, those cases were the exception, and even when they happened the drama was invisible unless you knew where to look or ran into the Channel Twelve news people in the hallways. Normal mornings at the courthouse meant regular people doing common things. Folks came to pay speeding tickets, atone for parking in unusual places, obtain restraining orders against people they used to have sex with, and perform the various amends that people owe for trying to get along the best they can.

The halls of the lower floors of the courthouse were always filled with young people. Young women came with their babies in strollers, strollers that got searched by the young guards with metal detecting wands. Young men came to suffer the consequences of testosterone-driven violence, a love of things that go fast, and an insatiable desire for sex. The young defense lawyers came to counsel their young criminal clients and earn their stripes in the courtroom. The young district attorneys argued with the young public defenders about what to do with young criminals and the only old people were the occasional grandmother, waiting anxiously to find out what would become of young William, young Edward, or young Jane.

Young people and noise go together. Put large numbers of young people in uncarpeted halls with marble floors and you have noise. The lower floors of the courthouse, where people tended to traffic matters, divorces, and petty crime, were loud dirty places. However, as you ascended the marble staircases to the upper floors the courthouse became calmer and quieter. The building was eight floors high, and on the top—the most serene floor of them all—was the door with the small brown sign, "Probate."

The probate department consisted of four people: Kate, Harmony, Olga, and the Honorable Devin Bohum. The probate counter was the place for filing probates, starting guardianships, opening conservatorships, checking files, and doing the legal work necessary to protect people who were too dead or too disabled to fend for themselves. Behind the counter sat Kate, Harmony, and Olga. They did the day-to-day work in the department. I imagined there were fastidious probate lawyers who avoided both mistakes and messy cases, thereby going years without ever setting eyes on Judge Bohum. I was not one of those.

Kate, Olga, and Harmony took filings, scheduled hearings, and sent nasty notices when a lawyer broke the rules. I received a lot of notices. Olga, head of the department and manager of the other two, knew everything there was to know about probate. When a lawyer had a question, he could use his law school skills to find the answer through research, or he could ask Olga. She'd seen it all. She knew the law and when the law left the question unanswered she knew how the judge would rule. You could argue with Olga, but it was not a wise thing to do. Even over the phone I could sense the amusement as Olga would listen patiently to my thoroughly researched legal theory and then tell me, "That may be, Mr. Larson, but I don't think Judge Bohum sees it that way." Invariably she was right.

On this day, however, I had a simple matter.

"Soooo. Mr. Larson," Olga said, exposing both her Minnesota roots and the dark roots beneath her blond hair. "What can we do for you?"

"Olga, I want to know if there has been an Oregon probate filed for Elmo Darius Twill." She consulted the computer screen at one end of the counter.

"Alrighty now," she said while putting fingers to keyboard, "Elmo Darius Twill. Spelled like it sounds, I assume."

"Yes."

She studied the screen for a moment. "Nothing, Mr. Larson."

I pulled my briefcase off the counter preparing to take the creaking elevator back down into the noisy lower floors when I heard the nasal voice of Judge Bohum.

"Mr. Larson. I'm glad I ran into you. Could I see you in my chambers for a moment?"

"Certainly Judge," I said, always obsequious in judicial presence. "What's up?"

"Nothing important, I just want to chat for a moment."

We went into chambers. Judge Bohum, at five foot two was a foot shorter than I was and smaller than any of the women who worked for him. With the exception of a few wisps of gray hair around either ear, he was completely bald. That day he was wearing a white shirt, tie, and sweater vest. He led me into his chambers.

The only thing that movies and television ever get right about the judicial system is judge's chambers. Chambers all look the same: large book-lined offices furnished in dark expensive wood. The judge sits behind a Texas-sized desk from which he or she can peer at the lawyers in the leather guest chairs. CEO's and those who rise to the top in the private sector work in offices that say wealth. Judges work in offices that say power.

I think it is the lure of chambers that drives lawyers into the political campaigns, onto the boards of charitable organizations, and into the locker rooms of the upscale health clubs in search of the political connections that lead to a judgeship. Chambers is where lawyers talk freely, where deals are made, and where settlements are hammered out. It is in chambers that the judge does the real work of remaking the world one case at a time. Lawyers making half a million a year as partners in the big firms will toss it all away in a heartbeat for judge's chambers. They say that power is the final intoxicant, the one people turn to when money, drugs, and sex have lost their allure. It wasn't my drug of choice, but when I sat in chambers I understood its attraction.

"It's about the fee petition in the Freeman guardianship," Judge Bohum said. I had recently completed a guardianship and conservatorship for an elderly woman named Wendy Freeman. Mrs. Freeman developed dementia and turned paranoid, accusing her daughter of financial and physical abuse. The daughter came to me. I got a professional appointed to manage the money and arrange for long term care in the dementia wing of a local care center. The daughter, the only person who gave a damn about Wendy Freemen, ended up hated by the entire family. Wendy Freeman hated her daughter because the dementia made her unable to distinguish friend from foe. The rest of the family hated her because the old lady's money was now being used for care instead of being saved for them. It was the curse of the dutiful daughter, a script played over and over again in the probate department and one that made me able to pay Peggi's salary.

The judge took the Freeman file from a pile of files on a work table and opened it on his desk. "You haven't been practicing in my court that long, Leo," he said. "May I call you Leo? I know the girls sometimes do."

By girls he meant Kate, Olga, and Harmony. Although none of the women were younger than fifty, to Judge Bohum they were girls. Devin Bohum had become a judge by governor's appointment on his sixtieth birthday and had been sitting on the bench for twenty years. He was older than demented old Wendy

Freeman. Age, however, treats us all differently. Bohum, in his eighties was as sharp as any judge in the building. I admired his staying power in a day when a lot of men look forward to hanging it up at sixty.

"My job is to make sure people get the benefit of their own money," Bohum said. "In a probate it's to make sure the heirs receive what became theirs at the death of the family member. In a conservatorship, it is to make sure that the money that belonged to the protected person is used for his or her benefit. People don't always like me doing my job, but most people don't see what I see. I see parents who think a personal injury settlement for one of their children is their money. I see dead people who continue to charge on their credit cards for months after the funeral. I have lawyers in here every day asking me to waive the performance bond so loving sister Wilma or cousin Edna can be the personal representative of dear old father's estate. They assure me that loving sister would never steal from dear old dead dad because she is, after all, a loving sister. I have to point out that strangers do not steal from the estates of the deceased. It's always a loving somebody."

"No one will be stealing from Ms. Freeman, judge. I had Booter & Welk appointed conservators. They are very reliable."

Judge Bohum looked up from the file and gave me one of those judicial just-between-you-and-me smiles. "It's not that, Leo. Another way an estate can lose money is to attorneys. You are entitled by law to be paid from the conservatorship assets. I am charged with the duty of making sure that your fees are reasonable and that the work you did benefited the protected person. I know that in some courts you can just ask your computer to print out the number of hours you logged on the case and the fee request is allowed." I didn't know of a court where that was the case, but I nodded as if that was common knowledge. "That won't happen in my court. Those print-outs don't mean a thing to me. I need you to explain to me in plain English what problems you faced in the case, what work you did, and how that work benefited the estate. You don't have to make it a major production, just a simple statement that I can understand."

"I can do that," I said.

"I don't want to be critical, and I am not in any way suggesting that you did anything wrong in the Freeman case, but if you are going to practice in my court, I think we ought to be in agreement about how things are done."

"Consider us in agreement."

Bohum rolled back his chair and stared at the bookshelves to my right. "Leo, I know that you've had some trouble in the practice of law. Trouble with the Bar, that sort of thing. The word gets around. When I started to see your name on documents coming into my court, frankly, I had concerns. In this business, there can be large sums of money sitting around that are not well protected. If a man is subject to temptation . . ."

"I've paid my dues and I'm clear with the Bar judge. There will be no trouble out of my office. I want a quiet practice."

"Bonnie Kutala from the Office of Morals and Ethics called me a couple of weeks ago. She had concerns."

This did not make me happy. "I have tried, unsuccessfully judge, to assure Ms. Kutala that the decision of the Bar panel to reinstate me was the correct one, but she continues to have her own opinion on the issue."

Bohum looked back at me and smiled. "She has firm opinions, doesn't she?"

"Rigid might be another word for them."

"If you have trouble with anything associated with my court, I want you to call me. The best hedge against trouble, I think, is to keep the phone lines open. If there's another attorney on the case, arrange a conference call. Talk to the girls often."

"I will, your honor." He pushed the Freeman file to the side of his desk telling me that our conversation was over. I stood and picked up my briefcase.

"I'll redo that Freeman fee petition, judge," I said.

"No hurry," he answered without looking up. *Not unless I want to get paid*, I thought.

After the conversation with Judge Bohum, I skipped the elevator and took the marble staircase down all seven flights. The exercise helped me work off my annoyance with Bonnie Kutala and the fact that I had to redo the Freeman fee petition. I had five grand into the Freeman case. It was money I was tired of waiting for.

In most probate cases I got paid at the end of the case. That could mean no income for months with it all coming due when the judge signed off on the final judgment. The key to not going broke was making sure at the beginning that there would be enough money left over to pay my fee at the end. That meant not signing on to do a probate if the dead guy was bankrupt when he died. It meant not doing conservatorships or guardianships for poor people, and it meant being patient. However, when payday finally came, I was not above being eager to see the check.

I left the courthouse and walked out into a gentle rain. My car was parked three blocks away in the metro lot where I could park for ninety-five cents an hour. I had an umbrella in the car but never carried it unless faced with a true downpour. For the most part Oregonians do not use umbrellas.

I was driving a 1982 Datsun that I had bought off one of Torkum's divorce clients for four hundred dollars. The thing ran well enough but had dents and or rust on every panel. I had planned to use the Freeman case money to get a better car. I would spend five thousand dollars for a five year old vehicle planning to drive it fifty thousand miles. I'd pay cash, insure for liability only, and live a life without car payments. The five-five-fifty plan, however would have to wait until I got the Freeman money. Up in the parking lot I cranked the engine of the Datsun and drove across the Willamette River to the east side of town. It was nearly noon, so I stopped at Murdock's to get a slip signed. No use giving Bonnie any further excuses for thinking about me.

I parked half a block from Murdock's and walked to the meeting. The rain hung motionless in the air. The storefront home of Murdock's was sandwiched between an Asian-owned grocery store that served up malt liquor and cigarettes to the street people and a used clothing shop run by two women who wore short black skirts and facial jewelry. That day most of the street folks had found somewhere to hole up and stay dry. One Mexican loitered in a doorway hoping to sell a little heroin should any of the local addicts decide to venture out into the rain.

I took a seat at the back of Murdock's shortly before noon. The back of the room was the nonsmoking section, but there was no more point to prohibiting smoking in one part of the room than there is to prohibiting peeing in one end of a swimming pool. Nevertheless, the choice of seats identified me as a nonsmoker, something I'd been for five years.

The meeting was led by Hardhead Steve. Although the group had no formal officers or governing body, its older members—those who kept the traditions and set the tone for the meetings—were given honorary titles based upon their prior professions or some personal characteristic. Hardhead Steve was so named because he had once been shot in the forehead with a twenty-two caliber pistol and walked away without serious injury. Hardhead Steve, Electric Dave, Little Annie and Copper John were the deacons of the noon and dinner-time meetings.

Steve sat behind the chairman's desk at the end of the room farthest from the street door. He opened the meeting with the Serenity Prayer. After a moment of silence to honor the alcoholic who still suffered we chanted in unison. "God, grant me the serenity to accept the things I cannot change, the courage to change the things I can, and the wisdom to know the difference." This homily, the first lines of a longer poem by Reinhold Niebuhr, had started every AA meeting that I had ever attended, and I had attended a lot of them. The prayer was followed by the reading of the Twelve Steps and Twelve Traditions, the catechism of AA. Thereafter, Steve read from the Big Book, *Alcoholics Anonymous*, and began calling upon people in the room to share their experiences in drunkenness and sobriety.

The rule—the group conscience, at Murdock's—

was that the chairperson was not to tell his own story or otherwise do a lot of extemporaneous instruction from the chair. Chairmen were only required to have six months of sobriety and could nominate themselves for the job by simply signing up on the calendar by the coffee pot. The rule was designed to prevent the attendees from being held hostage to the megalomaniacal ravings of some mentally disturbed chairman. Murdock's members tended to have mental problems above and beyond alcoholism. The rule against pontificating from the chair, however, was honored more in its breach than its observance, and Hardhead Steve was one of the worst offenders. He had mastered the lingo of AA and he was not about to let the rules of the group prevent him from demonstrating his AA virtuosity. He did read from the Big Book and call on people, but he filled the time between speakers with his personal interpretation of the AA gospel.

Over the months of attending Murdock's, I had gotten to know Hardhead Steve as well as anyone there. He was a tall, thin, cowboy-looking man of fifty or so who had found a home in AA and was desperately looking for a way to make a living there. A lot of people did that sort of thing. Most of them, grateful at being saved from addiction, went off to community college to get certified by the State of Oregon as a drug and alcohol counselor and then landed low-paying jobs in treatment centers. Hardhead was blocked from this post-sobriety career path by three felony convictions for armed robbery. He had for a brief time made good money by renting a large house and subletting rooms to recently released ex-cons. The men paid their rent by working for Hardhead's landscaping business. The enterprise fell apart when the government discovered that Hardhead was not actually paying his employees, or the taxes that go along with having employees, or for that matter, the rent on the house they lived in. He laid low for a couple of years after that, but when I met him he was trying to revive the idea of sober housing. After attending a seminar that cost him a thousand dollars of his most recent girlfriend's money, he became convinced that he would be able to start over with a grant from the government or the Gates Foundation or some other charitable organization that gave free money to ex-armed robbers. He regularly pumped me for legal advice about setting up a corporation to receive the windfall. I was willing to help him. Setting up a corporation was not so difficult that I wouldn't do it for a friend. He was, however, consistently unable to answer even the simplest of technical questions, such as who would serve as officers or who would have a say in corporate decision making. Every time I'd inquire about these things he would take the conversation into some netherworld of collective decision making based upon the Bible and the Big Book. I would tell him I needed a little more than that—a name perhaps by which the corporation could be called—and he would promise to get back to me. Then a week later we would have the same conversation again. He never did get his corporation, but whenever someone he knew needed a lawyer, no matter what the issue, he would swear up and down that I was the man to see.

Despite his odd personal life and his pontificating, Hardhead ran an entertaining meeting. Alcoholics Anonymous to me was church without the afterlife, a church in which the parishioners had taken over the priesthood, but a church nevertheless. We invoked God to keep us sober. We swore our allegiance to the Twelve Steps. We prayed. We confessed. We forgave our enemies. We did everything they did in other churches, but in our church the members smoked, swore, and swilled coffee during services.

I have never been religious. If anything, I fancy myself a Renaissance man, a man of science and reason. However, as people had pointed out often enough to me in rehab, my own views of the world had not produced great results. I wasn't sure I believed any of the AA stuff, but attending the meetings didn't seem to have hurt me any. I hadn't taken up drinking again and I'd met people like Hardhead Steve.

Fifteen minutes into the meeting Spiritual Ed slipped through the door and sat down two seats away from me in the back of the room. People at Murdock's didn't hug, didn't hold hands, and didn't sit next to each other unless forced to by the crowd.

Spiritual Ed wore the suit and tie required by his job as an investment advisor. Like me, he was on his lunch. Not all the Murdock's members were down and out. Spiritual Ed had a decent job advising people to put their retirement money in the investment that paid him the best commission. Electric Dave spent a lot of time unemployed because of an often treated but never cured anger problem, but when he worked he made good money as a union electrician. Copper John was a retired policeman with a good pension who had never lost his desire to hang with the criminal element. John spent a lot of time at Murdock's and always sat with his back to the wall in the corner of the room farthest from the door. The story was that he still carried his policeman's thirty-eight under his jacket.

Little Annie was more typical. She was a tiny dark-haired woman about forty years old who rode the bus each day to Murdock's from her one room subsidized apartment downtown and was the unofficial leader of the evening SSI crowd. She had parlayed her mental illness into a permanent albeit small income and made her way in the world with the help of the Social Security Administration, Section 8 housing, and the generosity of others. She was talkative, opinionated and quick to point out that people who worked were not the only people who needed recovery. Those who could not work, and therefore relied upon government benefits, had just as much to offer as anybody else. She said this often and even when there was no one around to disagree. She was also belligerently Jewish and would lament to anyone who would listen that her lack of a husband was due to the fact that all the eligible Jewish boys had been killed in the Holocaust. She was quite convinced of this even though she had not been born when the Holocaust occurred.

As usual, the chair called on Spiritual Ed soon after he sat down. He came to the noon meeting on a break from work and would not stay for the entire ninety minutes. Respecting Ed's status in the group as well as the fact that he had a job and wore a tie, Hardhead Steve made sure Ed got a chance to speak.

"I'm a member of Alcoholics Anonymous," Ed said. Many of the members used a similar introduction because somewhere in the Big Book it said that members of the organization are supposed to refer to themselves that way. I'd read the passage and didn't think it really applied to meetings. To me the traditional, "I'm Leo, and I'm an alcoholic," seemed fine.

But everything at Murdock's was a little different.

"I haven't had a drink today," Ed continued. "I haven't smoked any marijuana. I haven't taken any pills that weren't prescribed to me. I haven't thought about suicide today." After this introduction which was approximately the same every time he spoke, he was off and rolling into how the Twelve Steps of Alcoholics Anonymous had taught him how to live and how to find satisfaction in a world when prior to that the only satisfaction was that which he found in a bottle. He was an engaging speaker and was always good for ten minutes.

About half way through the meeting Hardhead Steve passed the donation basket with the admonition that it was an in-basket not an out-basket. I put in a dollar and my slip to be signed. When I had ten signatures I would mail the slips to Bonnie Kutala at the Office of Morals and Ethics.

I closed my eyes and slid back in my chair to catch a bit of a nap during the last half hour of the meeting, a rest that was disturbed when I heard Spiritual Ed say, "Leo. Leo."

I opened my eyes. "Yeah," I said.

"How's your relationship?" he asked.

"My relationship?"

"Yeah. Your relationship?"

"With who?"

"With God." He smiled, got up and slipped out of the meeting.

I closed my eyes and was returning to the reverie when I felt a cold burst of air from the door. When my eyes focused I saw the broad back of a black motorcycle jacket. The figure flopped into a chair and through the cigarette smoke I saw, in all her tattooed glory, Daisy Twill. Daisy looked at me, smiled and gave me thumbs up. The other people in the room noticed.

Shortly after the sign of recognition from Daisy, Hardhead Steve called upon me to speak. I passed. I always passed. Although I had been going to Murdock's for three years, mostly to the evening meeting but sometimes at noon, I had never spoken there. I sat in the back. I drank coffee but didn't make it or pour it. I passed when called on. I talked to people, but I didn't get to know them. I went to meetings, got my slips signed, and went home.

I'd been ordered to a lot of AA over the years but never really took to it. For a while I had to go the meetings run by Don Yerke at the Lawyers Helping Lawyers office. Everybody there was a lawyer. The place had soft couches and the other lawyers were nice enough, but I never had much to say there either. Most of the people there had never punched a clock at a blue collar job in their lives. So I went other places. Of all those places, I guess I disliked Murdock's the least.

Chapter 4

Sometimes my clients needed a detective more than they needed a lawyer, and I was not a good detective. Normal channels turned up nothing about Elmo Twill's money. He had died from a fall and head injury in January of that year at his place at Everland Village. He was seventy-nine when he died, owned no real estate in Multnomah County or any of the adjacent counties, and died owing less than a hundred dollars on credit cards. The State of Oregon reported that he never received public benefits. Not only had I failed to find any money to pass on to Daisy, I couldn't even figure out how he had made a living while he was alive.

"Peggi," I said, "get Daisy Twill back in here. Tell her we can't find her dad's money. She has to help us. In the meantime, find out all you can about her."

"You mean you don't know Daisy Twill?"

"Nothing more than what's on the client intake sheet and that she goes to the same AA group as I do."

"Leo, you are hopeless. Daisy Twill owns Coney Bennett over on Foster Road. It's the oldest and best hot dog place in Portland. If you are going to have your office out here you got to get in touch with the community. Coney Bennett serves Foster Road gourmet."

"She doesn't look like a business owner," I said.

"She doesn't, and nobody is really sure how she got to be one. The place used to be owned by this skinny Irishman. Daisy just worked there, and the Irishman was running the place on the cheap while he lived good in the West Hills. After a while he made her the night manager. She might have been, as some people said, his special friend." This was Peggi's delicate trailer-park way of saying she was blowing him in the back room. "But I can guarantee she wasn't bringing home a lot of money. Then what's-his-name is gone and Daisy is the new owner."

"What happened?"

"Nobody really knew. One day, about three years ago, he is gone and she is writing the paychecks. It was a minimum wage place and the first thing she does is give everybody who works there a raise. The food got better too. People where I live had been eating there a long time and they noticed. Nobody knew how Daisy ended up in charge, but nobody was complaining either."

"Build a better Coney and the world will beat a path to your door?"

"I don't know what that means, but they make a good one. My kids are always begging for them. The other thing about Daisy Twill is that she beats her husband."

"Churley?"

"Yeah. Bad sometimes. He belongs to a sober motorcycle club called Rebellion Dogs."

"I've met Churley," I said, attempting to prove myself in Peggi's eyes.

"Then you seen he's a little guy. He fixes bikes when he has work, which isn't that often. There are a lot of guys trying to make a living fixing Harleys. She gets mad, beats him, and kicks him out of the house."

"How do you know all this?"

"I know about Coney Bennett from living around here. Everybody knows. Same with her beating on

Churley. In my neighborhood a woman beating up on a biker is news."

"They have kids?"

"Two. I don't know if Churley is the father. She might have brought them with her from a different guy. The story is that she was pretty wild when she was using."

I told Peggi again to set me an appointment with Daisy. In the meantime, I thought it couldn't hurt to take my gossipy but nevertheless useful legal assistant out to eat. "Tomorrow," I said, "we are going out to lunch together."

"Really? Let me guess, to Coney Bennett."

"Nothing so mundane. We are going to Everland Village."

The next day Peggi arrived at the office dressed in legal assistant formal. She wore a dark jacket with matching skirt that just covered the knee; business-like, yet as feminine and as sexy as a freckled canta-loupe could be. The white blouse was sheer enough to hint at the bra beneath, and her black heels as high as heels could be without being pornographic.

"You are looking uber-professional today," I com-mented.

"What does that mean?"

"It means you look good."

"Thank you," she said. "While we are talking about clothes, Leo, I've been meaning to suggest that you should dress better, being a lawyer and all. Image does count, you know."

"Thank you for the advice, Miss Iverson," I said. "I shall give your observations all the consideration they deserve."

"Just try and dress better."

I had a three-tiered system for work attire. On document days, those days in which I would spend my time talking on the phone and creating legal documents, I wore blue jeans, a pull-over shirt, and whatever pair of comfortable slip-on shoes was closest to my feet when it was time to leave my apartment. On client days, any day on which I was likely to see a client or someone else who needed a lawyer, I wore my brown or black Men's Warehouse sports jacket with pants that were somewhere on the color spectrum close to the jacket. On court days, days on which I might be seen by a judge, my dress depended upon the length of the hearing. I treated hearings of half an hour or less as a client day and risked the sports coat. For hearings of over half an hour I wore the black suit I bought at the Meier & Frank yearly half-price sale. In addition to the dress code, I attempted to shave, comb what was left of my blond hair, and brush my teeth as often as the statistically average fifty-year-old white man.

The upshot of it all was when we left the office for Everland Village I looked like a balding six foot Norwegian draped adequately but unremarkably with the markings of a white collar occupation. Peggi, on the other hand, had done a good job with what little she had to work with, and had strangers been required to guess who was the lawyer and who was the assistant, Peggi probably would have gotten more votes. Peggi was right. Looks do matter, but I was the one with the law license.

Everland Village sat on a ten acre campus nestled into the residential avenues of Portland's east side. The broad driveway to the front door curved through eighteen well manicured putting greens. To avoid showing up in my dented Datsun, Peggi had borrowed a blue Honda Accord for the trip. The rain that day was hardly rain at all, more like droplets of water emerging out of thin air.

Inside the main entrance to Everland we found a mini-mall for old people. It had a central courtyard filled with tables, chairs, and the other necessities of tablecloth dining. Hispanic waiters and waitresses wearing white shirts and black slacks took orders and brought food to the tables. At the edge of the dining area wide walkways gave access to a gift shop, an ice cream parlor, a stationary store, a hair dresser, and several other niche businesses that served the needs of wealthy old people. I noticed a one-room law office tucked among them and felt a pang of envy toward the attorney who had wrapped up that lucrative location. Signs visible from the dining area pointed toward the music room, the chapel, and the health spa.

Peggi and I stood inside the front door looking lost until a pleasant young woman emerged from a back room and asked if she could help us.

"Two for lunch," I said.

"Are you meeting a resident?" she asked, politely letting us know through body language that we were not welcome unless we were connected to someone who lived there.

"Mr. Elmo Twill," I said. Peggi rolled her eyes.

"I will let him know you are here. Roberto will seat you." She disappeared into the back room.

"Right this way," Roberto said. Only five or six of the thirty or so tables held diners. Roberto seated us and put three leather bound menus on the table. We browsed the menu and waited. Peggi and I had three lunch choices: halibut, a lamb patty or the sautéed chicken breast. Each came with salad, potato, and vegetable and cost the princely sum of $3.95. Based upon the price alone, I resolved to begin eating there every day. We had yet to order when the young lady from the counter came to the table.

"Excuse me," she said, addressing herself to Peggi, "may I have a word with you?" Peggi and I simultaneously nodded assent and the young woman slid onto one of the empty chairs. She continued to address Peggi.

"I am sad to say that Mr. Twill has not been with us for some time now. He passed away last January."

"I'm so sorry to hear that," Peggi said. She looked at me and I returned the look without saying anything. The woman had addressed her, so I left her the job of answering. After too small a hesitation Peggi continued, "We had a delightful time with him a year ago and promised that we would meet again on the same day this year. Mr. Larson and I were afraid he might not remember. We had not thought that he might be dead." Peggi's ability to lie under pressure was a skill that I had neither recognized nor appreciated. "Mr. Larson here is an estate planning and elder-law attorney. He had hoped to be of some use to Mr. Twill, but it appears that he is too late."

"It appears so," said the young woman, "but please enjoy your lunch, and if I can be of any further help, just ask." She rose and returned to her duties.

"Well aren't you the clever little liar?" I said to Peggi after the woman left.

"We couldn't just say we were here to snoop around."

"We couldn't?"

"No."

We ordered our meal, and after a very brief wait our lunches arrived. I had ordered the lamb patty and when it arrived I understood the reason behind the low prices. My patty was the size of a silver dollar. The remainder of the undersized plate held three thin slices of potato and five green beans. In this restaurant all the servings were senior servings. We would need two of these lunches to get the calories in a decent hot dog.

"After we eat here, I'll take you to Coney Bennett," I said.

Peggi and I picked at our meals and examined our surroundings. At the few occupied tables around us, well-dressed elderly couples chatted and laughed over their lunches. The staff moved quickly and quietly among the diners. I asked one of them directions to the men's room and used the trip to make a quick tour of Everland. I looked into the Chapel, the music room with its grand piano, the ice cream parlor, the exercise rooms, and the other small businesses along the promenade. Then following a sign to administrative offices I found in another large room an eating area far busier than the nearly deserted one in which Peggi and I were eating. In this second dining room the residents ate from trays and took food from a buffet tended by haired-netted women in white uniforms. The diners in this room were not dressed for the event, and the room had the distinctive odor of old people. This was the room where the meal was free, or free in the sense that the monthly rent at Everland paid the cost. There may have been no waiters, but there was no out-of-pocket cost either.

I returned to the table to fill Peggi in about what I had seen. While we talked a tiny gray haired woman approached our table. She was thin, shorter than Peggi, and wearing an immaculate blue dress trimmed in white lace. Her silver hair formed a perfect gray bun on the top of her head. Although old and small, she was so perfectly balanced and so free of blemish that she seemed to me more like a large doll than a living person. She spoke to Peggi.

"Debbie said you asked to see my brother, Elmo."

"Are you Ms. Twill?" Peggi asked.

"I'm Mrs. Bainbridge. Mr. Bainbridge passed away in 1995. Elmo was my little brother."

"Please join us," I said. She took a seat and folded her hands in her lap. "My name is Leo Larson. I am an attorney. This is my assistant, Peggi Iverson."

"I am pleased to meet you both." She put out her hand, holding it limply in its white glove, and allowed both Peggi and I to shake it. She looked at me. "I don't recall Elmo ever talking about an attorney. Did you represent him?" Peggi watched me struggle for a story that might be consistent with what she had told the young woman from the counter. I had visions of Bonnie Kutala questioning me under oath about what lies I had told and what frauds I had committed in order to extract information from the helpless elderly of Everland Village.

"I never represented your brother," I said, attempting to return us to some version of the truth. "I am a probate attorney working for Daisy Twill."

"Oh. Dear Daisy. I haven't seen her since Elmo died. How is she doing? How are the children?"

"She is fine. The children are fine," I said, as if I had the slightest idea of the answer to either question. It was a lie, but not one that was likely to get me into trouble with the Bar. Peggi rolled her eyes at the fabrication, which I thought fairly hypocritical of her.

Mrs. Bainbridge leaned forward and lowered her voice, as if someone from one of the other tables, the closest person being probably twenty-five feet away, might overhear and pass on the information to those who would use it to do harm. "Daisy has had a very hard life," she said. "She used drugs and had trouble with the law. But that is in her past now."

"Mrs. Bainbridge," Peggi began.

"Dear," the tiny woman interrupted, "call me Anita. Everybody here does. Even the Mexican boys."

"And you call me Peggi."

"Peggi," she said.

"Anita, could you tell us about Elmo?"

"Elmo was my brother. But of course you already know that. He died last January. Oh, but you probably know that too if you talked to Daisy. Daisy could have said things, I suppose, about Elmo." She leaned over the table again and lowered her voice as before. "Elmo drank," she said. "He smoked too. They don't allow smoking here, but he smoked right in his room. He did it right up until he died. As you might guess, I don't at all approve of smoking."

"Me neither," Peggi said. I nodded. I was suddenly in love with Anita Bainbridge and wanted to take her home with me to keep as a pet.

"Anita," I said, "When did your brother move here to Everland?"

"It's a terrible name, Everland. Don't you think so, Mr. Larson? I always use the full title, Everland Village, so it doesn't sound as awful."

"Call me Leo," I said.

"Short for Leopold?"

"Yes. So when did your brother come here?"

"He moved here in February of the year 2000, just after he turned seventy-five. He said he was trying to avoid the twenty-first century."

"What did your brother do for a living before he retired?"

"He was in business."

"What kind of business?"

"He did whatever business people do. He bought and sold things, I presume. I know that he had a business suit and a briefcase like business people do."

"Do you know the name of the business he worked for?"

"My gosh, no," she said. "I think he may have had something to do with real estate, but I am not sure. I must admit to you, although Elmo and I both ended up here, we were not always close. We had disagreements when we were younger. But later, when the children were grown, we were able to set our differences aside and be brother and sister again. It was God's work to bring us back together, but even in the last years it was better for us if we didn't talk about the bad times."

"As I understand it, your brother had two children."

"You don't know about the tragedy then."

"The tragedy?"

Anita sat up, put her hands in her lap, and stared into space. "In 1951, Elmo married Darlene Weston. She was from a wonderful family that lived up in the West Hills. It was a beautiful wedding. I was so happy for Elmo and Darlene. They eventually had a boy, Andrew. He was an amazing little boy, so bright and vibrant. I remember his playing with my boy, Miley, out in the back yard of our house in Eastmoreland. Then when he was twelve he and his mother were killed in a car accident in the West Hills. It was a horrible accident on one of those dark rainy winter nights. Darlene and Andrew were killed. Elmo survived, but he was never the same again."

"So where did Daisy come from?" I asked.

"Elmo remarried not so long after that. Her name was Lena and she was much younger than Elmo. I didn't see Elmo often during that time and didn't get to know Lena. They had two children: Daisy and David. When David was little more than a year old, Lena just disappeared. It is a mystery what happened to her. Elmo raised the children alone after that. David is now a very successful attorney. Daisy, as I said, had trouble in her life, but has turned all that around."

"Do you still have contact with Daisy and David?"

"They used to come and see me sometimes. A few years before Elmo died Daisy gave up the drugs. She started to bring her children to see Elmo and me here at Everland Village. They are wonderful children. They don't seem at all affected by what Daisy went through. David doesn't visit, but he calls me a couple times a year to see how I am doing. He is a very busy attorney and I doubt he has much time to check up on little old ladies in nursing homes."

"I'd hardly call this a nursing home," Peggi said, waving her hand toward the plush surroundings.

"Assisted living, they call it. Everland Village is nicer than some, but it is still a place where old people go to die."

"You don't look very ready to die," Peggi said.

"I tend to my health. But what else is there to do here? It's not like I can work any more."

"What line of work were you in?" I asked.

"I was a home-maker, but that is work too, work that is never done. Mr. Bainbridge was a vice president for the gas company. My son Miley dedicated himself to the betterment of children by becoming a teacher. I don't think there is a higher calling than to dedicate oneself to the betterment of children, do you?"

"It is very noble," I said.

"Miley teaches English."

"A necessary skill these days," I said. "Would it be all right if I asked a personal question about your brother?"

"Well, that depends on the question."

"Did he leave a will?"

"I don't really know, Mr. Larson. I will call you Mr. Larson now because I think you are asking as an attorney. I know that when he died, David came over right away and went through all the papers in his apartment. But David never said anything to me about a will. I must admit I wondered the same thing. I wondered if Elmo might have left a little something to his big sister. I know that in those kinds of affairs they contact you if you get something. Nobody ever called, so I concluded he didn't leave me anything."

"Did he have anything to leave?"

"That I don't know either. He had a house once. That was before he moved here. I don't know if he sold it or not. He was, however, a businessman. Miley says business people have lots of money."

"Sometimes they do," I said, thinking that although I was technically a businessman, I seldom had two nickels to rub together. "Do you happen to know how he paid his rent here at Everland?"

"Everland Village," she corrected me.

"Everland Village," I said.

"I think he paid it out of the income."

"What income?"

"He just called it the income. I don't know where it came from. I think he'd had the income for a long time, the way he talked. It must have been substantial though. Paying for my little one-bedroom apartment here takes all my Social Security and most of the retirement I get from Mr. Bainbridge's work at the gas company. Elmo had one of the big separate cottages at the edge of the Village. They are very nice. Much better than my little apartment when you have grandchildren coming to visit."

"What else do you know about the income?"

"Nothing. I never felt it polite to ask about such things. You might talk to David. He has all of Elmo's papers. I'm sure there are papers that tell about the income."

"I will do that," I said.

Anita Bainbridge begged to be excused for her afternoon nap and the interview ended. I got her address, a phone number, and the promise that she would talk to me again if it would be any help.

Peggi and I paid for lunch and took a short walking tour around the outside of Everland Village. The complex accommodated a full range of retirement living so that once a person checked in he or she could deteriorate from independent living in a monitored cottage to full nursing care without ever leaving the Village. We saw the cottages that Anita had referred to. We walked though the halls of smaller one and two bedroom apartments where tenants received three meals a day, laundry service, and such other personal services as needed included in rent. The nursing facility, although nicer than most, was just that, a nursing home, a place to die. I had expected to find Everland depressing, but I did not. In the lounges and recreation rooms scattered throughout the complex the elderly residents read newspapers, played cards, watched television, and lived a life that appeared from the outside better than mine. I resolved that when the time came, if I had the money, I would move to Everland Village.

"So what's with the lying to the lady from the front desk?" I asked Peggi as we walked.

"That was detective work," she said. "It's what they would do on TV."

"On TV?"

"You don't get it Leo. We could be great together. We could be just like on TV. You are a good lawyer. I can see it, but you don't see it in yourself. I can help you. You need to dress better and get a better car. I can help you with those things. I can run the office and be your detective. This is opportunity knocking for you and me together; we have to answer the door."

"So what's in this for you?"

"I live in a trailer park. I got two kids by fathers who never stayed around more than six months. All my friends live in trailer parks. But look at me now, with you. Nobody would ever know. That lady in there talked to me like I was somebody."

"Okay, I'll try to dress better, but you can't do things because you see them on TV. Practicing law like you see on TV will get me disbarred. I can't lie to people any more. Every lawyer is allowed just so many lies and I have used mine all up. You work for me, and my quota is your quota."

"Okay," Peggi said, "but will you get a nicer car and

a new suit?"

"As soon as I can afford it." She looked at me with a satisfied smile.

"What about Elmo?" she asked. Does he have any money that we can get for Daisy?"

"I don't know."

"What about the income?"

"It could be a lot of things. It could be investment income. It could be an annuity or retirement plan. I don't think so, though."

"What do you think it is?"

"I think we are dealing with a trust."

Chapter 5

Peggi and I didn't talk a lot for the next couple of days. The conversation about the car and her living in the trailer park and looking to me for a better life scared me. I'd seen her trailer house. It had more room than my apartment. I was not the person to be leading anyone out of the white trash wilderness. Keeping to myself, I dinked around on documents for a couple of nondescript probates and watched it rain. Eventually, the Twill matter came back to the top of the stack. Many of my past difficulties with Bonnie Kutala and the Office of Morals and Ethics had come as much from procrastination as drinking, and this time around I was resolved to work on both the hard cases and the easy ones.

One time while I was suspended I went to a seminar sponsored by the Bar about all the things you can do with your law license other than practice law. The place was packed. One of the speakers pointed out that most lawyers like the beginnings and ends of cases. They like that initial client interview. They like filing the complaint. And at the end they like the trial, the settlement if it goes that way, and receiving the check. What they hate is the months of drudgery in between: the endless paperwork, the repetitive calls from clients they once loved but now cringe at the thought of talking to. Lawyers are thrill seekers. The thrills are at the beginning and the end. In the middle is tedium and boredom, but that's also where cases are won and lost. The seminar didn't help me. I spent that suspension painting houses. I don't know if I liked practicing or not. I suspected, however, that I would do it until they threw me out permanently.

"Miss Iverson," I said, sticking my head out of my office and finally breaking the silence between us. "I would like to treat you to a Coney dog for lunch. Do you happen to know any place that makes a good one?"

"As it happens, Mr. Larson, I know a place that makes an excellent Coney dog." An hour later we were pulling off Foster road into the parking lot of Coney Bennett.

Daisy's hot dog stand was a perfect fit for its neighborhood. Foster Road in the vicinity of Coney Bennett meandered through a neighborhood that was neither city nor suburb. It was a community of pawnshops, trailer parks, u-pull-it auto wrecking yards, rent-by-the-week motels, strip joints, taco shops, and a thousand different businesses that help with the care and feeding of motor vehicles. The culture there was self-contained and self-supporting, for neither the city dwellers on one side with their foreign movies and lattes nor the suburbanites on the other with their double garages and Cadillac Escalades wanted anything to do with that junk-yard world in between. In the center of that world was Coney Bennett.

The restaurant itself, if one dared call it a restaurant at all, was constructed of an odd, rough-textured clapboard that even when painted bathroom white gave the place an unfinished look. The building was the size of a double-car garage. One car's worth contained the food and the employees. The other car space held three Formica tables for the few in-house diners. The to-go orders were delivered to walk-up customers through two slide-open windows left over from the old days of burger joints when all parts of the food transaction were conducted at the level of a grown man's belly button. The real business of Coney Bennett was in those to-go orders, but Peggi and I had more on our minds than just food.

Peggi and I went into the small dining area. A hand painted menu on one wall of the dining room listed dogs, burgers, and fries. We ordered across a tiny wooden counter from a young woman with orange hair and a metal ring through her eyebrow. She wrote our order on an Office Depot note pad. On Peggi's advice I got a Coney and chili-cheese fries. Peggi stopped at the Coney. The orange-haired woman gave us a four of hearts from an old deck of Bee playing cards to identify our order.

"Is Daisy Twill here?" I asked the woman with the eyebrow ring.

"Does it look like she's here?" she said, waving her hand toward the room in which she worked.

Peggi and I took a seat at one of the tables. Posters for punk bands covered the walls. I have little knowledge of music in general and even less of punk music, but the posters made entertaining reading as we waited for our food. I judged the bands based solely on the cleverness of the names and decided if I was to patronize any of them it would be either the Dandy Warhols or Jesus Presley.

"Four of hearts," called the woman with the eyebrow ring.

The food was wonderful. Both the Coney and the fries were covered with the secret brown Coney sauce that kept people coming back. It wasn't chili in any sense that I'd ever seen in a bowl or on a burger before. It was a rich brown sauce that carried all the flavors of chili without the lumps. My foot-long dog was misted with onions, dabbed in mustard and covered with the wonderful sauce. The fries were sprinkled with shredded cheese, small chunks of fresh tomato, and the same chili sauce. The result was a rich French fry, cheese, and chili casserole that could only properly be eaten with a fork.

After the food I felt sleepy and figured to go back to the office for a quick nap behind the desk. I hadn't advanced the Twill case any, but I was well fed.

"Why don't we go to Daisy's house?" Peggi asked.

"That's a bit intrusive, don't you think?" Peggi stuck out her lower lip in a sulk. I continued, "Besides, I don't know where she lives."

"I do," Peggi responded, "and we will call first." Peggi dialed the number on her cell phone. I had been suspended during much of the tech boom in the nineties and had fancied myself a bit of a nerd when it came to electronics. For a while I subscribed to computer magazines, knew about memory, motherboards, the fledgling internet, and amazed my friends and neighbors with my technical savvy. But the technical world eventually passed me by. I could still build a desktop computer from parts if I had to, but when some kid would do it for forty bucks, it hardly seemed a worthwhile talent. While my skills languished the world moved on to cell phones and little devices people carried for reasons that were not clear to me. I didn't have any of those things. Peggi's little thing held her address book, took pictures, and made phone calls. On occasions I considered getting a cell phone, but my need had not risen to the level where I was willing to tackle the learning curve. So while the tech world moved on I relied upon my land line and Peggi.

"Ms. Twill," Peggi said into the phone, "I'm Peggi Iverson, Mr. Larson's legal assistant. We are at your restaurant hoping we might run into you." I listened to the rest of half the conversation with a grudging admiration for the manner in which Peggi wrangled an invite to Daisy's house and got thanked for doing it.

Daisy lived near the end of a short winding street off Foster Road. Her house was one of those boxy split-level homes built in the seventies to be the epitome of comfortable suburban living. Hers was one of about twenty, all built on the same theme; part of a developer's bet that the city would expand in the right direction to make the area a respectable bedroom community. Instead, the neighborhood had remained the refuge for the city's outcasts, and the developer's split-level houses with their faux brick fronts had become homes for those just rich enough to buy but not rich enough to escape.

The driveway in front of Daisy's two-car garage held three Harley Davidsons and enough parts to build a fourth. Peggi and I made our way through the clutter to the front door and rang the bell.

Daisy answered the door wearing a short sleeveless denim dress that would have looked great on someone ten years younger and half her size. It did, however, provide a good view of the rose and thorn tattoos that covered her arms and shoulders. The body art was new enough that it still had its color.

"Thank you for letting us come on such short notice," Peggi said. "I just love your dress." Daisy motioned for us to come in. She had been cleaning up, or at least straightening the clutter, before we got there.

The inside of the house was American middle class, volume one. The carpeted living room held the obligatory oversized leather recliner for the old man, and the flowered couch for the wife and li'l ones, all of which faced a massive rear-projection television. Barbies and plastic military gear lay piled together in the corners of the room. The homes I had lived in during previous marriages had looked very much the same.

"I love what you've done with your house," Peggi said.

"Thank you so much. It's nothing really." The compliment put her at ease. She did a Mary Tyler Moore spin in the denim dress. "Churley and I will make this place a home yet."

"Daisy," I said, "let's talk about your father." Peggi and I took the couch. Daisy pulled in a chair from the adjoining dining area. No one used the recliner, it being the chair for the man of the house. "I need help finding your father's money. That is if he had any."

"Oh, he had it," she said.

"What makes you so sure?"

"Because he didn't have to work."

"Tell me about that. You said before he was in real estate."

"My father was an asshole. Our mother left before either of us can remember."

"By 'us' you refer to you and your bother, David."

"Yeah. Elmo was a barfly. He had an office and claimed that he did investments and deals, but he never went to the office. He went to the bars. Me and David raised ourselves. Finally, David ran away. When he ran away so did I. David went to live with cousin Miley. I went to live on the streets. He done good. I didn't. Now, he's a big time lawyer and I ended up like you, at Murdock's."

I didn't appreciate the comparison, but there was some truth in it. "Tell me more about your father's office."

"It was off Morrison Street. He claimed to sell real estate, or appraise real estate, or invest in real estate, usually something with real estate, but there was never anybody there. He had a desk where he slept off the booze, but I never knew him to do real work."

"Tell me how he spent his days." She started to rub the thumbs of both hands against the side of her index fingers. One of her muscular legs began to bounce up and down with nervous energy.

"I'd get Davy off to school then go myself. Our father would get up about eleven, put on shirt and tie and head off to the taverns to meet his buddies. He was good looking for an old guy. He dressed good and talked good. He met his friends for lunch, then he met more friends for drinks in the afternoon. Then he met more friends for drinks with dinner. I'd put Davy to bed at night. If I had to wait up until he got home in order to get money or something, he'd be sloppy drunk. Sometimes it was a good drunk. Sometimes not."

"How did he pay for all those drinks?"

"He had the income. He pretended that he was making money in real estate, but Davy and I knew. On the tenth of every month he got a check. I never saw it. It never came to the house. Maybe to the office, but not to the house 'cause we looked. It must have been pretty big too, because we always had a nice car. He wore nice clothes, and even though we seldom saw him, sober or otherwise, he had money to spread around if Davy and I were in need. We used to steal from him in the morning. After the money came he would have a lot of cash, or at least it seemed like a lot of cash to us kids, and he never missed a twenty if we took one from his wallet."

"When did you leave?"

"I was sixteen. That was in 1986. Davy went to stay with cousin Miley and wouldn't come home. He was fourteen. I realized that I was going to be there alone so I moved to the streets."

"Where were you living before you ran away?"

"We had a house in Sellwood, a big house, but it was rented."

"How did you know that?"

"I asked," she said. "Elmo didn't make any effort to get either Davy or me back. After we were gone he moved to an apartment closer to the office and became the Duke of Morrison Street."

"What's that?"

"It was his barfly name. He knew every drinker up and down the street. Once there was even a newspaper article about him and how beloved he was by all the alkies on Morrison Street."

"Did he ever get sober?"

"Not really. Toward the end he couldn't drink much, but I think it was just because he was old and sick."

"But you got sober?"

"Yeah. At Murdock's."

"Your mother was Elmo's second wife?"

"Yeah. He had a kid by his first wife. The wife and kid were killed in a car wreck. He never said much about it, but Aunt Anita thinks that's what made him drink."

"Is she right?"

"I think he drank because he was an alcoholic. He was driving when his first family was killed. He was probably drunk. He drove drunk often enough with Davy and me. Davy thinks Elmo killed 'em. I don't know, and I don't care. They were dead before I was born."

"What other family did he have?"

"His sister, Anita."

"Was she his only sibling?"

"What's a sibling?" she asked.

"Sister or brother."

"Yeah."

"What about his parents?"

"My grandpa and grandma died in the sixties before either Davy or I were born. Grandpa was a baker."

"Baker, as in a guy who makes bread?"

"Yeah. Bread and rolls and stuff."

"Here in Portland?"

"I think so."

"Could the money have come from him?"

"Could be, but I don't think so. Davy knows. Anita probably knows."

"Anita says she doesn't know."

"Well, then she doesn't. She's the honest one in the family. Ask Davy. He knows." Then Daisy seemed to lose track of the conversation. Her head moved from side to side as if she had gone away and come back and was not quite sure where she was. She looked at Peggi and I like she didn't remember who we were.

"I've been so rude," she finally said. "Let me get you something to drink. Would you like coffee or a coke? I got some Ritz crackers in here too. I could make a turkey sandwich." Without waiting for an answer she disappeared into the kitchen. A few minutes later she reappeared with three cans of Coke and a plate full of tiny sandwiches made out of Ritz crackers and peanut butter.

"I don't know if you like these," she said, motioning at the crackers. "Davy and I grew up on them and now my kids like them just like I did."

"So do mine," Peggi said. She took a gulp of the soda and picked up one of the tiny sandwiches.

"How come you don't get along with your brother now?" Peggi asked.

"Differences."

"Differences about what?"

"It's a long story. When I was on the street I went to him for help and embarrassed him in front of his friends. I took care of him all those years and when I was in trouble he turned me out. I probably did some wrong too, like trying to get drug money from him because he was becoming a lawyer and all, but that's no reason to turn on family. Now he works up there in that fancy office and I sell hot dogs. He lives his life and I live mine, but he knows that it was me that took care of him when Elmo wouldn't. And, he knows that the money if half mine."

"Are you sure he has it?" I asked.

"I'm sure he knows where it is."

"How exactly do you know that if you don't talk to him?"

"We are connected. I feel it. When it comes to our father we can't think anything without the other knowing it."

The questioning was interrupted when Churley and two children came through the front door. He had in tow a red-headed girl who appeared to be about twelve years old and a boy probably four years younger. Churley saw me and sent both children upstairs.

"Mr. Larson," he said. "What a surprise." The miniature biker was polite, calm, and confident.

"Hi, Churley," I said. "This is my assistant, Peggi Iverson."

"Pleased to meet you, Ms. Iverson." Peggi smiled. He reached over and took one of the Ritz sandwiches. "Let me get a Coke."

Churley returned and took his place of honor in the leather recliner. The chair engulfed him. With Churley in the room our conversation veered away from the case. Peggi and I learned that Churley and Daisy had hooked up shortly after Daisy had gotten off drugs and the two of them had been working their way up the economic ladder ever since. Daisy had acquired Coney Bennett. Churley fixed motorcycles, or if need be, cars, and had switched his biker allegiance to a clean and sober motorcycle club. Having given up both drugs and the kind of activities that require jail time, there had been little else for them to do other than get jobs and acquire stuff. While Daisy seemed to struggle with the change, surrounding herself with middle class goods without really fitting among them, Churley struck me as being as oblivious to it all as he was to the strangeness of his appearance. He found neither humor nor irony in wearing motorcycle gang leathers while he ferried children to and from soccer in the couple's mini-van.

After an hour or so I claimed business back at the office. Daisy disappeared up the stairs to tend to the kids and Churley followed us out to the car.

"If I might have a moment," he said to Peggi and

me. "I want you to know that Daisy is not always well."

"How do you mean?" I asked.

"She has an anger problem, or some kind of problem. A few months ago we had to take her to the psych ward. She has to stay on medication. She is doing a lot better, but you can never be sure how she will be. What I'm trying to get at is that I am happy that you are willing to help her about her father and the inheritance, but sometimes she doesn't see things clearly. I want you to know that if there isn't any inheritance, if it is just part of the fight between her and her brother, then I will understand and you shouldn't feel bad about it."

"Do you think she's making it all up?"

"I don't know. I never knew her dad. I've never met her brother. I just don't know. But sometimes when she talks about it she gets so worked up that I wonder if it's really the inheritance or if there needs to be changes in her medicine."

"Is she violent?" I asked, remembering Peggi's tale about her beating her husband.

"She has been in the past. Scary violent. But she has been good for a long time. I don't want to frighten you. It just wouldn't be fair for you to try to do your lawyer thing for her and not know how she is."

I drove Peggi back to the office. She stared out the passenger side window at the city. When not watching traffic I watched her. I looked at the curve of her neck above her collar and had the urge to reach out and touch her.

That evening I stopped by Hal's and bellied up to the bar at my regular crossword-solving stool. Unlike on Sundays, I had to share the place with the after work crowd stopping by for a few doubles before going home or going out drinking. The juke box was playing old Rolling Stones; people were arguing about sports and complaining about the government. In the evenings Hal had a helper, a thin dark haired woman in her early forties with enough of her looks left to flirt with the patrons while filling glasses. She was about to wait on me when Hal waved her off and put a soda water in front of me.

"What are you doing here?" he asked.

"I had a minute to waste. Wanted to thank you for recommending me to Churley Dowd. I took his wife's case."

"Don't mention it. So did her old man leave her any money?" He wiped imaginary spots from the bar in front of me.

"Can't tell yet, but maybe you could help me?"

"How's that?"

"You been around here forever, what do you know about the Duke of Morrison Street?"

"Elmo Twill?"

"Yeah," I said, "Elmo Twill, the Duke of Morrison Street."

"Where did you hear about him?"

"He's the dead guy. Churley's wife is Daisy Twill. The Duke of Morrison Street was her father."

"And somebody killed him?"

"Nobody killed him, Hal. He just died. Why do you think somebody killed him?"

"I know a lot of people whose fathers got killed."

"He wasn't killed. What do you know about him?"

"What's to know? He was a guy who drank on Morrison Street. Now he's dead. That's what happens."

"Where did he drink?" I asked.

"On Morrison Street."

"Well, no shit. Where on Morrison Street? I need to find out everything I can about this guy."

Hal walked a few steps away and stopped. He turned around and said, "Ask around at Murdock's."

"What's Murdock's?" It was a test. I was sure I had never mentioned Murdock's to Hal.

"Don't bullshit me," he said. He turned his back on me and walked down the bar announcing in his own way that the conversation was over.

For a moment I thought about staying. The after work crowd would thin out about seven and the place would be quiet. A few regulars would drink through the dinner hour and into the night. Others would go out for a meal and come back. About nine the night crowd would form. Drug deals would get made; arguments would start and end. Men would become best friends and the women might let you feel them up in the booths.

I finished my soda water and went home to my empty apartment.

Chapter 6

Hal's advice to ask about Elmo Twill at Murdock's wasn't useful. Murdock's was not the kind of place where you could ask for information. The sane members were closed-mouthed about people, likely to remind you that "what gets said at Murdock's stays at Murdock's," and the crazy ones would simply make up whatever they thought you wanted to hear. Of all the members of Murdock's, I figured Spiritual Ed to be my best bet for good information about the Duke of Morrison Street, but Ed was a noon meeting guy. I hadn't seen him since the day he had questioned me about my relationship with God.

Then Ed appeared.

I was parking my car after work and saw Ed down the street from my apartment coming out of Avian House. He was the first person I had ever seen come or go from the building. I hailed him on the street and told him I needed to talk. He invited me to walk with him. Ed's plump pale body was packed into the usual investment advisor black suit and tie. He gave me the condescending look of an AA guru expecting to be consulted on how to get and stay sober, a subject on which he was an acknowledged expert at Murdock's and on which he was often asked for advice.

"I want to know about the Duke of Morrison Street," I said. He did not seem surprised at the question.

"Why?"

"For a case I have," I said. "It may be nothing, but

I'd like to find out about him." Ed put his hand on my shoulder, as if talking to a student.

"He was one of us. A drunk, I mean. He drank on Morrison Street years ago. Good looking guy, always in style. He wore white suits, something you don't see much here in Oregon, and managed to make alcoholism romantic. He carried a cane. He didn't need it to walk—it was part of his outfit. Drove a nice car, and developed drunken conversation into an art form. Guys like him normally work a sales job: cars, electronics, real estate. Something like that. The Duke talked in taverns."

"Did he sell real estate?"

"The Duke, his real name was Elmo Twill, didn't sell anything except dreams. He had deals about to happen and ships about to come in. Mostly they were real estate deals, but they all involved making lots of money by being in the right place at the right time. He had a million of 'em. I didn't drink a lot with him, but if you drank on Morrison Street at all you eventually got to meet the Duke. He mesmerized people. He could make you believe that easy street was just around the corner."

"What did he live on?"

"Don't know. Maybe he really did have some deals. Maybe he inherited money or was a trust fund baby. For a while there was talk he was a cocaine dealer."

"Do you think that was true?" I asked.

"I doubt it," Ed said. "I think he was just a drinker. As far as I know he never did get sober. He stayed the same but the neighborhood changed. The bars on Morrison Street grew old with their patrons. The patron's died off and the young people who came in to fix up the neighborhood didn't want to drink in old bars with old men. So the old bars closed and they opened up new bars for the new residents to grow old in, and it started all over again. In the changeover, there was no place for a Duke of Morrison Street. A couple places always linger, just so the old timers have a place to drink themselves to death. The Duke quieted down, found one or two places where he could still spin tales among old men on rainy afternoons, and as far as I know did that until he died."

"Did you ever try to get him sober?"

"I've never tried to get anybody sober."

"Did he ever try to get sober?"

"Not seriously."

"Did he have family?"

"Kids. Two I think. He adored them. The son became a big time lawyer. Daughter did something; I don't remember what. He bragged about them. To hear him tell it, he was blessed with the best car, the best clothes, the best booze and the best kids." Ed paused. We had covered a couple of blocks and stopped at his car. "Does this stuff help with your case?"

"I'm not even sure I have a case."

"How's your relationship?"

"With God, you mean?"

"Of course."

"It's good," I said. "It's good. One more thing, Ed, what is Avian House?"

"I've got to go, Leo." He slipped into his Mercedes and waved as he drove away.

The next day Peggi was finding excuses to be in and out of my office all morning. My bar journal, the monthly magazine for members of the Oregon State Bar, had come and I was reading the disciplinary summaries—the little stories of lawyers admonished, suspended, and disbarred for malfeasance. Discipline was the only part of the journal I ever read. Reading the summaries gave me a chance to take a little pleasure at the misfortune of others and to celebrate any month that my name wasn't mentioned. It was a pleasure I got only once a month, so when my journal came I liked to stretch out the event without my short freckled legal assistant inventing excuses to bother me.

Finally, Peggi just plopped herself into one of my client chairs and said it. "When are you going to talk to David Twill?"

"I'm going to talk to David Twill when I am ready," I said.

"When are you going to be ready?"

"I'm going to be ready when I'm ready."

"The lawyers at Evanson Tribe Elber and Williamson put on their pants one at a time like you do."

"One leg at a time," I corrected her.

"However you guys put on your pants. Just call him."

"It's not because he works at Evanson Tribe," I said.

"Yeah, right." She got up and went back into the reception area.

She was right. The fact that David Twill worked for Evanson Tribe made me want to do just about anything except pick up the phone and call him. He was big firm. I was not. Evanson Tribe was headed by Frank Evanson, the richest most influential lawyer in Portland. Still jogging a mile a day and practicing law in his eighties, his firm employed something like a hundred and fifty lawyers, the lowliest of whom made more in his first year than I'd made in any year. The firm occupied the top three floors of the tallest building in town with escalators between the floors. The legal assistants had been to college and then paralegal school. Evanson Tribe employed a full time grammarian just to make sure every written document that left the office was not only free of misspellings but free of split infinitives and hanging participles. Frank Evanson's firm represented banks, public utilities, professional sports teams, and the top echelon of Oregon businesses. I represented tattooed hot dog vendors like Daisy Twill.

I wasn't afraid of the big firm lawyers because they were smarter, or for that matter, better lawyers. In my youth, I'd been in a big firm. I'd had a knack for law school and graduated with the kind of credentials that convinced one of the high-end firms in Portland to give me a shot. I lasted about six months. As it turned out not only did they want legal talent, they wanted someone who could stay off the bottle long enough to put in a full eight hours a day. Mine wasn't a long stay, but it was long enough for me to learn that the guys there, as Peggi said, put on their pants one at a time. The big firms are bureaucracies representing other bureaucracies. The associates claw their way up the pyramid for the big money to be made when they get high enough that they can stop the clawing and make money off the new associates clawing below them. In my little office on Eighty-second Avenue, I had to take a case, do the work, get my piece of the action at the end, and then spend the money on groceries. My goal was to do the job in a way that made the client happy enough to recommend me to friends and make myself enough money to make the effort worthwhile.

In the big firms the goal was different. The associates were salaried and never saw the money they made or lost on the case. Their job was to impress the partners they worked for. Only partners talked to the well-heeled clients and those clients often had long term plans that were not apparent in a single case. The client, for policy reasons, might be willing to spend fifty thousand to defend a case that could settle for ten. Sometimes I could see what motivated the big firm lawyer, but in other cases the behavior was unfathomable. To me the big firm lawyers were polite, educated, and well connected crazy people.

There was also envy. I envied the incomes, the big downtown offices, the herds of well dressed secretaries, and the fact that these guys didn't have to advertise in bowling alleys. But the big firm guys envied me as well. They envied my freedom from the demands of asshole partners, my ability to run a case without the oversight of the oversight committee, and my ability to be able to lose a case without it being seen as a victory of David over Goliath. The final one, the inability to lose, was the worst for them. With all the paralegals, investigators, and grammarians, they were expected to win them all. Winning legal cases, however, is not dependent upon the quality of the lawyer, but the quality of the case. Judges have their own agendas, and those agendas do not include making sure that rich law firms always get their way. When I paired off against one of the big firm lawyers, and the inventory was taken for both sides, I sometimes got the better of it. He had the money, the resources, and the prestige. I had nothing to lose. Whatever you could take from a lawyer, whether it be the case, his money, his reputation or even his license, I had lost, gotten back, and then lost it again. Having been there made me fearless, and a lawyer without fear is a dangerous opponent.

I didn't feel particularly fearless, however, as I tried to negotiate the maze of receptionists, paralegals and voice mail that lay between me and Daisy's brother.

"David Twill," a thin male voice finally said, after I had explained who I was and what I wanted to several different underlings.

I introduced myself as Daisy's lawyer representing her in issues surrounding her father's death. I concluded the introduction with, "Daisy is concerned that there is an inheritance that should be coming to her and is not." David made no effort to hide his displeasure.

"First, Mr. Larson," he said, stretching out the pronunciation of my last name to emphasize that we were to remain on a very formal footing, "your client is insane, a criminal, and a drug addict." My conversations with big firm lawyers often started with them giving me a moral report card on my client. "Second, she isn't entitled to an inheritance from our father or anybody else. And finally, if she were entitled to an inheritance or money of any sort, I am the last person on earth to help her get it."

"Why is that?" I asked.

"I do not intend to discuss my family history with you, Mr. Larson. However, one of the many reasons that I do not feel like helping my sister is that more than once she has tried to kill me." I was appropriately surprised. Daisy had failed to mention this.

"That could make a person mad," I observed.

"I don't get mad," he said. "I take action."

I tried to move to a more productive line of questioning. "Did your father have any assets to pass on when he died?"

The attempt went nowhere. "I am not going to answer questions about my father. I am not going to talk to you at all about my family. Daisy is subject to a stalking order that prevents her from attempting to communicate with me in any way and subjects her to arrest if she comes within two hundred feet of me. I am perfectly willing to return to court to make you subject to the same restrictions."

I apologized for calling him and hung up. I asked Peggi to go on OJIN, the Oregon court data base available to lawyers on the Internet, and bring me what she could about Daisy. The results weren't pretty. She had the drug related convictions that you would expect from any recovering addict. She had several assault charges that had been dismissed or bargained down. She had been evicted from three apartments, had been sued by five collection agencies, and been restrained from contacting or otherwise coming anywhere close to David Twill.

My first urge was to call Daisy and beg off the case. It wouldn't have been the first time I'd taken a client because he or she was an interesting person with a good story only to have it all to turn out to be bullshit. Personal injury lawyers are plagued by a type of person who firmly believes that his comfortable retirement is just around the corner because he fell on his ass at a Chevron station. Probate lawyers are afflicted with the "grandma promised" people. Each of these characters tells some variation on the theme that grandma, grandpa, mom or dad had always promised to take care of them, leave them the family home, or do some other similarly generous act that would rid the person of that annoying need to find a job and earn a living. Grandma, of course, had left no written evidence of her generosity so the potential client needed me, the lawyer, to get what grandma had really intended the destitute relative to have and to pay my modest fee out of the proceeds. These folks have been around since Roman days, and long ago strict rules were enacted to make sure that wills were not undone by a lot of undocumented claims about what grandma did or didn't promise. The "grandma promised" folks made up about ten percent of my new appointments. I did a fairly good job of weeding them out and sending them down the road with an explanation that my refusal to take the case was not a rejection of the validity of the case, but an admission that I simply didn't have the skill to handle such an important matter. Every now and then, however, everybody gets taken in. It was beginning to look like Daisy Twill was not only a "grandma promised" client, but a violent one at that.

"We are fairly sure," I said to Peggi, "that the Duke of Morrison Street didn't earn money by the sweat of his brow. He didn't win the lottery. If he had money at all, a proposition that I am beginning to doubt, he may have inherited it."

"Who cares where he got it? Can't you get his records and just figure out where he kept it?"

"Anita says David got to the records. David says he's going to get a restraining order if I contact him again."

"So you can't even look at the records?"

"There are ways, but there is also the possibility

that Daisy is a psycho, and I am not going head to head with David Twill and Evanson Tribe over the ravings of a loon."

"She is not a loon," Peggi declared.

"Her brother claims she tried to kill him."

"Maybe he deserved it." Peggi's trailer park penchant for loyalty had kicked in on Daisy's behalf.

Although a depressive by nature, I was more depressed than usual that night. I stood in my front window watching the loading dock of Haven Appliance across the street from my apartment. A middle aged man on a fork lift was loading trucks. The orders for appliance parts had been pulled and were being shipped out to customers. Next to the parts place a single light glowed from a second floor window at Avian House. It was a light meant to suggest that the building was occupied, but all it did was emphasize the emptiness. The warehouseman smoked on the loading dock between trucks. During one of my suspensions, I'd worked in a similar warehouse. The place I'd worked sold the oversized hardware used to build industrial electrical systems. Warehouse work is hard dirty work. We took orders, pulled the product off the shelves with fork lifts, strapped it to pallets, and loaded the trucks. The only good thing about the job was that at the end of the day I was too tired to be depressed.

My nonsuspended colleagues in law used to opine that I must have suffered greatly from a lack of mental stimulation and educated conversation during my stints in the blue collar world, but that was not the case. I didn't know the warehouseman loading the truck in the loading dock at Haven Appliance, but I knew a lot of men like him. He didn't define himself by the job he was doing that afternoon. He may have been a fork lift driver at the moment, but he was also a musician, a motorcycle racer, a hunter, or a poet. Lawyers, including myself when practicing, are consumed by the job. When lawyers gather they talk about their jobs, their cases, and other lawyers. The blue collar world was different. The people in it talked about goals unrelated to earning a living and seemed to me more curious and creative than people in the professions. As I stood in the window, I felt nostalgia for that world. I liked industry, heavy machinery, and working with men in groups. Yet, when I did it I was always planning my return to the law.

The Haven Appliance warehouse had not been built for warehousing. It had the remnants of large storage containers on the roof and residual architecture suggesting that at one time some sort of product had moved by mechanical pathways from one part of the building to another. Something had once been manufactured there, maybe back when my apartment housed families and children.

I didn't know what to do about Daisy. I had no evidence that she was entitled to an inheritance, or even that her father had any money. Elderly men are well known for intimating a fortune as a method of getting care and attention in their last years, and more than one person had now suggested that Daisy's grasp on reality was not as firm as I might hope. Her diminutive husband, Churley, had warned me off in his own understated way. Her Aunt Anita had left hints of trouble, and her brother had suggested that she was a murderer. No one would blame me if I called her, told her I couldn't find the money and didn't want to continue the case.

Across the street the last truck pulled away in the dark, and the warehouseman pulled down the big rolling metal door to close up for the night. The routine was the same every evening. In an hour all the lights in the warehouse would go out and the street would be dark except for the decoy glow in the upper window of Avian House.

I went to Murdock's that night for the eight thirty meeting. Before the start, members sat around discussing sports, weather, news, each other, and the crap of everyday life. Hardhead Steve collared me again for advice about grant writing, a subject I still knew nothing about. Copper Bob was walking with a cane after a recent heart attack and was railing against smoking, a horrible habit he had forsworn six days earlier while in a hospital bed. Little Annie was sulking in the corner over some slight having to do with her need for public assistance or her Jewishness.

For all of us, Murdock's replaced the taverns. With its smoke, bad coffee, and posters on the wall the room looked and even sounded like the places I drank. There is a phrase in the Big Book about there being a sufficient substitute for alcohol and it being membership in Alcoholics Anonymous. In my case AA was very much a substitute. I drank quietly in the back of shit-hole bars like Hal's. When sober, I went to AA and listened quietly in the back of shit-hole meetings like Murdock's.

Electric Dave was sitting against one wall arguing with another man about the results of a recent business meeting. At business meetings the members made decisions about money, meeting format, and the minimal behavioral requirements for Murdock's membership. I had only attended one business meeting. At it the members voted down a motion to have a summer picnic on the grounds that picnics did not serve the primary purpose of AA: carrying the message to the alcoholic who still suffers. They voted in a rule requiring that anyone who physically attacks another member in a meeting be expelled for sixty days. An ex-member who had stolen money from the group by fishing with a hook and line through the deposit slot in the safe apologized and was readmitted to the group.

Electric Dave was angry because he had been on the wrong side of a vote about an anonymous donation. Someone had put a cashier's check for five thousand dollars into the deposit slot of the safe. Dave stabbed his finger at the text at the back of the Book and read to the others at the top of his lungs, "We view with much concern those A.A. treasuries which continue, beyond prudent reserves to accumulate funds for no stated A.A. purpose. Experience has often warned us that nothing can so surely destroy our spiritual heritage as futile disputes over property, money, and authority."

Hardhead Steve moved in to answer. "We have an AA purpose, Dave. We need the money for expenses in case we have to move when the lease runs out." Except when discussing grants, Hardhead Steve was one of the more reasonable members of Murdock's. "The group has voted. We will send one hundred dollars to New York and keep the rest in prudent reserve for emergencies."

"Emergencies are not an AA purpose," Dave protested. "We are required to be self supporting. We can't solicit, we can't advertise, and we can't take outside contributions. What the hell kind of contribution do you think that is? You think maybe Little Annie saved it up from her SSI?" Copper John came over looking to get in on the argument.

"It was a member or ex-member who wishes to remain anonymous," Steve said, "Maybe it is somebody doing a ninth step amend. Maybe somebody here got an inheritance or won some money gambling. We don't know that it was an outside contribution, and being we don't know, we have an obligation to use it to remain self supporting."

Electric Dave countered with, "Being self supporting doesn't require another five thousand in the bank over and above our operating costs."

Copper John saw his opening and took up the argument for Steve. "Five thousand is not that much, Dave. If we have to move we could burn through that in no time."

Dave turned even redder and started pulling at the gray hairs above his ear. "We are not moving. We have been in this place for fifteen years. You are ignoring the traditions."

"We had a vote, Dave," Copper John said. "You may disagree, but the group conscience rules."

"This ain't the only fucking group in town, John. I can go where people pay attention to the Book and do what it says rather than give it lip service and then go ahead and do whatever the hell they want." He stuck his fist in Hardhead Steve's face and slowly lifted his middle finger.

"Calm down, Dave," Steve whined.

"I quit," Dave yelled. "You hear that? I quit this group." He swooped his oversized coffee cup off the table and marched to the doorway. Halfway out the door he stopped, turned to a room full of quiet observers and shouted, "Keep your goddamn money you fuckers. I'm going to find some real AA." He slammed the door and was gone into the night.

After the commotion, Hardhead Steve sat his long cowboy body next to me.

"What do you think, Leo?" he asked, "Do we keep the money?"

"Sure," I said, "keep the money, but what do I know?"

"Did the money come from you?"

"No, Steve. I don't have that kind of money. I'm a lawyer but not a rich lawyer. Does that kind of thing happen often—big contributions from anonymous sources?"

"Every year we get a big one. Usually for five thousand. It's the maximum the group can accept from any one source. Sometimes there are smaller ones. People get sober here, go off and make it in the world. Then they come back and show their gratitude."

"Did Electric Dave really quit?"

"Sure, just like he did last month and the month before that. He has nowhere else to go. None of us do."

"That's sad," I said.

"Not as sad as living in bars. Not as sad as the Elks Club or the Golf Course or Union Hall. Here we get a chance at a spiritual life."

"The Elks Clubs and the Union Halls have nicer buildings."

Steve stood and faced me. "Material goods, Leo, material goods. They are as enticing and deceptive as alcohol. They are the false prophet. If you want a nice building there are a lot of places you can go. Churches. They have great buildings. You could go to the high-end AA meetings in Lake Oswego or the West Hills." I thought of the well upholstered couches downtown at the Lawyers Helping Lawyers meeting run by Don Yerke. "You are a normal looking guy. If you want nice buildings why do you come here?"

"I like it here," I told him. "I hear things here."

"The truth, you mean."

"I suppose so."

"And Leo," he asked, "how do you know that it's the truth?"

"What I hear here? How do I know it's true? I don't know. Maybe because it doesn't sound like the same old crap, like everybody trying to look good and out-shine the next guy. At most places I hear about victims. At this place I hear from the people who create them."

"Abusers and victimizers lie too. How do you know what you hear is true?"

"I don't know," I confessed.

"Because you feel it." He slapped himself in the chest with his hand. "You feel it here when the truth gets said. After years of destroying yourself with alcohol you are learning to feel again." He sat back down, smug in his conclusion. Copper John took the chairman's seat and asked for a moment of silence to be followed by the Serenity Prayer. About half way into the meeting John called on me to speak. I passed.

Chapter 7

The next morning Peggi was at her desk when I arrived at the office.

As I hung up my coat I said to her, "Prepare me a draft of an intestate probate petition asking that Daisy Twill be appointed the personal representative of the estate of Elmo Twill." I walked through the reception area into my office, and turning back just for a moment I saw Peggi giving me a thumbs up.

In my little two-room practice nearly everything involving court started with a legal document called a petition. The petition was the formal legal paper that opened a probate, began a guardianship, or started a trust case. The petition to appoint a personal representative for the estate of a dead guy who died without a will is a document that tells the court where the person died, who his relatives were, and what he might have owned when he kicked the bucket. It also requests that someone be appointed to be the dead guy's legal representative. It is the filing of a lawsuit, and the filing of the petition means that the wheels of justice are about to move.

No matter how long I practiced there was still a thrill in the filing of the initial papers that bring a matter before the court. I'd write them up, ponder the consequences, rewrite them, ponder some more, and rewrite again. When satisfied, I'd take the papers down to Olga at the probate counter. She accepts the filing fee, stamps the thing with a case number, and the deed is done. Over the days that follow the affected parties are served with copies and the process of law begins. What had been a private matter between citizens has become a public dispute before the court. If one is inclined to view a legal action as a battle, the filing of that first paper is the opening shot.

Within an hour Peggi had written a draft of a petition stating that Elmo Twill had died without a will, that Daisy and David Twill were his only heirs, and that Daisy should be appointed his representative to collect, inventory, and distribute his assets according to Oregon law. I had been unable to find any assets for Daisy to distribute other than the few personal effects Elmo had left behind in his apartment. What I really wanted was the power to collect and inventory. If granted, the petition would allow Daisy to become, for legal purposes, her father. She could get into his accounts, assume control of his property, and most importantly, take possession of everything he owned when he died. That would include his personal papers. Daisy's Aunt Anita had said that David had the papers. I wanted them.

After lunch Peggi left with the petition to get it signed by Daisy. Although written by lawyers, the allegations in the petition had to be sworn to by the client. Daisy had little interest in the contents of the document or its legal effect. She signed it because Peggi told her to and Peggi represented her lawyer.

After filing the petition, Peggi met me in front of Everland Village. The only person in the case who seemed both willing to talk and possessed of useful information was Anita Bainbridge. If I was going to tangle with David over Elmo's papers I needed everything she knew. Earning her keep, Peggi had managed to get me a meeting in Mrs. Bainbridge's apartment at Everland.

Anita lived in a simple one bedroom apartment on the second floor of the main building. When we arrived she appeared at the door as attractive as ever, and her home showed the same meticulous attention to feminine detail as did her person.

"Mr. Larson, Miss Iverson, please come in," she said.

She wore a blue dress patterned with small white flowers. Her hair was pulled tightly into the same gray bun. The apartment matched her ensemble, a subdued flower décor with lace doilies protecting a few pieces of delicate high quality furniture. The room held a couch, an upholstered chair, two small lamp tables, and a television. A single book about chicken soup and the soul lay on the coffee table. She motioned for us to sit on the couch and took the upholstered chair for herself.

"How can I help you today?" she asked.

"Ms. Iverson and I are still working on the estate of your brother, Elmo. We are trying to find out what Daisy and David and even you might inherit from him."

"I think I have told you all I know."

"When we met before, you mentioned that David may have come over and gone through your brother's papers. Do you know when that was?"

"I believe it was a few days after Elmo died. David is a lawyer. He has to do things like that."

"Do you know whether he took any papers with him?"

"I think he took them all. He never said that, but when I went in later, after the funeral, to clean up Elmo's apartment, Elmo's file cabinet and his desk drawers were all empty. Not even a note pad or a pencil. As a businessman, I know that Elmo kept papers. All businessmen do."

"Did anyone else go in there who might have taken papers?"

"Oh, I can't say. Any number of people might have gone in there after he died. Some friends of his came over at one point and went inside his apartment. Daisy went in. But it was David's job, he being a lawyer. You should talk to David; he could tell you for sure."

"Mrs. Bainbridge," I said, "could you tell me a little bit about your father and mother?"

"What would you like to know?"

"Where they lived. What your father did for a living."

"My father was Bergan Twill. He came to Portland from Ames, Iowa in the twenties. He was a baker. He met my mother, Emily, here in Portland and they were married. Father was very industrious. He left for work at four in the morning every day to bake bread. It was hard work and mother had to raise Elmo and me. We were poor at first, but father made a good life for us. Eventually, he had his own bakery with other bakers working for him. I would sometimes go down and watch the bread being made by the men in their white uniforms. It was very exciting for me and I was proud that my father could make bread for people. Then we got a nice house on this side of the river. It was not fancy compared to what people have today, but it was plenty for mother, father, Elmo, and me."

"What happened to the bakery?"

"Father retired. Elmo did not want to be a baker and it was not proper work for a woman. Father sold the business. Later he sold the house. The new owners of the bakery were not as industrious as father and a few years later it closed. Elmo went into business. I married Mr. Bainbridge. Mr. Bainbridge was a vice president with the gas company and very well respected in the community."

"I do not want to pry, Anita," I said, "and I wouldn't ask if it weren't important, but did your father and mother leave you anything in their wills when they died?"

"There was nothing left," she said. "Father still held stock in the bakery, but it was closed. Elmo and I each received half of the stock, but it had been worthless for years. There was still a few thousand dollars for us to divide. We think it was left over from the sale of the house, but we weren't sure. I turned my portion over to Mr. Bainbridge who invested it for me so that we could put Miley through college. Mr. Bainbridge was talented that way."

"Why didn't Elmo take over the bakery?" Peggi asked.

"He didn't want to be a baker. He and father argued over it. They argued about other things as well."

"What did they argue about?" she asked.

"Elmo drank, and father did not approve."

"Your father did not drink?"

"Father had a glass of beer now and again, but he never got drunk. Elmo got drunk. But in the end, it didn't matter. The bakery had to close. Elmo went into business. The less said about all that the better. They are both gone and there is no reason to speak ill of the dead they say."

"I suppose not," I said. "Did your father and mother always live here in Multnomah County?"

"Oh yes. At least since coming from Iowa."

"Mrs. Bainbridge, have you ever heard of the Duke of Morrison Street?"

"No. I don't know any Dukes, from Morrison Street or otherwise."

"Tell me about when David came to get your brother's papers. Were you there?"

"No. I called David and asked him to help. After all, Elmo was his father. He said that he would take care of the matter. He works for a very respected law firm. I trust David and the lawyers he works with completely."

"I have talked to David, Mrs. Bainbridge. He says that he does not have your brother's records." Anita folded her hands in her lap and stared at them.

"Perhaps you are mistaken about what he said," Mr. Larson. "Or perhaps he was not completely forthcoming because you work for Daisy. There has been a lot of trouble over Daisy in the past. But I cannot help you any further than to tell you what I know. You and David are both attorneys. I would think the two of you can work something out." She raised her gaze from her hands and looked me square in the eye. The conversation was over.

Peggi and I thanked Anita for her time, made a courteous exit, and headed back to the office. Back home, I asked Peggi, "Do you know what to do?"

"The probate files for Bergan Twill?"

"Right."

"The documents will be on microfilm."

"Get copies."

"It will be expensive."

"I'll pay," I said. "I want to see what Bergan left for his kids."

"Don't you believe Mrs. Bainbridge?"

"I believe everybody," I said. "I also check things out."

Peggi opened the Twill file. I went into the office, paused, and then stepped back into the doorway to watch her at work. She was in a dark skirt, jacket, and white blouse, all of which were well made and tailored to her body. She wore highly polished black heels with a single strap. Peggi was changing. The black skirt had a slit up the right side revealing an inch or so of the darker patterned top of her stockings. Although what I saw was probably the top of some workaday panty hose, I took a moment to imagine more exotic under-garments.

At the end of the day as we were closing up shop I went out into Peggi's part of the office and reclined with my hands behind my head in one of the waiting room chairs. We could hear the rain beating on the roof.

"It will be a soggy drive home," I said to her.

"Yeah." She turned in her steno chair to face me. Her skirt had ridden up. She tugged it down, then pushed her red hair away from her face.

"Peggi . . ." I didn't know how to continue.

"Yes." She tugged again at the skirt, this time out of nervousness rather than modesty.

"You did a good job today . . . with Mrs. Bain-bridge, I mean. Very professional."

"Thank you. I like going with you for things like that."

"I will buy a better suit."

"You don't have to, Leo. You look fine. I shouldn't have said that."

"No. You should have. We are in this together. I

don't know why you work here, why you stay here, I mean. But I like it that you do. If I can change things to make it better for you, I will try and do that."

She looked at the floor. "Thank you," she said. "I like working with you. I like what we do."

I wanted to hold her in my arms. "I know you don't get paid like some—."

"The money is fine, Leo. It is not about the money."

"If the practice picks up some—."

"It's not about the money." She stood, turned her back to me and began cleaning her desktop. She was doing it so she didn't have to face me.

"Peggi . . ."

She turned her head but not her body. "Yes."

I hesitated and again couldn't say what I had intended. "Do you need some days off for Christmas?"

"Whatever you want, Leo. What are you going to do?"

"I have nowhere to go. I will work, or maybe go out to dinner."

"I just need some time to spend with my kids. My sister will be in town. But if you need me, I can be here."

I wanted to say that I did need her, but not for anything to do with practicing law. I wanted to take her to dinner, and to a movie and to bed. But instead I said, "Let me know. You can have all the time you want. Nobody sues people during the holidays anyway."

"Thank you. And if you have nowhere to go my sister and I could have you over to the house."

"I don't think so, but thanks."

"If you change your mind I would love to have you."

I'd love to have you too, I thought. I felt as if she were waiting for me to speak, but I was struck dumb by the fear that everything I read in Peggi was out of my own head, my own imagination. She was simply being polite to a boss at Christmas time, a boss twenty years older than she was, a boss who was a fool to think that she could see him in that way.

"Stay dry out there," I said.

I pondered the Peggi problem that night as I waited for the evening meeting at Murdock's to begin. I made a resolution. Peggi and I had known each other for years and there had never been any trouble in the man-woman department. No matter how I felt about her, I needed it to stay that way.

I was a half an hour early for the meeting. Little Annie was making coffee and talking to herself in very earnest tones. People wandered in and out. Copper John came in and took a seat beside me. John was a small man, maybe a hundred and thirty pounds, somewhere in the range of sixty years old, and still every inch a cop. He came to Murdock's every day in pressed blue jeans, a starched work shirt, and a brown leather bomber's jacket. It was as close to a policeman's uniform as he was allowed to wear without getting arrested himself. Although he'd been gone from the Portland Police force for twenty years, fired for a series of alcohol related offenses that even the powerful police union couldn't make go away, he never gave up his loyalty to the force and to force in general. He was always ready to kick someone's ass, or get a friend on the force to do it for him.

"Leo," he said to me, "did you know I can spot a con the moment he walks in the door just by the way he walks? They learn a certain walk in prison, and it never goes away. I can point 'em out on the street."

"That's good, John."

"You're a lawyer, aincha?"

"Yeah, John," I said. "I'm still a lawyer."

"Do you know Dennis Harlington? He's a lawyer." People at Murdock's tended to think all lawyers knew each other.

"Don't know him."

"Damn good criminal defense lawyer. I never had much use for lawyers. Most of 'em just out for the money, but Harlington was Cracker Jack good if you were in trouble with the law. I'm surprised you never heard of him."

"I'm a probate lawyer, John. No cops and robbers; just wills and trusts and stuff like that." He looked disappointed. People often were.

"What you doing coming here all the time?"

"I got to get my slips signed for the Bar."

"Tavern keepers will sign those slips for you. You don't have to come here."

"I know that. I could sign them myself too. I'm trying to do it straight this time. Besides, I like it here."

"How long you been sober?"

"Three years and change. I went to the East County Alano Club for a while when I was just out of treatment."

"Bunch of pussies," he said.

"They're okay. Then I whored around to a bunch of groups. There is a group just for lawyers that I go to some times, but this place is close to my apartment. I like it."

"Have you done the steps?" Murdock's was not the kind of twelve step program where the steps were posted on the wall like the Ten Commandments in a courthouse and thereafter ignored. Members were expected to actually do the steps. People with a lot of time and guilt did them over and over. I'd done them once in the first year of my last sobriety. Doing them was a pain in the ass, but it had made me feel better. The effect, however, wore off and I hadn't worried much about them for a few years.

"I've done them. I suppose I could have done them better, but I gave it a good try."

"Step one is the only one you can do completely," Bob said. It was common AA advice. "Have you admitted you are powerless over alcohol?"

"I have, Bob. I was probably the last one to become convinced. I had a couple of wives and more than one boss who figured it out before I did, but I eventually got it." Bob smiled.

I had lied to Bob. The whole 'powerless' thing still bothered me. One of the passages of the Big Book described the alcoholic as a victim of the delusion that he could wrest satisfaction out of life if he only managed well. I didn't accept that it was a delusion. All I really wanted was to manage well, or at least better. My job was to manage other people's stuff. I had to run the probate, get the guardianship, or as in the Twill case, find the inheritance. If I managed it all well I made money, kept Bonnie Kutala off my back, got to drive a better car, and even got laid once in a while. There might be more to life than that, but I wasn't sure I wanted to know what the more was.

"How are you with God?" John asked.

"That's what Spiritual Ed always asks me."

"So how are you?"

"Okay, I guess. I'm not a religious man, John."

"It's not about religion, Leo. It's spirituality. It's

the fact that you aren't in charge."

"I'm convinced I'm not in charge, John."

"That's a start then."

"Yeah, that's a start."

That evening when I got home I made myself a dinner of scrambled eggs with cheese in microwaved corn tortillas. I owned six plates, six glasses, six sets of silverware, one eight inch non-stick frying pan, and a toaster. I had a small television on the counter in the kitchen and watched the never ending cable news as I ate. In theory I could serve six people in my apartment, but I never had. I could also cook things other than egg and cheese burritos, but I seldom did.

I thought I might take a walk after dinner, but when I looked out the front bay window rain had started coming down hard. I stared into the open loading bay of Haven Appliance and tried not to think about Peggi.

Chapter 8

I had lawyer dreams that night, the kind in which I find myself at the start of a jury trial in my bathrobe, or learn that a case I hadn't prepared is set to start in a few hours. I'd had these kinds of anxiety dreams on and off all my life. Sometimes they weren't about law, but they all had to do with something that I couldn't manage. Sometimes in the dream I was drinking again. Those were even worse.

I got up early to escape the dreams and went to the office. Peggi was not in. She had scheduled her morning at the court house to look up the probate of Bergan Twill. I did some legal research on the internet and swilled coffee.

The first unpleasant event of the morning was a visit from Torkum Masoogian. I heard the front door open and having no one scheduled went into the reception area to see who it was. Masoogian was standing there in all his obese grandeur.

"*Buenos dias*, Leo," he said. He didn't actually speak Spanish but took a perverse humor in peppering his language with Spanish phrases he'd picked up from television. "How's life among the dead and dying?"

"What do you want, Masoogian?"

"I want to see my buddy Leo, find out how the practice is going and help out any way I can so that my old buddy continues to be able to pay his rent."

"The practice is fine," I said, "raking in money hand over foot."

"So who is the Amazon with the tattoos?"

"A client," I said, "an heiress."

"Heiress, whatever. She is a big woman. Fuckin' mean tits on her. I like them big ones, Leo. From the looks of her she ain't no stranger to being on her knees, so if you was to send her down to my office for a little slurp and swallow, I'd be sure you got something out of it."

"Torkum, get out."

"C'mon Leo, I know you ain't getting any off her."

"Torkum, get out." He leaned against the wall showing no inclination to leave.

"What kind of case is she?"

"Probate. Maybe trust administration. I don't know."

"Who kicked the bucket?"

"Her father."

"How much was he worth?"

"I don't know that either."

"What do you know?"

"Not much. I don't have a lot to go on. I have a hunch."

"A hunch about what?" he continued.

"That she's entitled to enough money to make the case worthwhile."

"As I recall, your hunches usually suck. They not only suck, they get you suspended. I can't say for sure, but it seems to me you don't have too many more suspensions before they start talking the 'D' word."

"The word is 'disbarment,'" I said.

"Yeah, that's it," he said. "By the way, have you nailed Peggi yet?"

"Torkum, get out."

"She's a squealer, Leo. Put that freckled ass of hers

up in the air doggie style and she squeals like the prettiest little trailer trash you could ever imagine."

"Like you know."

"Oh, I know," he said. "The more I had to discipline her, the more typos she made."

"Out!"

"All right. All right. Good luck with Twill. You will need it." He spun his flabbiness around like a ballet dancer and left the office.

I went back to my desk and reconsidered whether Torkum might be telling the truth about Peggi. Things are not always what they seem. I took Peggi's trailer park Puritanism at face value. It made sense to me that people struggling in the backwaters of the economic world would hold faster to personal virtues than those who could base their self esteem on what they could buy. On the other hand, not all the evidence pointed the same way. Peggi had two children by men who never stayed long enough to wear out a pair of blue jeans. Although she had refused to put up with Masoogian's workplace harassment, she never pretended to be any stranger to the bedroom. Maybe doggie style on the desk was what she expected. I tried to put the whole thing out of my mind, but had a hard time getting rid of the image of Torkum having sex with her. I was also troubled by the fact that Masoogian knew the name of Daisy Twill.

I might have continued to ponder Peggi Iverson's sex life if had not been for a phone call from another of my least favorite people.

"Law office," I answered.

"Mr. Leopold Larson, please." It was Bonnie Kutala from the Office of Morals and Ethics.

"It's me Bonnie and you know it."

"When are you going to get a receptionist?" she demanded.

"I have a receptionist and you know that too. She's out at the moment."

"Peggi Iverson is not a receptionist, she is an accomplice."

"Ms. Iverson is an experienced legal professional."

"Leo, the only lawyer she has ever worked for is you and Torkum Masoogian. Thus, putting the word professional in the same sentence with Peggi Iverson ought to be an ethical violation on its own." Bonnie was an advocate of professionalism. I could take it or leave it. To me, professionalism was for people too lazy for morals.

"Bonnie, what do you want?"

"I've got another complaint about you."

"From who?"

"I don't have to tell you unless we proceed with a formal investigation. I just wanted to let you know that we have received a complaint."

"What is your anonymous source complaining about?"

"Filing an action, a probate, that has no foundation in law or fact."

Although lawyers are allowed to file fairly speculative, strange, and even weird cases, they are not permitted to file a case, even a probate case, unless the petition has some reasonable legal basis. In practice, it simply means that the lawyer has to make his argument with a straight face, but the Office of Morals and Ethics had on more than one occasion gone after a lawyer for filing frivolous cases. Maybe the Bar office actually cared about preventing frivolous cases, but it was equally possible that the office used the charge to go after lawyers they wanted to get for other reasons. Al Capone, after all, was sent up for tax evasion. Things are not always what they seem.

"I am not filing frivolous cases," I said.

"Somebody says that you are, and we have to look into it."

"It's bogus, Bonnie. How long has it been between us? A frivolous case charge is a nothing. When I play poker with the guys, a man needs jacks or better to open. A frivolous filing charge isn't enough to even start the betting."

"This is not a poker game, Leo," she said. "We are here to protect the public. We have information that you are seeking to have a personal representative appointed who is not only unqualified to serve, but has actually attempted to kill one of the other heirs."

"My review of the law," I said, "suggests that attempting to kill other heirs does not disqualify one from becoming a personal representative unless there is a conviction."

"If she wasn't convicted, it must be the only thing she hasn't been convicted of. There are specific prohibitions about putting felons in charge of estates."

"Actually, Bonnie, if you'd ever practiced real law you might know that there is only a prohibition against felons if the underlying conviction involved dishonesty. My client very honestly wanted to kill her brother, very honestly possessed and sold drugs, and very honestly beat up her husband. I have her court record right here in the file. Not a single one of her convictions involved dishonesty. Thus, she has the same right as any other citizen to serve as the personal representative of an estate."

"Are you suggesting that possession of

methamphetamine with intent to distribute is not dishonest?"

"It's entrepreneurship, pure and simple. Illegal yes. Dishonest, no."

"Unless you want to try making that argument to a disciplinary trial panel you should withdraw the petition."

"Bonnie. This is a straightforward family dispute. My office is full of them. I have brother against brother. I have sister against sister. This one happens to be sister against brother. I make my living off of sibling rivalry. Mom or dad dies and it is the kids' last chance to even old scores and get compensation for the fact that dad never loved 'em enough. This one is no different from any of the others."

"When one of the siblings is a member of Evanson Tribe, it is different from the others. Have you ever in your life had to face off against a firm like that, Leo?"

"Bonnie, I eat Evanson Tribe lawyers for lunch."

"Leo, you can't afford to eat lunch *with* an Evanson Tribe lawyer."

"We are all equal before the law."

"No we're not. Why don't you just save yourself some trouble, drop the case and disappear back in your hole. If you withdraw the petition, I'll drop the investigation."

"Bonnie. I will give it some thought. I really will. If you'd ever had real clients you'd know that quitting a case is not that easy to do. I develop relationships. Daisy Twill is devastated at the death of her father and is now left out in the cold unable to care for her children because of the mishandling of his estate. How can I look her in the eye and say, 'I can't help you. Your brother is just too powerful.'"

"Oh, stop," Bonnie said.

"You say stop, but your eyes beg for more, Bonnie. When are you going to let me take you out for a drink?"

"You are not allowed to drink."

"You can do the drinking. I'll ply you with liquor, and then . . . "

"I'm hanging up now. I expect you to withdraw the petition in Twill."

"I know a romantic little place down by the river."

"Goodbye, Leo."

I put on my gortex and went out into the rain for a couple chicken tacos from Pedro's. The Hispanic woman behind the counter didn't speak English but recognized me as the white guy who always orders two chicken tacos. With a mustard squirter full of tomatilla sauce and my tacos, I sat in the window to watch the traffic.

I was just a few days into it and the Twill case was out of control. Maybe Bonnie was wrong about Daisy, but she was right about one thing—I had no business going up against Evanson Tribe.

The tacos made me feel better. When I returned to the office, Peggi was there with copies of the Bergan Twill probate file. She came in and took a seat in my office, waiting for me to read the file and comment.

"You looked at this stuff," I said to her. "What do you think?"

"It looks to me like he died broke. Gave his stuff to his kids, half to Anita, half to Elmo, just like she said."

I thumbed through the documents. It was a whitebread probate of an old man who had nothing.

Bergan Twill's last will and testament had been written in 1946 giving everything to his wife, or if she did not survive him, as she did not, to his children in equal shares. It was right out of the form book. The probate petition was filed in July of 1964, an appropriate two months after Bergan died. It stated that his wife, Emily Twill, had died three years earlier and that his sole heirs and devisees were Elmo and Anita. In the time between the writing of the will and the death of Bergan Twill, Elmo had married Darlene Weston and had the boy, Andrew, both of whom would be lost in the car accident a couple of years later. Anita had married the vice president of the gas company and given birth to Miley Bainbridge, the English teacher. At the time of the probate, the remarriage of Elmo and the birth of Daisy and David were still several years away.

The inventory was as uneventful as the petition. Bergan had owned the furniture in his house, a savings account worth eighteen thousand dollars, and stock in Emily Foods Inc., with the notation "no value." The stock was what remained of the bakery.

"What do you see?" asked Peggi, eager for something I might see that would help Daisy.

"Nothing. Same thing you did. It's the probate of an average man."

"Does it help Daisy?"

"No. But there is something."

"What?"

"The will was written by Dan Evanson. Then twenty years later, Elmo Twill, the heir and executor was represented by someone from Evanson Bainer & Yowth."

"Who is that?"

"Bainer and Yowth are dead, but Dan Evanson remains and the place is called Evanson Tribe."

"The firm where David works?"

"Bingo."

"What does that mean?"

"Let's see. It means the head of David Twill's firm knew David's grandfather and probably Elmo Twill as well."

"Does that help Daisy?"

"Not really. There is no reason Dan Evanson wouldn't be writing wills in 1946. By 1964, however, the Evanson firm was already big. We might wonder why a firm that size would do the probate on such a small estate. But there could be a lot of reasons. Maybe Evanson got sentimental about an old client."

"It doesn't tell us where Elmo Twill got his money?"

"No it doesn't."

I called Daisy and told her that her grandfather's will didn't answer any questions for me. I made copies and said I would give them to her that night at Murdock's.

I arrived early for the five thirty meeting. My stress level dropped just walking through the door, much in the same way it had in the old days when I walked into Hal's. I sat close to the chairman this time, despite the smoke. Daisy arrived and plopped her tattooed torso into the chair beside me. "Wha'cha got?" she asked. I handed her copies of what Peggi had copied at the courthouse. She glanced at the packet with no intention of trying to read any of it.

"What does it say?"

"It says that your grandfather died broke. Your dad and Aunt Anita each got a few thousand. Your father's money didn't come from him."

"Then where did it come from?"

"I don't know."

"Have you talked to David?"

"Yes," I said. "He threatened to have me arrested."

"Welcome to the club."

"Do you know he has a restraining order against you for stalking him?"

"So?"

"Do you stalk him?"

"I have, I guess. Not lately."

"Why do you do it?"

"Because he's what's wrong with the world. Because he left me to the streets. Because I'm angry. There are other reasons that make more sense when I'm manic." She smiled at me.

"While I'm your lawyer you need to leave him alone. I can't have you trying to kill him while I'm arguing that you should be the executrix of your father's estate."

"What's executrix?"

"In charge of," I said. "It's a legal way for me to get your father's papers. Your brother, I'm pretty sure, has them."

She cocked her head sideways and looked at me. "Leo," she asked, "are you up to this case? Can you win it?"

I hesitated. I was about to go into marketing mode with my spiel about how I was better than any downtown lawyer could ever be and how she was lucky to have found me, but there is something unseemly about blatant lying right before the start of an AA meeting. Bullshit was still my first response to stress, but it was no longer my only one.

"I don't know," I told her. "I don't know if you have a case, and if you do I don't know if I can win it. The other day, I almost called you and quit."

"Why?"

"Because I don't know what to do next. I could end up looking like a jerk in this case. Your brother is big time. I might get my ass kicked."

"By my brother?"

"In a legal sense, not in a fist fight."

"And if you get your ass kicked what happens to me?" she asked.

"You get no money."

"I have enough money. Just do what you can. If you don't want to do this case, you don't have to. I like you. If you want to do it, I will stick with you, even if you lose."

"Thanks Daisy," I said. She got up and took a seat next to her husband. The diminutive Churley Dowd, always in his motorcycle leathers, waved and smiled at me. The two of them had brought the children. The red-headed girl was old enough to be annoyed at being dragged away from the important issues of her preadolescent life to attend a boring AA meeting with her parents. The younger cherubic brown-haired boy was happy to be anywhere. The girl had school work; the boy, paper and crayons. Murdock's, to my way of thinking, was no place for children, but as more than one of the members had pointed out, children were better off at Murdock's than locked in a car outside a bar, a place that many of the members had spent their childhoods.

The meeting was chaired by Electric Dave who, as Hardhead predicted, had rejoined the group within a day or so of his outburst about the group finances. We opened with the Serenity Prayer, read the Twelve Steps and the Twelve Traditions. I was a good listener at AA meetings. I liked people's stories. In day-to-day life, I seldom got to hear people tell where they came from, how they came to be where they are, how they live their life, and how they feel about it. In the regular world, talking about those things leaves you defenseless against the charge of being human. At Murdock's I learned how other people lived.

On this day my mind wandered. I began hearing only the sounds of the voices and letting the meaning of the words escape. Listening only to the raw notes of human voice, I could hear the emotion but not the sense of what was said. This way of listening makes me sleepy. Although it was not unheard of, Murdock's was not a good place to fall sleep. I was yanked back to attention when Spiritual Ed sat down in the seat beside me. He nudged me and winked, as if we were conspirators.

"How's your relationship?" He whispered.

"It's fine, Ed," I whispered back, "and yours?"

"Good," he responded. "I'd like to talk to you about something serious. Can I buy you a cup of coffee after the meeting?"

"Sure Ed," I answered.

Ed wore his usual white shirt and black suit. It never changed. He never had a striped shirt or brown suit or any other variation in his uniform. He appeared fit and active, despite being overweight, but if you hung around Murdock's you learned that he was plagued by arthritis. He needed pain medication to make it through the day and his stories about being able to use pain meds as prescribed, rather than a bottle at a time washed down with whiskey, were lessons for the rest of us on dealing with physical pain without booze.

Electric Dave called on Ed to share almost immediately.

"I have not had a drink today," Ed began in his sonorous AA voice. "I have not considered suicide today. I have found a new way of life and I am happy about that." I had heard it hundreds of times and it still made me smile. People have knacks for things. Some people are good at tennis. Some are good at math. Spiritual Ed was good at AA.

I met Ed for coffee at the Fat Rooster a few blocks from Murdock's. Under the white fluorescent bulbs I talked with a different Ed. His eyes were harder. We were there to be serious.

"How long are you sober this time?" he demanded.

"Three years and some," I said.

"How long have you been around AA?"

"Oh, twenty-one, twenty-two years now, I guess. Since after my first stint in treatment. But there were long periods in there that I was away from it."

"And how did those years go for you?"

"The years I was away from it?"

"Yes."

"Not good."

"How are things now?" he asked.

"Better. Or getting better."

"Are you interested in something that might cause things to get a lot better?"

"Sure Ed," I said. "What do you have in mind?"

"Some people have taken an interest in you. We looked you up. It's not hard with Google and a record like yours. Want to know what we found?"

"I'm not sure."

"We found a man who has God given gifts, completely undeserved gifts, but God given, that are being wasted. Tell me if I get any of this wrong. You came out of college hot as a pistol, double majors in linguistics and economics. You published articles in both subjects and got a full ride to law school where you were a top academic performer and editor-in-chief of the law review. After graduation you went to one of the elite Portland firms and performed brilliantly until drinking brought you down. Since then it's been treatment centers, shit hole offices with catch-as-you-can cases, suspensions, stints painting houses or driving forklifts, lost opportunities, lost wives, and a wasted life. Now you are holed up three nights a week at Murdock's making a social life out of conversations with Copper John and Shithead Steve."

"I'm sober," I said.

"Sober is good, but you know as well as I that classmates of yours with half your intellect, half your drive and creativity, are senior partners driving BMW's and living in big houses in the West Hills. What did they have that you didn't? They were not born alcoholic, that's what. You got the disease and they didn't. You fucked up. That's true. You drank too much and you fucked up some cases because of it. But it doesn't have to be a life sentence. In fact it shouldn't be a life sentence.

"You've read the Big Book. It has a lot about how to get sober, but where does it say that you can't get back what you should have had. It says, 'A man is a fool if he thinks sobriety is enough.' It says, 'We know only a little. God will reveal more.' The truth is, Leopold Larson, more was revealed. More is being revealed. The Big Book carries a blueprint for how to quit drinking. For those who want to quit living in bars and start living in places that look like bars but don't serve alcohol, that blueprint is enough. But the Big Book has more than just the program to quit the booze. It has road signs, pointers to something beyond, something bigger than you will ever hear about at Murdock's."

"What are you talking about?" I asked.

"Let me ask you this. The first chapter of the Big Book is Bill's story, the drunkalogue of our founder, Bill Wilson. You've read it many times by now. What do you think of Bill?"

"I've never been fond of him, as a person I mean. I give him credit for starting AA though."

"He stole the credit for starting it and through his own egomania prevented it from ever getting beyond a refuge for losers and mental cases like him. You've heard the crap, 'Nobody is too dumb to get the program, but many are too smart. The Big Book says it, I believe it, that settles it.' That's Bill Wilson, and it's all fine for the drones, but not everyone was born a drone. Look at you. You go to treatment, you hang around AA for a while, and in the meantime, your practice and your life goes nowhere. Eventually, the pure boredom of it all drives you crazy and you drink again. It doesn't have to be that way.

"Certain of the first hundred, the hundred founders of AA, never accepted Bill Wilson's domination or the limits he put on the program. They continued the work. They developed ways for those afflicted by the disease not only to cast away the addiction and return to respectability, but to claim the positions in society they would have occupied had they not been laid low by the disease."

Ed had a white knuckle grip on the paper napkin that had come with his coffee. His face reddened as he spoke.

"We learned in getting sober that we could not stop drinking on our own. We needed the help of those who had gone before us. When it came to taking our rightful place in society we needed the same kind of help. But that kind of help would not come from the kind of people who can't see beyond weekly AA meetings in old store fronts and church basements. It would not come from people whose idea of a good life was Social Security and subsidized housing. It would come from people who had demanded back what their addiction had taken away. We refused to be held down. We refused to be held to the ground. We chose to soar."

"Soar?" I said. "Avians?" He had started to flush as he made his plea. When I said "Avians," he smiled, as if my figuring out the connection was proof of my worthiness.

"We are a group of recovering men and women who demand more than just sobriety. We start with the Twelve Steps of Alcoholics Anonymous, but we go beyond it. And just as in AA where the old timers sponsor and mentor the new members, we ensure our own positions in society by sponsoring and mentoring those we choose for new membership. There are important people in this city willing to help you. They know your talents and they can provide you a place to practice them. All you have to do is be willing to accept the help, do what you already know how to do, and when you have reaped the rewards pass on what has been given you to those who follow."

"What about humility, worker among workers, and all that?" I asked.

"We do not repudiate or change anything you have learned in AA. For us sobriety is still the most important thing in our lives. Bill Wilson built a foundation and then spent the rest of his life preventing anyone from building on it. We have developed what is the natural outgrowth of what the original one hundred started. If we could offer it to everyone, we would, but at this point in our evolution we cannot. We must choose those who can benefit the most and who, by joining us, will enrich us further. In AA we are taught to help the new man recover, not for his benefit, but because helping others ensures our own sobriety. It is the same with say, wealth. There are people willing to help you, powerful people, because they know that in helping someone like you to wealth they will increase and protect their own. This is an opportunity that is offered to few. I want you to consider very carefully the decision you will be asked to make. The right response to our offer can open doors for you that you didn't even know existed. But the offer is only made once, and if you turn it down, the offer will not be made again. The doors of AA are always open. The doors of Avian House open only once, and if you do not go through, they shall forever close."

"What do I have to do?"

"Tell me that you are willing," he said, "that you are willing to do what it takes to resume your rightful place in the world, the place that you would have earned had you not been struck down with our disease."

Ed was flushed and sweating by the end of his talk. Thinking of my old Datsun, which despite Peggi's nagging, I had yet to replace, I said, "Okay, I am willing."

Ed threw out his hand like I'd just agreed to buy a high-commission annuity. "You've made the right decision, Leo. I hope that, like me, you will someday look upon the day you became an Avian as the most important day of your life."

"I hope so too, I guess."

"Go about your business as usual. I will report your decision to the others. One of us will contact you. There is much to do and much for you to learn before doors begin to open, but they will open, and you will be amazed before you are half way through."

The two of us shook hands in front of the Fat Rooster and left for our respective homes. He drove off in his Mercedes. I walked back to my apartment in the rain and was soaked to the skin by the time I got there. I made a cup of tea, turned on the cable news for background, and thought about what Ed had to say. On one hand, it was flattering to be invited—to be considered smart, creative and worthy of joining a group of people who fancied themselves a notch above. On the other, the invite suggested that without help I was, and would always remain, a failure.

I stayed up late that night thinking and occasionally walking to the front bay window to look at the lone light in the upstairs window at Avian House. When I finally went to bed, I slept hard. I overslept the next morning and got up with what felt strangely like a hangover.

Chapter 9

Christmas was on Sunday that year. I made myself an egg and tortilla breakfast and ate it at my kitchen table while watching a Christmas parade on the little television. I wondered what Peggi was doing. I figured I'd go over to Murdock's for one of the pot luck dinners they held on the holidays where alcoholics find themselves alone, but I never made it. Spiritual Ed called me at my apartment that afternoon, waking me from a Christmas nap, and scheduled my first meeting with the Avians for the following Friday night.

The day of the meeting it rained hard all day. I left work in the early afternoon, took a nap, had a delightfully greasy patty melt at the Fat Rooster, and waited. I was scheduled to arrive at seven thirty. Because of heavy cloud cover, the street lights came on early that night. About seven o'clock, I turned out the lights in my living room so I couldn't be seen from the outside and watched Avian house from my bay window. For a while the only movement was the forklift driver loading trucks on the dock of the Haven Appliance. It was a late evening for him, and a Friday to boot. Shortly before seven thirty people began to arrive at Avian House. The first arrivals were two men who came together in a blue minivan. Next was Spiritual Ed in his Mercedes. A man I didn't know arrived on foot. And then someone I did know showed up riding a tricked out Harley Davidson. It was Hal from Hal's Place. He got off the bike, covered it with a rain tarp, and walked casually up the stairs to the front door.

I considered wearing my black suit just because I had never seen Spiritual Ed in anything other than a black suit, but out of fear of being overdressed I decided on a corduroy sports jacket. Estimating my walk time to be about two minutes I waited until exactly seven-thirty to leave the apartment.

I rang the bell at Avian House and Ed answered. "Right on time," he said. "Very good." He waved me inside. Ed was wearing a heavy blue robe that was cut like a graduation gown. In his hand he held a matching blue fez with an attached mask.

The front room of the old Victorian contained a library furnished by and for men. There were books enough on the walls, but the emphasis was on the overstuffed leather chairs and reading lamps. In the same way that AA halls often look like bars, Avian House looked like a private club where old men might meet to read the paper, drink, and smoke.

"Take a seat," Ed said, pointing to the largest of the leather chairs. "I will see if your welcoming committee is ready. Fill this out while you wait." He handed me an intake form and disappeared down a hall that led to the back of the building. I filled out the form with my address, phone number, sobriety date, and my agreement to keep secret everything I saw or heard there. When I finished the form I set it on the arm of the chair and browsed the reading material on the shelves around me.

Most of the books on the shelf were the standards of AA literature. There were several editions of the Big Book, including an original first edition from when it was physically a big book. There were several copies of William James's, *Varieties of Religious Experience* and other works by James. There were histories of

AA, both sympathetic and not. The Avians had books by Emmett Fox, Og Mandigo, Dale Carnegie, and Napoleon Hill. There was a copy of Scott Peck's, *A Road Less Traveled* and a copy of *Atlas Shrugged*. There was a copy of the *I-Ching*. Some of it, like the William James and the Emmett Fox, had historical connections to AA. The rest was the old and the new of good living from Marcus Aurelius to Zig Zigler.

I had seen most of the books before and read a few. However, one set of books was new to me. They were apart from the others in a closed glass case. The case held about forty small blue volumes bearing the Avian House imprint. The shelves held multiple copies of books with names like, *The Nature of Wealth, Thriving with God, Tapping the Power of the Spirit.*

My wait at Avian House reminded me of the time I tried but failed to become an Episcopalian. I had been attending the morning services at a local Episcopalian Church, first because I thought I might find clients there, but later because I took comfort in the repetitive early-morning ritual. Not many people attended the morning service and eventually I was noticed by the minister. He invited me to begin the classes necessary to join the church and I accepted. At various times during my religious education I spent time in the small library attached to his office. He had a similar selection of books. There were the Bibles and prayer books, the theological treatises, and quite a bit of general reading on the religious issues of the day. Then there were the special books. In his case they had brown covers and were published by the church itself. That's where the secrets were, or so I thought. At Avian House, the secrets, I surmised, were between the blue covers and locked in the glass cabinet.

I never did become an Episcopalian. I made it to the Sunday on which I was to be sworn in or whatever they did and I simply failed to show up. I never went back, and I never attempted to join another church. That was not the first or the last organization where I got to the altar but could not take the vow. I once told the story to Bonnie Kutala. She suggested I had the same problem with being a lawyer.

Ed came back into the room. "We are ready for you." He motioned me to follow and led me down the hall to a small but elegantly furnished conference room. Ed pointed me to a seat at one end of the table while he took the chair at the other end. Four other men sat at the table, each wearing the same kind of blue robe, fez, and attached mask. The blue masks had eyeholes and extended from the front rim of the fez down to the end of the noses, leaving the mouths visible. As Ed sat he put on a headpiece of his own, leaving me the only bare-faced person at the table. The masks protected the identity of all of them except Hal, whose big white beard made him easily recognizable even with the mask. Each man had a sheaf of papers in front of him. Ed introduced them in the AA tradition of using initials for last names.

"Leopold Larson, this is Ted H., Andy M., James P., and Hal S." I nodded to each.

"I know Hal," I said. Ed ignored me.

"Gentlemen, this is Leopold Larson," Ed said. I looked at Hal and smiled. Hal remained taciturn. The meeting began with the serenity prayer, the same prayer that begins every AA meeting. At the end of the prayer Ed took control of the proceedings.

"Gentlemen," he said, "we have been called here to consider the nomination of Leopold David Larson to be one of us. This is the First Consideration, one of five events that may lead to the induction of Mr. Larson into the ranks of Avian House."

The men around him responded in unison, "Let it be so."

"Mr. Leopold David Larson," Ed continued, "You have been nominated for membership in Avian House. Avian House is a group of one hundred and eighty-five men and women who, having been struck down in their prime by the curse of alcoholism, and having recovered through the grace of God from that hopeless condition, have banded together to explore the furthest reaches of the spiritual life." This speech was something Ed had memorized and said more than once before. I recognize ritual.

"Leo," he said. You will become the one hundred and eighty-sixth member of Avian House. Avian House is the name for a group of people in recovery who have refused to turn their backs on the true path that the first one hundred began. We have seen that God's grace—that grace which manifested itself in the miracle of our becoming sober—did not end with sobriety. We have learned how to use the simple tools given to us by those who went before us to become leaders in our churches and our communities and in our workplaces. We have been taught the secrets of personal power and the secrets of wealth. Over the next year, God willing, we will transmit these secrets to you. During this apprenticeship you will be helped by those who have gone before you.

"I am not at liberty to reveal to you the process by which you were selected for this honor, but I want to assure you that it is not related to your success or failure in any other organization, including Alcoholics

Anonymous. Thousands of AA members in our community have lived sober honest lives for years without ever being given a hint of our existence. The selection is not based upon your skills or your accomplishments, although it turns out that most of our members are capable of remarkable things. Your selection, like your continued sobriety, was a matter of God's will, and your continued receipt of the benefits of the Avian way shall be dependent upon your acceptance and adoption of a few simple precepts."

"I am honored," I said, because it seemed the appropriate thing to say. I was really wondering when I would get a key to the building.

"Do you accept your nomination?" Ed asked.

"I do," I said.

The spectators around the table chanted, "Let it be so."

"Today we will provide you with the first of several important books we want you to read. We demand that you give each of them your full attention. The content of these books and the books themselves are to be kept completely secret. You shall discuss the contents with no one and shall allow no one access to the copy in your possession. All matters related to Avian House are confidential. You may tell no one about this meeting, your nomination, or anything related to your membership. Soon we will have a Second Consideration to discuss with you the matters you have learned and we will assign you a sponsor for the purpose of creating your life plan. That plan will consist of things spiritual, things practical, and, things economic. You should be aware that for most of our members wealth is an important part of the life plan."

"Wealth sounds good to me," I said. Ed frowned. Levity about money, it seemed, was not encouraged.

Ed reached into a briefcase beside his chair and withdrew a blue book like the ones I had seen in the glass cabinet. He took a key and placed it on top of the book. I was confident that it was the front door key I had been hoping for. Looking at the book on the table in front of him he said, "This is the first step in your journey. As of today you are a novice in the ways of Avian House and entitled to all the rights and privileges attached thereto. The first of those rights is access to the first volume in *A Program for Life*. I suggest that you read it several times. I am also giving you a key to this building where you may take refuge from the rush of life and avail yourself of the many good books in our library. For the time being only the first volume in *A Program for Life* will be available, but once you have been fully accepted into our ranks all of the volumes will be yours for study.

"All members of Avian House have been advised of your nomination and asked to support your progress. For now, most of the members will remain unknown to you, but they will reveal themselves as your progress warrants. I am personally proud to have been chosen to preside here at your First Consideration, and want you to know that I am very pleased for Avian House that God has chosen you to be one of us."

"Let it be so," the others chanted. Ed slid the book and the key down to my end of the table. The committee members stood and filed out.

With the exception of the prayer at the beginning and the various chants of "let it be so," no one except Ed had said a word to me. When the others were gone, Ed came up and put his hand on my shoulder.

"Leo," he said, "this is going to change your life. You are going to see and experience things that you have never imagined." He walked me to the front door. "Study the book," he continued. "Study it like you did the Big Book when you first came to AA. Study it like you did your law books. We know your talents and we have great plans for you, but first we have to be sure that you are bringing yourself fully to the program."

"I will study," I promised.

Ed ushered me out the door, turned out the last of the lights, and locked the door behind us. I watched his hands. His key fit the lock but was different from mine. The rain had turned to a light drizzle. The minivan and Hal's motorcycle were gone. I walked Ed to his car and said my goodbyes. From there I walked home, the small blue book safe in my jacket pocket.

Back in my apartment I put the new key on my key ring, brewed some weak Folgers, and settled in the front room of my apartment with my new reading material. The first volume in *A Program for Life* was titled simply *Introduction*. It had no author, no copyright information, and no ISBN number. Beneath the words "Avian House" on the title page, bold faced type warned the reader that the book was the private property of Avian House and should be immediately returned to the organization unless the person in possession of it was authorized by Avian House to possess it. The warning went on to provide severe legal consequences for anyone who failed to obey the secrecy restrictions.

The book had been privately published, and whoever commissioned the work had paid for quality. The pages were sewn, not glued. The title and the Avian

House name were stamped in gold leaf onto the smooth blue leather spine. My copy, however, was not new. It had been read before, probably more than once.

I spent the next few hours reading. The program inside the covers was Alcoholic Anonymous on steroids, promising that the reader would not only be able to put down the bottle but would also get a good job, drive a nice car, and bag the hot girlfriend. The trick was to believe in God, be moral, help others, network, and pay attention when God's bounty came your way. A lot of it had to do with visualization and the power of the mind to make the world conform to its vision. If you were sober and pious you could imagine yourself in a BMW—believe that you will have a BMW—and thereby end up with a BMW.

The *Introduction* to *A Program for Life* set out a principal for success and followed it with inspiring stories of how that principle had worked in other people's lives. The stories were about people down in their luck who finally found that perfect combination of God, healthy living, and positive mental attitude that allowed them to rise from misery and get what they had always wanted out of life. The process for developing that perfect combination was to be revealed in its purest form in the coming volumes. Sitting in my dark empty apartment the book made me feel good about life and where I might be going. By midnight, I was inspired.

For the most part the AA I had seen limited itself to helping getting a person off the bottle. It had a few general rules for living, such as cutting back on the felonious behaviors closely associated with drinking, but it didn't even pretend to do major life enhancement. At Murdock's they didn't loan you money, find you a place to sleep, give you rides, or get you a job. That was for your relatives or social service agencies. The program in the little blue book, however, was not one that accepted limitations. The book said that the miracle worked by God and the Twelve Steps—the miracle that had freed millions of people from the chains of addiction—could also free a person from the chains of poverty, the oppression of social class, or the humiliation of obscurity. Money, fame and power, whatever you desired, were obtainable by a few simple but secret tweaks to the program we already knew. It made clear, however, that the introduction I was getting in the first volume was just a teaser. The real secrets, the secrets of wealth and the secrets of the universe were in the later volumes—the ones I would get once I had proven myself worthy.

What the Gnostics of old had done to Christianity, the Avians had done to Bill Wilson and Alcoholics Anonymous. They turned the tables on Bill Wilson, the founder of AA. In the world of the Avians he was not the founder, spokesman, and promoter of the original twelve step program, but a despot who had distorted the work of others and suppressed both the real content and the importance of what the founders of AA had discovered.

To a lot of people in AA, me included, Bill Wilson was not a likeable guy. I never had much of an urge to study his life, having gotten about as much I wanted of Bill Wilson from reading his story in the opening chapter of the Big Book. There were rumors that he cheated on his wife many times in sobriety and may have embezzled from the organization he founded. I never knew if those claims were true, but I knew for sure that he ultimately smoked himself to death. One of the code phrases to find AA members is to ask "Are you a friend of Bill's?" From what I knew there was nothing in Bill Wilson's sobriety that made him the kind of friend I would actually want to have.

Although I was no huge fan of Bill Wilson's, I had never heard, as the *Introduction* to *A Program for Life* suggested, that he had not stayed loyal to the people and the program of recovery that became AA. Religious movements and AA are filled with people who carry the message without ever being able to apply the tenets effectively to their own lives. Over the years I had been profoundly influenced by lessons in sobriety given me by people who never managed to stay sober themselves. I had been taught most of what little I knew about honesty by people who could not themselves be honest. Some people, for reasons unknown, can make those around them better people without becoming better themselves.

The fact that the Avians were a bit off the map in regard to mainstream recovery didn't much matter to me. The Avians had a nice club house just down the street from me with big leather chairs. My favorite bartender was already a member, and they were promising to put some money in my office account. I was more used to getting kicked out of organizations than invited in, so if an established group promising salvation, sobriety, and riches wanted me to read a couple of private label self-help books and learn a secret handshake, I was not only willing, but thankful for the offer.

Monday morning at the office I was still feeling positive. When I got into the office Peggi said that David Twill wanted me to call him. I called the number Peggi gave me and David Twill answered. It was a number that bypassed the banks of receptionists and other intermediaries.

"I have had a change of heart," he said, "and I want to apologize to you. I do not always think clearly in matters that involve Daisy. I realize now that you are simply doing your job, representing your client to the best of your ability, just as I do with our clients here." His cadence and choice of words was precise. It was a perfectly phrased apology.

"No apology necessary," I said. "I do probate. High emotion among siblings is the lifeblood of my practice."

"I suppose it is," he responded, sounding sorry that anything he did would be considered common by me. "I called to propose that we get together and talk about the petition you filed. I will answer whatever questions you want, and maybe at the end we can put the whole thing behind us. I know I have better use for my time and I'm sure that you do too."

"Hey," I said, "if there's no case, there's no case."

"Would you mind coming to my office? I have a public offering that I am working on which makes it very difficult for me to get away." Neither of us minded that. He had no desire to see my little two room office and I had no reason to want him to see it. Similarly, he would not willingly give up the intimidation factor of Evanson Tribe.

I stuck my head out of my office and said to Peggi, "Put on your frilly knickers, girl. We are going to Evanson Tribe."

"What happened?"

I filled her in on the conversation and the fact that we had a meeting with David Twill in two days.

"Am I invited?" she asked.

"Well, not exactly. In fact, I never mentioned you. But no person in the law business should ever pass up a chance to visit Evanson Tribe. You will probably have to sit in the waiting room while I talk to David, but that will give you a chance to ride the escalator between floors, explore the restrooms and, best of all, marvel at the view. With any luck at all it will be one of those days when the offices are above the cloud cover and you can look out at the wrong side of rain clouds."

"Is he going to give you the Twill papers?"

"We are going to talk. That's all I know. And, despite the fact that I am not actually going to court, I will be wearing a suit."

"As well you should, and I will wear my frilly knickers."

"Give me a peek if you do," I said.

She smiled. "If you are good, I just might."

Chapter 10

Peggi and I met at my office dressed for our meeting with David Twill. I was wearing my gray suit. Peggi was crisply professional in a navy blue skirt and jacket with a shiny white blouse beneath. She carried a black leather folder too small to be a briefcase and too businesslike to be a purse. It looked very legal, although I had no idea what practical items it could contain. She twirled on her black high heels in the front office to give me a three hundred sixty degree view of her preparations and then proceeded to adjust my collar and tie. We stuffed ourselves in the Datsun and headed downtown.

Evanson Tribe Elber and Williamson occupied the top floors of a downtown skyscraper commonly called Big Pink. The pink marble building was tall enough that it swayed in heavy winds. Peggi and I parked the Datsun in Smart-Park, the cheap city lot, and hiked the several blocks that lay between the parking lot and Big Pink. Downtown was clean and cold that morning. Delivery trucks were loading goods on the kind of outside elevators that appear miraculously out of the sidewalk. Hispanic restaurant workers were preparing for the day while the pan handlers and gutter punks were still sleeping off the previous night. The men on the street wore suits and ties. The women wore dresses and heels. My gray Meier & Frank suit felt good on my body. Peggi looked confident, determined, and happy.

The ground floor of Big Pink was a grand promen-

ade of restaurants and shops. This bottom floor mall
was large enough to hold several of Torkum Masoogian's Eighty-second Avenue office buildings. The skyscraper above, constructed of glass and pink marble,
was as impressive inside as it was on the Portland
skyline.

Peggi and I took the express elevators to the top
floors, exited together, and breathed in the rarified air
of Evanson Tribe. The doors of the elevator opened
onto the windowed north east corner of the top floor
of Big Pink. The waiting room had the square footage
of an average home and was sparsely furnished with
couches stationed so that visitors faced a grand view
of northeast Portland. The big open waiting room said
that Evanson Tribe had enough money to lease the
most expensive office space in Portland and leave it
empty. The receptionist held court over her minimal-
ist domain from a small desk and console in the center of the room, allowing her to greet visitors without
distracting them from the view. On the day we arrived, the clouds had cleared enough to reveal the
Willamette River disappearing over the horizon on its
way to the Columbia. I had seen it before. Peggi was
transfixed.

"Leo Larson," I said to the receptionist, "here to
meet David Twill." She consulted the flat computer
monitor built into her desk. Whatever she saw there
confirmed that I was expected.

"I will inform him that you are here," she said in an
authentic English accent. "Please take a seat." She
motioned toward the couches. "Would you like coffee
or tea?" I looked to Peggi.

"We are fine," I said. "Thank you."

We took a seat and gawked at the city through the

big windows. Behind us was a glass-walled room that held a thirty foot mahogany conference table. I leaned over to Peggi and pointed. "Check out the escalator. The people who work here don't even have to walk between floors."

"Are you taking me along when you talk to Mr. Twill?" she asked.

"I don't think I can pull that off. You'll have to wait here. But make sure to ride the escalator and check out the bathrooms when I am away."

"Oh, I will."

After a few minutes, I was separated from Peggi by a well dressed young woman and ushered into the office of David Twill. The office was exactly what I expected; a comfortable but small pastel office with a sufficient allocation of the city view to remind the young associate that he was part of a very prestigious firm, but cramped enough that he would not confuse himself with a partner. The office was what I had imagined, but David Twill was not. Daisy was a large woman, muscular and finely chiseled. Her brother was large too, and I had no difficulty in seeing the family resemblance. David, however, had soft rounded corners. He moved slowly, almost clumsily, and in a certain unexpected way looked oafish and stupid. On this day he wore a brown wool suit that struck me as being a size too small. I expected Evanson Tribe lawyers to be thin, intense, obsessive-compulsive, and slightly threatening. David Twill looked like someone who should be singing songs to toddlers on children's television.

David motioned me toward the seats in front of his desk. His desk and office were adequately but not overly messy. Offices that were either too cluttered or too neat scared me.

"So how is Daisy?" he asked.

"She is fine," I lied. I had no idea how she was.

"Tell me. Why do you want to probate my father's estate?"

"Daisy has a document from your father stating that he made arrangements so that she would be taken care of after his death. She knows that he was able to live a fairly comfortable life without working and she thinks that whatever income he was getting should now be coming to her."

He looked up from his desk. The only thing hard about David Twill was his eyes. They were cold, empty, and masked him in the way that sunglasses do for other people. "She told you that I have the money?"

"You have it or you know where it is."

"As usual, she is wrong. I don't know where our father got that money. I don't have it, and if I find it I am willing to give it all to Daisy. I want nothing that was his."

"Do you have his personal papers?"

"I do not," he said. My case, if I ever had one, was disappearing before my eyes.

"Anita Bainbridge says that after he died, you went to his place at Everland Village and took them."

"I went there. Aunt Anita called me and asked me to take possession of them. She thought because I was a lawyer I should be the one to do it. I am not a pro-bate lawyer, however, and wouldn't have known what to do had I found them. I took an experienced paralegal from our probate department with me to the apartment where my father died, but when I got there everything was gone. I thought Daisy took them and at the time was glad she did. I wanted nothing to do with my father when he was alive, and I want nothing to do with him now that he is dead."

"Daisy doesn't have them."

"Then they are gone, I guess. I really could care less."

"Where do you think his money came from?"

"I told you. I don't know. Maybe one of his deals actually paid off. Maybe it was drug money or black-mail money." David Twill sat motionless with his hands palm down on the desk in front of him. He looked directly into my eyes as he spoke.

"Was he a blackmailer?" I asked.

"Possibly. The amount was such that it could have come from blackmail."

This was new to me. "Do you know how much he got?"

"I saw a check once, money order actually. I found it while going through his wallet to steal lunch money after he had passed out on the couch. It was for six thousand dollars. I believe he got one every month."

"I thought it was more."

"You listen to Daisy too much. To her everything he did was oversized. To me everything he did was small, mean, and pathetic."

"Other than being a drunk, what did he do that was so wrong?"

"Mother ran out on Daisy and me once, when we were too young to remember, and eventually the hurt went away. My father ran out on us every morning. He had another family in the bars on Morrison Street. Every day he walked out on us anew. When I was old enough, I ran away to live with my cousin, Miley Bainbridge."

"The son of Anita Bainbridge, who was married to the vice president of the gas company?"

"You have been talking to Anita. Bill Bainbridge was one of many vice presidents of the gas company. Those were the days when any manager with more than fifteen years of service was made a vice president in charge of something. It was a good stable job, but he was neither rich nor powerful. He was, however, a good father to Miley."

"What did Miley think of your moving in with him?"

"Miley had children of his own by that time. You have to remember that my father was fifty-six years old when I was born. When I was nine, he became eligible for social security. When it came time for him to be a parent he had been drinking hard for thirty years. The suave and witty Duke of Morrison Street was gone. When Daisy and I were growing up our father was a pathetic, old, late-stage alcoholic."

"I get it," I said. "So you moved in with the Bainbridge's, studied hard, went to law school and ended up here?"

"Yes."

"When did your trouble with Daisy begin?"

"As soon as I moved in with the Bainbridges. She had an obsession about family and loyalty, no matter how horrible it got. I didn't share her point of view. Daisy does not handle dissent well. She stayed loyal to our father and he drove her mad. She ended up a junkie."

"Tell me about her trying to kill you."

"Which time?"

"All of them."

"That might take a while. The first time was in high

school. I was going to Cleveland High School and living with Miley's family. Daisy had dropped out of school and moved to the streets. While I was in school she was on the run or back with our father, depending on the month. Then she decided that her problems were all my fault for abandoning the family. She got all drugged up, sneaked onto school grounds, and attacked me while I was out on the track during gym class. I'm no athlete to begin with, so you can imagine my humiliation when in front of the whole class I got beat up by my sister. She had to be pulled off me by the teachers and I had to be taken to the hospital for stitches.

"After that I never knew when or where her attacks would come from. Sometimes she would walk back and forth in front of wherever I was living. Once, when I was home from college she tried to run me over with a car. Other times she would leave me alone for years at a time. The most recent one was a couple of years ago. She came here, walked right into reception carrying a kitchen knife, and told the receptionist to get me so that she could slit my throat. We called the police. The firm then stepped in and got the stalking order. She can now be arrested for just being around me."

Despite my best efforts to stay loyal to Daisy, David was gaining my sympathy. "Have you considered that all of that behavior might have been connected with her drug use?"

"I'm sure it was," he told me. "The booze and cocaine and methamphetamine drove her crazy. But you have to be fairly crazy in the first place to do all that stuff, so what came first, the chicken or the egg? At the end of the day, when someone wants to cut my throat I don't care about the underlying cause. I had a tough childhood. I didn't turn to drugs. I don't try and kill my relatives. I'm sure the underlying reasons for her behavior are of great interest to psychologists and social workers, but they aren't to me."

"She is sober now," I said. "She attends AA; she runs her own business."

"I know. I hear about her from Anita and Miley. At one point she was trying to make contact with me in order to 'make amends' or some such nonsense related to her getting straight. I am not very interested. I don't know the intricacies of drug and alcohol recovery programs, but I know they consider addiction a disease and to a certain extent they lay responsibility for the misdeeds of the addicts on the disease. That is a valid approach, I think. I, however, have a different set of beliefs. One of those beliefs is that I can choose what I will do today. A very religious person might say I am mistaken in that God has predestined everything, and what I experience as choice is the unfolding of God's plan. A scientist who sees me as a soggy bag of electrochemical reactions might find me equally mistaken asserting that what I experience as choice is actually predetermined by some complex calculus of stimulus and response. I, however, choose to believe that what I experience as choice is exactly that, a conscious reasoned decision to select one behavior over another. I choose that belief because that's the way I want the world to be. Similarly, I choose to believe that you have choices and Daisy has choices and so does everyone else. When it turned out that our father was a worthless piece of shit, I found another place to live, went to school, followed the law, and worked my way up in the world. Daisy took to the street and took drugs. Every drink she took, every drug she stuck up her nose or in her arm, was a choice she made, and she suffered the predictable consequences. If she now wants to trade in drugs for an AA group, God, and a story about how it wasn't really her fault, that's her own choice. Maybe I'd make the same choice if I were in her place. But I'm not. And no matter what she decides to believe, she has to live with the consequences of the things she has done in the past. One of those consequences is that she will be arrested if she comes near me again."

I shifted in my seat, smarting on Daisy's behalf and my own from the lecture. "One of your choices could be to forgive her. She is, after all, your sister."

"Okay," he said, "she's forgiven, whatever that means. You can pass on the message. If, however, she comes near me, forgiven or not, it violates the law, and she will still go to jail. As to her being my sister, that is a curse that I was born with. I doubt I will be rid of it soon. I fully acknowledge that we are bound to each other by being family and growing up together. However, I am not, because of that, compelled to like her, be around her, or keep her out of prison."

"No mercy?" I said.

He leaned forward in his chair, the black eyes even colder in his plump round head. "I show her mercy by choosing not to cause her harm. I have every justification for revenge, and I rise above it. Do you understand? It is because of this choice, this conscious and difficult decision, that she is alive today."

His tone announced that this line of questioning was at an end. "Let's return to the question of your father's probate," I said.

"There is no probate. My father died with nothing."

"But," I said, "there is still the fact that he supported a high-end apartment at a high-end old folks home until the very end. There was an income stream and I have no reasonable explanation of where it came from or where it went."

He leaned back in his chair. "I hope you find it," he said. "I truly do, and if you do I will cooperate in having it transferred to Daisy. But I will not be part of the court proceedings you have begun. I will not have my family history made public for no reason. If need be, the firm here will represent me and we will resist your efforts in court by all legal means."

This was no meager threat. My case was weak, and even a good case had problems when Evanson Tribe was intent upon opposing it by all legal means.

"On the other hand," he resumed, "my firm has always been very supportive of me in the difficulties surrounding my sister. The lawyers here have helped me in several instances both before and after she came here threatening to kill me. They are continuing to be supportive. Evanson Tribe understands that Daisy has probably incurred a significant debt to you for attorney fees in pursuing this matter. The firm is willing to offer you twenty-five thousand dollars to be allocated between you and Daisy as you see fit. Some of it, maybe most of it, would go to you so that you are adequately compensated for the time you have put into the case. The remainder, if there is any left after your bill is paid, could be distributed to Daisy as a small compensation for the trouble she has gone through."

"And what do you want for this money?"

"You will withdraw the petition to probate my father's estate. You keep Daisy, me, and my firm out of the court system and out of the newspapers. The case goes away. You get some money. Daisy gets some money, and we never see each other again."

"It is a generous offer," I said. "What I don't understand is why you would pay to get rid of a case you don't care about. If your father had no money and you don't have his documents, what difference does it make whether she gets appointed personal representative and pokes around."

He smiled. "First, I don't care as long as I am left alone. Second, I'm not paying a cent of this. My firm feels that I will be a more satisfied employee and more attentive to my job if it relieves me of any distractions related to the activities of my sister. Lawyers here stepped up and got the stalking order that protects me from her. I imagine the legal fees for that were more than twenty-five thousand. We are not an inexpensive firm."

"I've heard that."

"Please discuss this offer with Daisy. And when you do, be frank about the realities of her position. Our father had income, but by today's standards it may not have been that much. He was after all a pathological liar prone to pretending he had skills, contacts, and assets that did not really exist. I have little idea what he may have done or earned in his youth. However, a lot of income sources, whether they be pensions or blackmail payments, end at death. You have no evidence that there is anything to probate except for his furniture. My offer puts a reasonable sum of money into both of your pockets. You should take it."

I leaned back in my chair and did my best at acting like I had better options than his measly twenty-five grand, but behind the look I had decided to accept the offer. Daisy got some money and I got paid. I'd done a lot worse many a time.

"I will give it serious consideration," I promised.

"Thank you. Please let me know your decision as soon as possible. If you decide to take it we will have a check delivered to you the same day."

David and I stood and shook hands goodbye. His handshake was gelatinous and warm. I returned to the reception area. Peggi was sitting on a couch talking to an old man in jeans and a plaid loggers shirt. They were laughing together. Peggi caught sight of me approaching and pointed me out to her companion. He stood as I approached.

"This is Leo Larson," she said. The old man smiled and stuck out his hand. As I shook it, Peggi continued, "Leo, this is Dan Evanson."

After she said his name, I recognized him from his picture. Peggi had been chatting with the eighty-year old senior partner in Evanson Tribe.

"I'm honored to meet you, Mr. Evanson," I said. Despite his age, he was still a vigorous man. His blue eyes sparkled with humor and old western friendliness. David Twill's eyes protected and defended him. Dan Evanson's eyes engaged the world around him.

"Call me Dan," he said.

"That might be hard for me," I responded. "You are a bit of a legend."

"I put my pants on one leg at a time." Peggi mugged at me with her I-told-you-so look.

"I suppose you do," I said.

"Miss Iverson and I have been passing the time while you talked with David. Pursuant to your instructions, we rode the escalator."

"Oh, good."

"I think you are very lucky to have her in your office."

"I feel the same," I said.

"It's has been a pleasure talking with you," Peggi said to him. "I've got something to brag about now."

As we walked back to the car I told Peggi about my interview with David Twill and she told me about her interview with Dan Evanson. She had spent the entire time talking to old man Evanson about everything under the sun except the Twill case. According to Peggi he was just a down home good old boy who happened to get lucky in the law business and, although not really understanding how it all came about, felt as blessed as a pig in shit. He had asked briefly about her work with me, but according to her didn't make a big deal of it. Mostly they talked about the view, the places they could see, and how the city had grown and changed over the years.

"So what are we going to do with Daisy's case?" she asked, finally returning to the subject of our trip.

"It's over," I said. "I have no evidence that old Elmo Twill really had any money when he died. Evanson Tribe is paying us twenty-five thousand to go away. I split that with Daisy. She gets something, I get paid good white-collar wages for the time we put in and we move on to the next case."

Peggi eyed me suspiciously. "Are you okay with that?"

I told her I was. In fact, I was overjoyed with that. The case had begun to look dark and stormy—a case in which I could waste hours and hours of work struggling against a firm that had more money, more talent and more time than I did. I'd had plenty of those kinds of cases in my life and they had never worked out. Sometimes, however, in the middle of one of those stormy day cases the clouds would open for a moment allowing the sun to shine and letting a little money fall in my pocket. When that happened, I knew enough to breathe easy, take the money, and live to fight another day. I was putting to bed a case I probably should never have taken and getting paid well for it.

When I arrived back to the office I had a message from Spiritual Ed on the answering machine and I returned the call.

"Have you read the book?" Ed asked.

"Twice," I said. "Treated it like a text book."

"What did you think?"

"Made me want to read more, Ed." I knew how to be ingratiating when I had to.

"I thought that might be the case. Your next meeting with the committee is this Friday. Same time."

"I'll be there," I told him. When I hung up Peggi was standing in my office. She had her hands on her hips.

"Shall I call Daisy about settling her case?"

"No," I said. "Not yet. We need to let the offer rest first."

Chapter 11

Friday evening I ate a cheeseburger and fries at the Fat Rooster, went back to my apartment, and waited for my meeting with the Avians. Again I turned out the light in the front room and watched Avian house from the bay window of my apartment. As the meeting time approached two men arrived together in a late model Toyota. Just before it was time for me to leave, Spiritual Ed showed up in the silver Mercedes. This time I wore a raincoat over my sports jacket to give me some protection against the winter cold. The coat wasn't much help, and by the time I got from my front door to the steps of Avian House, I was feeling the chill.

Spiritual Ed answered my knock. "Welcome to round two," he said as he shook my hand salesman style and helped me off with the overcoat. "Tonight we start on the real program."

"I am looking forward to it," I said. The room was exactly as before. I surmised that the library, like most libraries, was seldom used.

"Did you read the book?" he asked.

"I told you I did."

"You will be quizzed."

"I'm ready."

Ed had me sit in one of the chairs in the library while he went back into the conference room, presumably to make preparations. I bided my time perusing titles on the shelves around me. After about ten minutes Ed returned and invited me into the conference room. Once again I was directed to the chair at the end of the table. This time there were only two men other than Ed, both wearing blue robes and masks. Hal was not among them. Ed put on his own mask and took the seat at the other end of the table.

"Gentlemen, we are here for the second consideration of Leopold Larson. His nomination has been presented to the membership and no person has exercised the right of rejection. He presents himself here today as having followed the instructions given him in the first consideration and ready to prove his compliance. Leopold Larson, have you read the first book in *A Program for Life*?"

"I have," I said.

"And what is the name of that volume?"

"*Introduction*."

"What are the four principals that we will study in the Program?"

"Sobriety, spirituality, integrity and satisfaction."

Ed proceeded to quiz me on the contents of my first little blue book and I breezed through. I am good at tests, particularly ones where the people administering the test want you to pass.

After about fifteen questions Ed switched to his most sonorous voice and asked, "Shall we conclude that this applicant has successfully crossed the first bridge?"

"It is concluded," the others chanted.

"Avian Henry," Ed said, "Please mentor our applicant on the nature of belief."

The man to my right took a small card from his lap, put it in front of him, and began to speak. "We came to believe," he said, "in Step Two of the first program that a power greater than ourselves could re-

store us to sanity. And as we came to believe the belief
became reality so long as we continued upon the path.
This was no coincidence, for in believing that we
could be saved from our addiction we made it possible. In believing that a power greater than ourselves
would return us to sanity we brought that power into
our lives. It is not a myth. Believing can alter the material world around you." The man had started out
stiffly, referring to the notes on the paper in front of
him, but as he continued, the power of his convictions
gave him confidence. He turned to look at me directly
through the eyeholes in the blue mask.

"Your faith—your belief—can change the world for
you. It brought you sobriety and it can bring you the
stuff of your dreams. Humans were designed to believe what is true. You cannot believe that black is
white no matter how hard you try. Even if your life
depended upon it, you could not believe it. If you can
believe, however, you make it true. You make it true
for you. I learned in the first program how to use belief to escape addiction. I learned here in the second
program how belief could bring me whatever I
wanted."

The first program, I surmised, was traditional AA.
The second program was in the little blue books.

"In the first program we learned to be grateful for
what we had. People learned even to be grateful for
the fact that they were alcoholic because the alcoholism led them to the first program. Here you will learn
to be grateful for the treasures that you have yet to receive, for you will believe that they are coming, and in
that belief you make their arrival inevitable.

"The power of belief, that power inherent in each
of us has formed the world we live in. Christianity,

Judaism, Islam, communism, capitalism, monarchy, democracy; they are all manifestations of mankind's ability to believe and cause the world to conform to the system of belief. What works for mankind can also work for each of us. If we believe that we shall be possessed of riches, that we shall arise from poverty and obscurity, and then enforce that belief with action, what we believe will come true.

"In the first program we learned that courage comes through faith and that fear ought to be classed with stealing. Fear is the age-old enemy of belief. In our addictions fear drove us, and the first program taught us methods of setting aside fear. We inventoried our defects of character, we listed our fears, and we cleaned up the wreckage of our past so that we could begin life anew without the burden of guilt. We learned to pray and meditate. We learned to take our personal inventories on a daily basis. The result was recovery from addiction, from a hopeless condition of mind and body. We saw the miracle of the program first hand.

"But that is where many of us stopped. Our fears had been listed but the fear problem had not been solved. We had learned to believe in a power that would return us to sanity, but we had failed to follow the natural implication of what we had learned. We were delivered from addiction by the most powerful force in the universe and then were taught that we should cast it aside, being forever grateful for what we had received and forever forbidden from using the power again. We as Avians reject that boundary.

"Leopold Larson we offer you a pathway to wealth. We invite you to define wealth in your own way. For many of us it means material things. For some of us it means respect or fame. For others it means political power. The first program allows you to define God for yourself, asking only that it be a power greater than yourself. We allow you to define wealth according to your own desires. Once you can do that, once you can see wealth in your own mind, we provide you with a way to believe that you shall obtain it, and when you truly believe, the achievement of it will be inevitable." The man stopped and looked at his notes. He then looked at Spiritual Ed and the other masked man across from him. Both gave him nods of approval.

He continued, "This may all sound fantastic to you. We do not expect you to believe it all right now, but soon you will see things in your life that may convince you. Now all we ask is that you be willing."

My instructor made eye contact with the other two and they chanted in unison, "Leopold Larson, are you willing to believe?"

The setting didn't leave much room for discussion. I answered, "I am willing," and in fact I was. I was always willing to believe. I had been willing to believe the Episcopalians. I was willing to believe in the law the way Bonnie Kutala did. I was willing to believe in AA. I was quite convinced that I would be better off if I could believe in all of those things, but when the day was over and I was all alone with my thoughts, belief never came for me.

"I am willing," I said again. Spiritual Ed looked at the other masked man. The second man began the next part of my lesson and working without notes spoke more confidently than his predecessor.

"Leopold Larson," he said, "ours is a program of action. To believe in a way that will change your life will require that you focus your mental and spiritual energies. *A Program for Life* teaches you to do this. The first hurdle you face is to identify what you want to achieve. If you want money, write down how much. If you want a new car, find a picture of the car you want and keep a vision of it in your head. In the first program you took an inventory of those things that held you back from the sunlight of the spirit. In this program you will create an inventory of the blessings you are about to receive. You will not receive them if you cannot see them.

"During the next week you are to take paper and pencil and begin to inventory the blessings that you are soon to receive. You are to write them down. Do not skimp on this step. It must be as thorough as your fourth step under the first program. You may have desires that you do not want to fully acknowledge, that you would not want others to know of, desires that you are ashamed of. Be brave and put them down, for you will not receive what you cannot envision, and to the extent that you omit things out of fear or shame, you deny yourself true wealth. When making this list you should include material things; you should include positions of power or influence you want to achieve; you should include the relationships you want to develop; and in sexual matters you must be explicit about your needs. Remember that you are creating your future. If you skimp on this step you diminish what you shall receive and in the end you diminish yourself." He leaned back in his chair, comfortable and confident with his words.

"Once you have identified and described each of your desires, I want you to make an outline ranking each of your aspirations in order of importance. The outline should be brief, but sufficient to allow you to bring up a mental picture of each aspect of the wealth that awaits you. Each morning and each evening you are to review the outline. You will visualize yourself having each of the things on the list. You are not to wish for them. Desire and want are not your friends. You are to believe that they are yours, that each of them has already been received. In your mind, see the new car, the new bank account, the new lover, the new relationship with God. See yourself having them and being happy with them. This will draw these things to you, and what you have envisioned will become reality." He stopped and looked at Ed, then back at me. "Are you willing to do these things?"

"I am," I said.

"Let it be so," they answered in unison.

Ed then spoke. "You may ask questions now."

"Can I envision world peace?" I asked.

"You can," he said. "You can also do the steps of Alcoholics Anonymous and expect someone else to get sober. Your question tells us that you are far from understanding the journey you are about to take, but each one of us has been where you are. It will be clear to you in time. We do not offer a way in which you can remake the world around you. You will remain as powerless over the world and the people in it as you have always been. Instead, through the power of faith, the power of belief, used in a benevolent yet disciplined fashion, you will obtain from that world the things to fulfill you."

"So keep it simple?" I asked. "Don't over think it?"

"Precisely, at first. The power is to remake *your* life, not to remake the world around you."

"What happens when I have my list?"

"You will learn more at the next meeting. Eventually you will be asked to share your vision with another member. That member will be your mentor and may make suggestions. Often people do not know what they really want. You will find it useful to have help from someone who has been through the process, someone who has made mistakes, sought out a kind of wealth that in the end did not satisfy and had to start over again. You would do well to listen to what your mentor has to say. It is not our job to tell you what goal to seek, what wealth should mean to you, but it is our duty to let you learn from our mistakes."

"I appreciate that," I said.

"Do you have more questions?"

"How about the networking thing—where we help each other out in our businesses and stuff like that?"

"You have enough to do getting started on what we have talked about tonight. And the truth is you don't have much to offer right now. Your time will come, but for now work on your program. To keep you on track we are giving you the second volume in *A Program for Life.* It is called *The Power of Belief.* It will explain in more detail the things we have told you tonight. Have you brought the first volume, the one we gave you last time?" I took if from the breast pocket of my coat. "Lay it on the table. For the time being you must concentrate on one volume at a time. We will return the first one to the case." Ed looked at the other two men and asked, "Do you have anything further for Leo?" Both of them indicated by head nods that they did not. "Our meeting then is adjourned."

I could see what was coming and without being asked joined in the closing chant of "Let it be so." Ed indicated with his hand that I should remain seated while the other two left the room. When they were gone, Ed took off the blue head covering. His voice dropped to the familiar. "How are you doing Leo?" he asked. "Is this scaring you?"

"A little, Ed," I said. "I'm not sure about the robes and the masks. It is a little spooky."

"It seems unnecessary at first, but it serves a purpose. You will understand later. Try not to judge too quickly. The robes and the masks remind us that what we do here is not business as usual. It is apart from the rest of the world. It is something special and important, something to be treated with respect. No, it is more than just respect. What we do here is sacred and should not be profaned with the normal trappings of worldly matters."

"I suppose," I said. "The Shriners wear fezzes too."

"Yes Leo, but we are not the Shriners. You will never see these robes or these masks outside this building."

When we returned to the library the other two men were gone. Ed turned out the lights and walked me down the stairs to the street. "Do you know what you are supposed to do now?" he asked.

"I do," I said.

"We will contact you soon with more directions."

I walked back to my apartment in the January cold. In the dark front room I could see the security lights on across the street at Haven Appliance. I turned up the heat in the apartment and sat in my front room thinking about the evening. I read the first twenty pages in the new blue book. They were right. It was the same stuff they had talked about in the meeting with a lot more examples and inspirational stories.

How would I define wealth? What did riches

mean to me? I hadn't the slightest idea. Start simple, I thought. I looked around the room. It was furnished with the old flowered couch and a green chair my last wife had given me because she didn't want me to leave the marriage with nothing. Neither the couch nor swivel chair belonged to me or to the room. The picture of Mount Hood on the wall had been left by the last tenant. I didn't like it or dislike it. I left it up because it was easier to leave it there than get a different one.

I closed my eyes and tried to visualize the room as my own, with my own furniture and my own pictures on the wall. It would be a brown couch. No flowers. Not leather, but something sturdy and masculine. The chair would be larger and there would be an ottoman for my feet. The wall would have three pictures. Nothing realistic. Just patterns. There would be a television here so I didn't have to sit in the kitchen to watch. And the kitchen would be different. I wanted stoneware plates, light brown, and heavy silverware with forks that only had three tines. Out front I would have a green Ford Explorer with four wheel drive.

I sat and imagined myself with those things, and as I did so, for a moment, I could believe that I had them —that I was sitting on the brown couch and that the Explorer was waiting for me outside. The visualization put me to sleep and when I woke up at two o'clock in the morning on the couch it still had the flower pattern my ex-wife had been so fond of. I slept in late on Saturday morning. After breakfast at the Fat Rooster I took the Datsun to Schleifer Furniture, opened a charge account and bought myself a brown couch, a chair, and three abstract paintings for the wall. The young sales woman at the furniture store fawned over me and complimented me on my taste. I chalked the compliments up to the commission she was about to get, but felt oddly proud of myself for finally doing something about the front room. After lunch I bought new silverware. The pieces were heavy and comfortable in my hand and the forks had only three tines.

When I got back to the apartment after the shopping trip I called Don Yerke, the godfather of Lawyers Helping Lawyers.

"Leo," he said, "where you been? You haven't been at meetings."

"I've been going to Murdock's," I told him, "but I'm thinking of coming back to lawyer meetings."

"Why's that?" he asked. Don had always had a soft spot in his heart for Murdock's. Whenever he had a pigeon who couldn't seem to get sober despite the best efforts of the treatment centers and the other lawyers at the Lawyers Helping Lawyers program, Don would take them to Murdock's. On occasions I would see Don there, and when I did I would look around the room for a new face, some well dressed but frightened lawyer being shown how he might end up if he didn't get with the program soon.

"I'm tired of Murdock's," I said.

"Go anyway," he told me. "You aren't going to find better AA at a lawyers meeting." Maybe not, I thought, but you will find more intelligent people. I had called to ask him about the Avians but the conversation had taken a turn that made it seem like a bad subject. "Don't over think this stuff, Leo. How is the practice?"

"It's okay. Paying the bills."

"Good. Come see me some time. We'll have lunch."

"Yeah Don, I'll do that soon." I'd been promising to have lunch with Don for three years and it had never happened. I had also been promising myself to start going to the lawyers meeting again. The lawyers meetings were not the greatest places to get AA, but they were good places to meet and talk with other lawyers. A person could make contacts there and get referrals. I had the feeling that if I was going to ever be fully accepted in the profession I needed to do more with other lawyers and less with the folks at Murdock's.

They didn't hold lawyers meetings on weekends, so that Saturday night I went back to Murdock's. The place was crowded and smokier than usual. All the reasonably comfortable chairs had been taken by those members with so little to do that they could come to the meeting an hour early to get a good seat. Lawyers meetings at least had decent furniture. I decided to wait outside on the sidewalk where I ran into Copper John.

"John," I said, "have you ever heard of a place called Avian House?"

He looked at me blankly and thought for a moment. "Can't say as I have, Leo. What is it?"

"Are you sure? Spiritual Ed never mentioned it to you?"

"Not so much that it made an impression. You might ask Hardhead." He leaned against the outside wall and lit a cigarette. "Leo, how come you never speak in meetings?"

"I have nothing to say."

"I never heard of a lawyer with nothing to say."

"I never heard of a cop who couldn't keep his nose out of other people's business."

"Talking in meetings is part of the program."

"And where," I asked, "in the Big Book does it say that?"

"It doesn't, but those slips you get signed are not going to keep you sober."

"And talking will?"

"It might."

I went back inside, asked Hardhead Steve about the Avians, and got the same answer I'd gotten from John. I took a seat in the back and waited for the meeting to start. Just before the meeting began, Daisy and Churley came in and took seats close to the chairman. Little Annie was chairing. That night she was stable and managed to lead the meeting in a fairly standard manner, but I still could not follow the proceedings. Copper John was chain smoking. Diane, one of the street people, had arranged cosmetics from her grocery bag on the table in front of her and was meticulously applying what appeared to be her third or fourth layer of makeup. Hardhead Steve was walking around the room pushing bad coffee on anyone who had emptied more than a quarter of his cup.

Before my second wife threw me out, we lived in a small ranch home on the edge of Portland. It was the least expensive house in an expensive neighborhood. During that marriage I had become enamored with home maintenance and took great pleasure in getting up early every Saturday morning to mow grass, clean gutters, and fix fences. One fall I decided to rid my lawn of various agricultural blights by killing the grass completely and starting from scratch. I sprayed the lawn with herbicide, and once the grass was dead, rented the power tools it took to remove the dead grass, turn the earth, and replant. The new rye grass came up thick, green, and beautiful. All was well until the following spring when the crabgrass in neighboring lawns began to bloom and send out tiny explorers whose job it was to establish colonies. Some of those explorers embedded themselves in my new lawn. And thus my war against crab grass began. Every night I would come home from work and before changing my clothes or taking off my work boots I would examine my lawn and dig out any crab grass that had grown that day. At first it was fun. I could lay on the cool rye and crawl around tending it, keeping it pure. But after a while things changed. Whether in my own lawn or other people's lawns, all I could see was the crabgrass. I would visit other people's houses and instantly notice if they had crabgrass. At the park or the baseball field I could no longer see the expanse of green, but only the patches of clawlike crab grass in its midst. In my effort to eliminate imperfection, I had become incapable of seeing anything else. This Saturday night it was that way at Murdock's. All I could see was the dirt and the smoke and the crabgrass.

After the meeting Daisy came over and took the chair next to me.

"So how's our case?" she asked, smiling. She put her hand on mine. I found the gesture irritating. I couldn't bring myself to tell her about the settlement.

"No change," I said. "I'll let you know if anything develops."

"Okay," she answered, "I trust you."

Sunday afternoon I was back at Hal's Place with the New York Times crossword. Hal was in his usual spot behind the register. The bar was empty. He barely looked up as I pulled up a barstool next to his spot by the register.

"What'll it be?" he asked.

"Soda water," I said, "and a few answers."

"No answers," he said.

"Come on, Hal," I pushed. "I didn't even know you were in the program and now you show up at Avian House. How long have you been sober?"

"Twenty-two years?"

"So what's with the Avian's? When did you join them?"

"Twelve years ago."

"What am I getting into? The way I see it I get invited by Ed who is some kind of stock broker with visions of grandeur. I get told that I have been anointed by God to join the rich and powerful and the first person I meet who I know is the guy who owns the dive bar I used to drink in."

"It's not about being rich or powerful, Leo," Hal said, "it's about having the life you want and helping others to get what they want. This dive bar provides me with a comfortable living. I wouldn't have it without Avian House. But it is not about making a lot of money. This is the life I wanted. This is what I would have chosen had I not become an addict. I am not like you. I have no education. I know the army. I know bikes, bikers, drunks and hookers. All I ever wanted was a place like this, a dive bar with my name on the front where I make a little money, pay my taxes, and grow old among the people I know. I had nothing, even in sobriety. Then one day I was asked to join Avian House. I did what they asked and my life changed. Now I own the bar I used to pass out in."

"So why me?" I said.

He looked at me. "I don't know. I had nothing to do with that. Somebody nominated you. Other people checked you out without your knowing. I wasn't part of it."

"So who else is in? Anybody famous?"

"You will learn that when you learn it. All I can say is that you don't want to fuck around with this. Follow directions. Do what you are asked to do and don't be a smart ass."

"What about AA?"

"Be patient and keep an open mind. I got sober in AA and I will never forget that. You may find some of the things you learn at Avian House shocking. Or at least I did. I watched. I investigated, and I have seen how what you learn in AA in the beginning sets you free from the disease, but it also holds you back. We believe the one hundred founders meant AA to be more than it is. Bill Wilson and others, mostly others I believe, have changed AA from the road to the destination. Go to Murdock's. Look around you. Murdock's does not have to be the end of the road for you."

Monday morning I was back in the office paying bills when Peggi came in. "Olga just called from Judge Bohum's court. He signed off for payment in the Freeman case."

"Call Booter and Welk," I said. "Have them cut me a check." Carl Booter was the professional conservator in the case. He knew what side his bread was buttered on and was always quick to cut the check for the lawyer who got him the job.

I called Bonnie Kutala at the Office of Morals and Ethics. "It looks like I will be dismissing the Twill probate," I said.

"Very wise of you, Leo. Are you finally taking my advice?"

"Absolutely. There was also the fact that Evanson

Tribe was so terrified of facing me in court that they gave in to my every demand."

"You are lying to me again."

"It's the truth, Bonnie. Call and ask them."

"I may just do that."

"And now that I am dropping the Twill matter, can I take you out to dinner?"

"That's still a no, Leo, but thanks for asking."

"You have me under your spell, Bonnie."

"Goodbye Leo." She hung up. I turned to the skills I was learning at Avian House and visualized Bonnie Kutala giving me a blow job.

Later that morning I got a call about my Datsun. A dealer down Eighty-second Avenue had noticed it parked every day in front of the office and wanted to buy it. According to him, he had a customer who was rebuilding a Datsun and was willing to buy one for parts. At Peggi's insistence that I grab any chance to dump the Datsun we found ourselves a mile or so down Eighty-second Avenue shopping for cars at World of Wheels.

Eighty-second Avenue is Portland's auto row where used up jocks go to make a living when their athletic days are over. Driving down Eighty-second you see them waiting for prey on the steps of the white double-wides the dealers use as offices. When Peggi and I pulled into World of Wheels, however, none of the young white shirted vultures approached us. Instead, we were directed to the rotund and jocular owner of the lot, Mr. L. J. Horton. Mr. Horton, dressed in plaid pants, suspenders, and red penny loafers, barely mentioned the Datsun. He gave my hand a vigorous shake, winked a flirtatious wink at Peggi, and waved his arm toward the lot full of cars.

"Don't worry about sticker prices," he said, so we didn't. Peggi, consistent with her trailer park upbringing, gravitated toward the American sedans with big engines. I liked the Subaru's with their Northwest tree hugger connotations, but when I saw the gently used green 2002 Ford Explorer I couldn't resist. It was the one I had imagined in front of my apartment the night after the meeting at Avian House. I internally reprimanded myself for not imagining a brand new one and told L.J we would take it. He was detached and seemed unconcerned with either car or the price he got.

"Give me the Datsun and two grand," he said. This was a deal even I could afford. We did the paperwork, I wrote him a check, and I drove away in the new Explorer. I liked the car and liked being seen in the car. I had emotionally connected to the dented and rusted old Datsun because it worked and because I was as dented and rusted as it was. In the Ford I felt clean, new, and a part of the world. As I began to feel noticed, I began to notice other cars. It seemed, suddenly, that every third car in Oregon was a green Ford Explorer.

"We should've got a Lexus," Peggi said, imputing some sort of joint ownership to the vehicle.

"Why's that?"

"A lawyer should drive a Lexus."

"Next time we'll get a Lexus." I looked surreptitiously down at Peggi's legs. I thought that a Lexus would be nice but there was more room to lift her skirt in the back of the Explorer.

We took the new car back to the office and settled back in to work. That afternoon I signed two new probate cases, good cases with enough money involved that the heirs wouldn't begrudge a few thousand going to the lawyer. Just before quitting time, Peggi came in the office.

"Are you going to tell Daisy about the settlement today?" The offer from Evanson for the Twill case was another nice piece of fruit hanging out there just ready to be picked.

"Maybe tomorrow," I said.

Chapter 12

One of my probates went to hell on me when my client disappeared with all the estate money, so for a few days Peggi and I had no time for Daisy and David Twill. No one called me from Avian House. My new furniture arrived. The couch didn't fit the room, and the pictures had been a lot more attractive in the big furniture showroom than in my abused Victorian flat. I was impressed, however, by the fact that everything I had visualized that night after the second meeting at Avian House had come to be. I had new furniture and a green Ford Explorer. I was a beginner. I had not visualized well, but I had visualized and believed, and everything had come true.

I read my little blue book a couple more times and visualized more things, trying not to feel stupid as I did it. It was hard to be convinced of the cosmic power of belief because I wanted something and went out and bought it, but I remained willing to give the blue books a chance.

At night I kept an eye on Avian House from my apartment window. No one came or went. I had a key to the front door, but I didn't feel right about going in there alone. Instead I sat on my new couch and thought about stuff. I thought about commitment and whether, after my experiences in law, marriage, and Episcopalianism, I had it in me to be an Avian. I had blown my two marriages. I had been suspended from my profession for about as many years as I had practiced. I had no long term relationships with anybody except Peggi Iverson. My commitment to AA and Murdock's was not going to win me any prizes and the Avian House thing was screwing with my head.

Ed and the Avians were offering everything that had been missing from my life. What Hal said about Murdock's was true. It was a dead end for people who had so screwed up their lives that there was no place else for them to go. When I considered myself one of those people, it didn't seem so bad, but if I wasn't, if I really could do better, then how could I refuse to take up my bed and walk again? Or was I simply destined for places like Murdock'? When crunch time came would I quit and limp back to Murdock's because at the end of the day that is where I belonged?

After waiting two weeks for someone from Avian House to call, I decided to go there on my own. Late one evening, I checked my key ring, took a small flashlight from the kitchen, and headed to Avian House. A heavy cloud cover blanketed the city, and the warehousemen had gone home long ago. Although I had a key and permission to enter at any time, I didn't want to be seen.

The key fit and I slipped through the door. I considered leaving the lights off and using the flashlight but decided that from the outside the light from a moving flashlight would attract more attention than the reading lamps. With the lamps on the room was exactly as it had been the evening of my initiation. I stood at the shelves in the library and browsed through the books again, largely so that if anyone appeared I would be found doing exactly what one is supposed to do in a library. I tried to feel comfortable in the room, to make it mine, but I could not. I went over to the glass case containing the blue books. It was locked. Enlightenment, it seemed, would be doled out one volume at a time. Locked out of the glass case I began exploring the rest of the building.

The lone hall led away from the front door, past the conference room where the Avians had held my two instruction sessions, and ended in a small kitchen. The building had at one time been a residence and the kitchen had never been remodeled for commercial purposes. It had a refrigerator, gas range, and microwave that would have looked at home in my apartment. I checked the cupboards and found the predictable collection of cups, spoons, and saucers. They had enough kitchen gear to serve coffee and donuts but nothing for the preparation of real meals.

At one side of the kitchen was a door to a stairway. The door was locked. I returned to the library, took a copy of James's *Varieties of Religious Experience* from the shelf, and opened it to a random page. I had no intention of actually reading, but I felt like I ought to be holding a book. I sat there for half an hour fidgeting and trying to convince myself to go home.

Instead of going back to the apartment, I began to search the room. It was a tactile search. I ran my fingers over the door frames, across all parts of the window frames, anywhere where one might hide a key. The key to the glass case was easy. They had hung it on a small hook on the back of the book case leaving just enough space between the case and the wall to allow the key to be retrieved by a flat hand. Finding the key to the upper floor took longer. It turned up in an empty coffee cup behind the cleaning supplies underneath the kitchen sink.

I turned out the lights in the library and used the key and my flashlight to get safely up the stairs. On the second floor there was a small landing area with another chair and a reading lamp. To one side of the reading area was a storage room with old furniture, janitorial materials, and a stack of cardboard boxes. Some of the boxes were the shipping containers for the books that made up *A Program for Life*.

Opposite the storage room was an office. The front window of the office faced the street and next to the desk was the lamp that was always on. Like the other furniture at Avian House, the teak desk looked expensive. Behind it sat a genuine Aeron office chair that had put someone back a pretty penny. I had a two hundred dollar counterfeit version of the same chair in my law office. I sat down behind the desk and booted the computer. The hard drive whirred and the Microsoft audio logo boomed through the speakers. The sign-on screen showed login's for two users and a guest. One user was Ed. The other was someone named Ian. Both of the user logins required a password. I tried a few obvious passwords—'avian,' 'bill-wilson,' 'password,'—and gave up. I logged on as 'guest' but was locked out of Ed and Ian's files. I turned my attention to paper.

A bookshelf on one wall held twenty-five or so ring binders that looked like organizational records. I checked the spines and took out the one labeled 'membership.' It appeared to be exactly that, the membership of Avian House with names, addresses, admission dates, and sobriety dates. I thumbed through. I knew Ed, and Hal. Dan Evanson was a member. The rest were strangers to me. I had no doubt that, as Ed said, the names represented the rich and powerful in Portland, but I had never paid enough attention to the rich and powerful in the city to recognize them by name. I remembered also Hal's observation that it was not all about becoming rich. Becoming rich was Ed's dream, not everybody's.

I put the membership binder back and looked at the other folders. One of them held the corporate records for a corporation called Food for Life Inc. The corporation had been created in the sixties. The bylaws were boilerplate bylaws from that era and were printed on paper from the law firm that was the predecessor of Evanson Tribe. I would have expected the Avians to be organized as a non-profit, possibly even tax exempt, but Food For Life Inc., if it was part of the Avians, was a standard for-profit corporation. I thumbed through the minutes. Most of the minutes consisted of some director who I had never heard of resigning and being replaced by another director who I had never heard of. I skipped over most of it and turned to the back, to the section tabbed as 'stock transfer ledger." There was only one entry. All of the stock was owned by the Bergan Twill Charitable Trust.

For a moment I just stared at the entry. There was a trust. Or there had been a trust. Somehow in the past, old Bergan Twill had hooked up with the Avians.

I went back to the bookshelf and examined each binder. The Avians had been busy over the years. There were records of corporations, partnerships, trusts, and all manner of business transactions. I figured out that the records were shelved loosely by date, with the most recent at eye level near the computer and the older ones lower down and farther from the desk. On the bottom shelf near the corner of the room with the oldest of the documents I saw an old spineless binder held together with metal posts. The title page inside declared it to be the Bergan Twill Charitable Trust. The trust document was about fifty pages long and was written in the old style legalese with all the "forthwiths" and "heretofores."

I found a legal pad in the drawers of the desk and sat down to take notes. The parties were Bergan Twill, trustor, the creator of the trust, and John Murdock, Trustee and "a member of Alcoholics Anonymous." It was dated July 15, 1955. I read and scribbled notes on the legal pad. As I worked I tried to remember the law-school definition of burglary. I wasn't sure if what I was doing qualified, but I knew that it could get me disbarred.

I had about half a page of notes when I decided my method was too time consuming. Although there was no copier in the office there was an inexpensive printer with a scanner. I returned to the computer and logged in as guest again. From there I could scan, print and access the internet. I put the first page of the trust into the scanner, and while it scanned, went to one of my throwaway email accounts on the web. I planned to scan the trust and mail it, page by page if I had to, to my office.

The computer was old and progress was painfully slow. One at a time I placed the pages of the open trust document onto the scanner, scanned it to a file, and emailed it to myself. By the clock the work went well, but in my head every scan was taking hours. I was down to the last three or four pages when I heard the downstairs door open. I knew that I had locked it behind me when I came in. Whoever was down there had a key.

"Who's in here?" yelled someone from the first floor.

I was trapped. The only way down was by the stairs. I sent the computer files I had created to the computer recycle bin and emptied it. I held down the off button on the computer, causing it to shut down silently, then put the trust back in its place on the shelf. I could hear the person downstairs as he moved from room to room. There wasn't much to search down there. He would soon be on the stairs. I tip-toed out of the office and into the back room to look for a hiding place among the boxes and cleaning supplies. As I moved about the room by flashlight I saw something that I had missed when I first passed the room. In one corner were three cardboard boxes about the size of apple boxes. They were taped shut, and someone had written upon them in black marker the words, "Elmo Twill." The downstairs door to the stairway opened.

The storage room had a single window. It was one of those double hung windows used in every Victorian house ever built. I turned the latch, grabbed the handle at the bottom, and the window slid open. Outside, no more than three feet away, I could see the roof of Haven Appliance. Like most Victorians, the side of the building was as plain and unadorned as the front was ornate. There was, however, a small ledge between the two floors, just wide enough to support me on the outside. I awkwardly maneuvered my six foot body through the window and held onto the window frame with my fingers to keep me anchored against the outside of the building. Holding on with one hand, I was able to use the other to pull the window almost closed. The gap between me and the roof of the warehouse was one long step for a man of my size, but I had never been brave around heights. The searcher from downstairs came into the back room and turned on the light.

It was a dark night, cloudy but not raining. In one movement I threw myself across the gap and landed on the gravel studded tar roof of the warehouse. As I landed, my ankle gave way and pain shot up my leg. Close to me a square vent emerged from the warehouse roof. I rolled behind it and lay still.

After catching my breath I peeked out from behind the vent. A large man was searching the room. He came to the window. It was Hal. He stared out into the darkness at me for probably a full minute. Peering from the lit room into the dark, however, rendered him incapable of seeing anything in the night. Finally, he closed the window and locked it. He moved away from the window and turned off the light.

I lay still for a few minutes and then began to explore the warehouse roof in the dark. With the exception of the space cut for Avian House, the building occupied the entire city block. Skylights in the roof gave off a dull glow from security lighting inside the warehouse. My eyes adapted to the dark, and the light escaping from skylights was sufficient to let me see my way without the flashlight. I made my way along the edge of the roof looking for any safe descent. My ankle was swelling in my shoe as I walked. I knew sprains from my youthful attempts at basketball. I would be okay as long as I kept the shoe on, but the moment I took it off I would be crippled.

On the opposite corner from Avian House I found the rounded handrail of a ladder leading down the warehouse wall to the street. It was about midnight and there was no traffic. The ladder ended about ten feet above street level. I climbed over the edge and descended. My ankle throbbed and sent a jabbing pain up my leg each time I put weight on it. When I got to the last few rungs I let my legs hang and lowered myself with my hands. I descended the last three rungs using only my hands and then dropped to the street. On hitting the ground the ankle collapsed. I lay against the wall to catch my breath and let the pain subside. I took out the flashlight and used it to look at my foot. The swelling above the shoe was already straining the laces on my Oxfords. As I put the flashlight away the beam fell on writing carved into the cornerstone of the building. It said, "Emily Foods."

I realized as I sat there that old Bergan Twill's bakery had been right across the street from me the whole time. The abandoned bins and silos on the roof had been storage for the ingredients that go into bread. Today, the warehousemen filled the trucks on the loading dock with appliance parts. In the past, the building had been filled with bakers and the trucks filled with bread.

I stood up and limped down the street in the dark. At the corner where I could look down toward Avian House I saw two cars and Hal's motorcycle parked in front. I crossed the street and limped to the next block. My apartment had a rear entrance accessible through an alley used by garbage men. I grimaced, clinging to the handrail on the way up to my back door. Once inside, I collapsed on my bed and took off my shoe. The swelling, no longer contained by the shoe, engulfed the rest of my foot, encasing it in a flesh cast. I hopped to the kitchen, emptied the ice trays into a plastic bag and returned to the bedroom. There I raised the throbbing foot above the level of my heart, and lay perfectly still. The pain receded. A sprain, I knew, would not hurt as long as you did what it asked of you. Keep it cool, keep it above your heart, and no matter what, don't move it.

As I lay there I thought about how stupid it had all been. I had been invited to join Avian House, had been recognized for my talents, and been offered a chance to come up in the world. I had returned the favor by burglarizing the building. I could not recall the mental process that led me to do it. One moment I was at Avian House as an invited guest and the next I was going through locked doors with a stolen key. I reached into my pocket. The key to the stairway door was still there.

I tried to recall everything that had happened. Had I put the corporate minute book and the trust back on the shelf? Had I left files on the computer? I remembered the legal pad. I could see it on the desk next to the computer, a perfect writing sample to compare to the intake form I had filled out the night of my interview. They probably knew it was me already, and if they didn't they would know it within a few hours. Hal might not figure it out. Ed would.

With the throbbing foot and my self-recrimination, I didn't get to sleep until about four in the morning. When I woke I felt better. In the morning light I accepted that I had screwed up my chances at Avian House, that opportunity had come knocking, and once again I had failed to answer. On the other hand, it didn't seem like I was really any worse off than I had been. Avian House could simply be counted along with the Bar and the firms where I'd worked when adding up the number of places I was no longer welcome. No matter what people were going to do or think in the next few days the rain would still fall and the moss would still grow.

I limped out to the green Explorer and drove myself to the emergency room. X-rays showed no broken bones or torn tendons. It was a simple but painful sprain. I would be fine in a few days. The hospital issued me one of those high-tech black walking casts with Velcro straps. The boot was a great improvement over the plaster casts they had tortured me with in my basketball days. The doctor offered me pain medication, and I declined. The foot hurt, but I was still an addict. It didn't hurt enough to risk pills.

I limped into work with my Darth Vader Velcro cast just before noon the next day. "Where have you been?" Peggi demanded.

"I fell down the stairs at my apartment."

"Does it hurt?"

"Yes, it hurts. But we have to work. Get me a trio on 1486 SE Seventh Avenue." A trio was a short report the title companies offered for free. It would tell me who owned the property under Avian House.

"What's that?" she asked.

"It's the address of a club I might join. I want to know who I'm getting involved with." She came into the office ten minutes later holding a fax. "The property is owned by Food for Life Inc.," Peggi said and handed me the paper.

"Look it up."

"I already did. It's an Oregon corporation. President is a guy named Adam Borland, address here in Portland. Registered agent is Dan Evanson."

"Your buddy, Dan."

"The one and only."

"Fascinating," I said. "My social circle may be expanding."

"About time. By the way, Daisy called. She wants you to call her back." Peggi looked at me disapprovingly.

"Call her and tell her it will be a couple more days before I have time to talk to her."

"Are you going to settle her case or not?"

"I don't know any more. Find out what you can about Emily Foods and put me in touch with Miley Bainbridge."

"Anita Bainbridge's son?"

"Yeah, the school teacher."

"Okay. Whatever you say." She left the office. The sight of her butt going out the door reminded that I still wanted her. Peggi went downtown to do research and returned that afternoon.

"It's pretty much what we knew," she said. "Bergan Twill started a small bakery here in Portland in the twenties. He named the business after his wife. It grew and made money. For a while Emily Foods provided bread for most of Portland. In 1955 he sold the business to a group of employees. Everything went down hill after that. There were disputes with the city, scandals about what was going in the bread, lawsuits among the owners, and in the end, bankruptcy. The new owners wiped out everything he had done. When old Twill died, any stock he held in Emily Foods was worthless."

"Where was the bakery?" I asked.

"Down by the river where you live."

"Get the address and find out who owns the property now." She looked at me quizzically.

"I thought you settled Daisy's case?"

"I did," I said, having no idea what effect my foray

into the records of Avian House might have on my deal with Evanson Tribe. She turned to leave and then hung on the door frame for a moment facing me. "Well, it doesn't sound very settled to me."

"Shut the door. And no phone calls."

I logged on to my computer and downloaded email. Amidst the spam and notices from the Bar were forty-six emails, each containing a single page of the Bergan Twill Charitable Trust. I transferred the pages into a single file, printed the trust, and sat down to read.

In 1955, the same year that Bergan Twill was selling his bakery he created a charitable trust that attempted to name Alcoholics Anonymous as its beneficiary. The trust was to provide his son Elmo with sufficient income to support himself and help him overcome his alcoholism. At his death all of the trust assets were to be distributed to Alcoholics Anonymous. Should Alcoholics Anonymous not be in existence or otherwise unable to accept the sums, the corpus of the trust was to be distributed to the children of Elmo Twill. During Elmo's life, income not needed for Elmo's support was to be used to advance the activities of Alcoholics Anonymous as the trustee saw fit. The first named trustee of the trust was John Murdock.

Due to my hurried departure from Avian House, the last few pages of the trust were missing. I did not have the signature page. I could not be sure that Bergan Twill had signed it, but it did not seem likely that the folks at Avian House would have kept the document for fifty years if it had been a rough draft. The other missing part was the attachment that would include the funding. A trust is only as valuable as the assets you put in it.

Peggi came back into the office holding a legal pad. She was wearing her knee-length navy blue skirt and matching jacket. She took a seat in the office and crossed her plump legs in front of me.

"Bergan Twill's bakery is now Haven Appliance," she said. "The business is owned by the Haven brothers, Damon and Arnold. They wholesale appliance parts to repair shops throughout the Northwest. The underlying land is owned by Food for Life Inc., the same folks who own the other building you asked about."

It was all about the land. Portland, like most cities, was in the process of gentrification. Money was moving from the suburbs back into the city. The poor neighborhoods were being torn down and being replaced by high priced condos and art galleries. The process had not yet reached the industrial area where I lived, but it was only a matter of time. Eventually Haven Appliance and I would be driven away. The warehouse would have to relocate in one of the suburban industrial parks. I would have to relocate into one of the big apartment buildings with an oval pool and exercise machines. The land underneath Haven Appliance wasn't worth millions today. But it would be.

"What about Miley?" I asked.

"I have a call into him," Peggi said.

"Get Daisy in here. Or get Churley, whoever you can get."

"So we're not going to settle?"

"Probably not."

"Why?" she asked. In that second things between the two of us came to a turning point from which there was no retreat. I could lie to her. I could withhold what had happened. And if I did that in this case, a case that we had truly worked on together, it would always be like that. I would be the employer and she would be the employee. I stared at her. She was looking at the legal pad in front of her, and I sensed that we both knew the next thing I would say was important.

"I did something last night that I am not entirely proud of," I began. I told her everything. I told her about the Avians, about Hal, about limping across the roof of Haven Appliance, and about the trust.

When I was done she just sat there. We were quiet for a moment. Then she rose, smoothed her skirt, and said, "I'll let you know as soon as I get in touch with Daisy."

Chapter 13

Legal cases, like sports, have a random element to them. My first wife introduced me to bowling. Under her influence, I bought myself a custom fitted ball, good shoes, and learned to curve the ball into the pocket with reasonable efficiency. However, in bowling the perfect roll is not always a strike and the most awful of rolls can, once in a while, knock down all the pins. The better bowler, the one who has practiced, prepared, and bought the best equipment, will normally beat the bowler who hasn't done those things. But not always. There is a randomness to it. And that is what makes it a sport. That wife left me, but I still like to throw the bowling ball.

In the law, the better-prepared lawyer, the smarter lawyer, the richer lawyer, wins more often than the poorer, dumber, and unprepared lawyer. But not always. Witnesses disappear or simply don't say the things everyone expected them to say. Motions are allowed that shouldn't have been because the judge was too busy to read the briefs. Motions are denied that should have been allowed because the judge didn't understand the law. I once won a case on a legal theory that I didn't present because the judge thought it was better than the one I did. Things happen.

The randomness is what attracts risk takers to the law. Over the years I'd spent a fair amount of time in meetings of Lawyers Helping Lawyers. Once or twice a year some newcomer suggested that he or she drank because of the pressures of the profession. Upon closer examination, however, it always came out that the person had been drinking excessively prior to becoming a lawyer. Alcoholics are risk takers. They are thrill seekers, and because of that they are attracted to the randomness of the law. The public abhors the randomness. Lawyers revel in it.

I knew where Elmo Twill got the monthly checks, and it looked like there was plenty more where that came from. If his father's trust owned Food for Life Inc., and Food for Life owned a city block or more of inner city Portland property, then there would have been enough income to keep several Elmo Twills drinking on Morrison Street. The question was what had happened to the rest. It certainly hadn't been spent on Murdock's. The trust had named John Murdock as trustee to use the income for the benefit of Alcoholics Anonymous. Down at the meeting hall that carried his name, the story was that Murdock had been a grumpy old man disgusted with the way AA in Portland was headed. He bought himself a coffee pot, rented a room, and started his own meeting. The group had thereafter taken on the personality of its founder. But did John Murdock, the infamous founder of Murdock's, have a secret life? Was he the trustee for the Bergan Twill Charitable Trust, writing out checks each month to keep the Duke of Morrison Street in spending money? Had he been an Avian? If so, what happened when he died? Who was the trustee now, and where was the money?

Then there was my Avian problem. David Twill, Dan Evanson and whoever else was involved at Evanson Tribe had twenty-five thousand on the table to buy Daisy and me out of the probate I'd filed for her. I had a new car, new furniture, new clients, and Bonnie

Kutala was playing nice for a change. Taking the offer from Evanson, apologizing to the Avians for the break-in, and letting the good times roll seemed like a reasonably good idea.

I stood in the office looking out the window toward Eighty-second Avenue. The rain was beading up on the window. I thought about the blue collar jobs I had held during my suspensions and the satisfaction I got just showing up, doing the work in front of me, and collecting a paycheck at the end of the day. My law practice consisted of two rooms in a run down office building off auto row. Peggi shared one of the rooms with the office machines and the reception area. I shared my office with the file cabinets, my computer, and the two client chairs. Our neighbors were collection agents, financial planners, therapists and the always delightful Torkum Masoogian. The only redeeming quality to my practice was that I was my own boss. In the two rented rooms I called home I handled the jobs the way I wanted. I was accountable to no one except my clients. Freedom is an intoxicant of its own.

I dialed the phone. "David Twill here," the man on the other end of the phone said.

"Leo Larson," I announced. "Have you ever heard of a charitable trust set up by your grandfather, specifically the Bergan Twill Charitable Trust?" I was using information that I had obtained in the commission of a felony, using it in a conversation with a lawyer from the biggest and meanest firm in Portland. The announcement had its effect. David Twill was silent.

"Never heard of it," he finally said.

"Well, you are a remainder beneficiary," I continued, "You and Daisy. The way it looks is that the trust owns some prime Portland real estate. If you are entitled to some of it, it would be from your grandfather, not your father, and unless grandpa has also offended you in some dire way, you and Daisy could pick up a serious chunk of change."

After another pause he said, "Are you turning down our offer?"

"Probably not. I have to talk to Daisy. I'll take the offer to dismiss the probate case. As far as I can tell, your father really did die broke. His income was from a trust. I can dismiss like you want, take your twenty-five thousand, and refile the thing as a trust administration case."

"I do believe," he said, "that your plan violates the spirit, if not the letter, of the offer we made."

"In what spirit was that offer made? Was it a spirit of good will in which we all, and by we all I mean Daisy, are to get what justice says we should get? Is that the philosophy at Evanson Tribe—to make sure that every person gets his or her fair share?"

"Probably not," David said, tacitly admitting to Evanson's general reputation as ruthless advocates for its corporate clients. "But in this case it was a generous offer to end an annoying situation. The situation does not end if you refile with a slightly different legal theory."

"But what about you?" I asked, "Don't you want to know whether you are entitled to a couple million dollars worth of real estate?" I was making up facts as I went along. I had no idea whether the trust had any assets at all, much less millions of dollars worth of real estate, but I figured it probably still had something in it and if it had something, why couldn't that something be a couple million in real estate.

"I suppose I am curious," he answered, "but I have very little interest in having you look into it for me. I think we at the firm are completely capable of handling any legal issues surrounding either my father's or my grandfather's estate plan. I think the fair thing to do is to accept our offer of the twenty-five thousand, sign the appropriate releases, and turn over the information you have to my firm."

"Are you sure Dan Evanson has your best interests at heart?"

"I am confident that he does."

"I wouldn't be so sure if I were you."

"You are not me. You are nothing at all like me. I don't need your help or your advice. You represent Daisy. As to me, I ask you to provide me with any information you have relevant to any inheritance or other expectancy to which I might be entitled and allow me to evaluate the information with counsel of my own choosing. If you like, I will make this request in writing, and thereafter I will expect it to be honored." He had gone into litigation mode. There was nothing more to say.

"I look forward to your letter," I said. I hung up. I knew that there would be a certified letter to follow. It would be couched in respectful terms, but would carry an unpleasant message.

I left the office early that afternoon and when I got back to the apartment there was a letter taped to the door from the management company that collected the rent on my apartment. I was being evicted. Eastside Property Management was giving me thirty days to get out. I called the contact number for my landlord and got a pleasant young lady who explained that the owner had other plans for the property. It was not eviction for cause, but a thirty day notice for no reason, the kind for which there was no legal defense. I stood in my bay window watching the warehousemen at Haven Appliance load the afternoon trucks. Down the street, Avian House was as lifeless as always.

Later in the evening I limped in my Velcro boot over to Hal's. It was a warm winter evening and Hal was standing in the doorway enjoying the break in the cold weather.

"Hi, Hal," I said.

"Hi, yourself," he responded. "You are no longer welcome here. Find some other bar to not drink in."

"Why? What'd I do to you?" I protested, but I had a pretty good idea, considering that the last time I'd seen him had been through the upstairs window of Avian House as I hid behind the venting on top of Haven Appliance.

"Don't matter why," he said. "If you ever set foot in here again you are trespassing."

Being that I was crippled and he was a biker reputed to have weapons close at hand, I chose not to argue. I limped the few blocks to Murdock's for the five thirty meeting. It was the usual collection. Although being evicted from my apartment and expelled from my favorite dive bar, I was still welcome at Murdock's. I made nice with Hardhead Steve and Little Annie by telling them lies about my foot. At meeting time I took a seat in the back. This night at Murdock's I could listen. The Avians wanted to make me all I could be. At Murdock's they left me alone.

After the meeting I got a bite to eat at the Fat Rooster, went back to the apartment, and called Don Yerke. Don had pulled the strings that got me the apartment. I explained about the eviction and whined. He immediately assumed that I had failed to pay the rent or done something else to piss off the owners. I assured him that I had not. I didn't tell him I was kicked out of Hal's. He didn't need to know I sat in bars doing crosswords. He grilled me about why I hadn't shown up at a lawyers meeting after our last conversation and what I was doing to stay sober. In the midst of this conversation I let slip something about Ed and the Avians.

"Jesus Christ," Don complained, "don't tell me you got hooked into those assholes." He always talked to me as if I was an idiot.

"They asked me to join and I said yes."

"Fuck, Leo," he said, "I thought you were smarter than that. When did this happen?" I told him about the invite from Ed and the two meetings at Avian House. I omitted the part about the trust, the Twills, and the midnight romp across the roof of Haven Appliance.

"We need to talk," he said. "Not on the phone. Here in my office. Not tomorrow. I'm busy. Come Friday. And in the meantime stay away from the Avians."

I said I would steer clear but knew I wouldn't. I had already decided that I would go back to Avian house that night. I waited until nearly midnight. After making sure the neighborhood was deserted, I put on a dark hoodie sweatshirt and slipped out the door. I limped down the street and up the stairs to Avian House. The key went in but it didn't turn. They had changed the locks. That was all I wanted to know. The next morning I had Peggi find out who owned my apartment. Eastside Property Management managed the property for Food for Life Inc. My apartment was owned by Bergan's Trust.

Things were quiet for a couple of days. I worked on some of my paying cases and let my ankle heal. Then Thursday, when I left the office, my green Explorer was gone. It had been stolen.

Peggi and I spent ninety minutes with the Portland Police explaining that the car had been there at lunch and now it was gone. They were sympathetic but said that most stolen cars in Portland were never recovered. Peggi made a call over to Heartland Mobile Estates where old motor vehicles were always in good supply and managed to borrow an abused 96 Honda Civic to get me around town until I had a more permanent solution.

The Civic was faded blue with a missing rear bumper and a right front fender the color of modeling clay. It belonged to a neighbor of Peggi's who had picked it up for a few hundred dollars because it had a blown engine. He replaced the engine but had not completed the body work. The Explorer had been a car with potential. It had four wheel drive, high clearance, and the ability to take me into the Oregon wilderness. Portland was filled with hunters, fishermen and Ford Explorers. The Civic was the kind of car the Mexicans drove. Portland was filled with those too.

I parked my new ride at Smart Park downtown an hour early for my three o'clock appointment with Don Yerke. The offices of Lawyers Helping Lawyers were on the tenth floor of an aging office building across from Portland's Pioneer Square. The square is the cultural center of the downtown area, a city block of red brick where office workers eat lunch, gutter punks gossip, panhandlers beg, Jesus freaks preach, and politicians make speeches. You can buy a gargantuan veggie burrito or a plate of pad tai from the food carts.

You can play five-minute chess with the chess hustlers. You can drink expensive coffee or sit and watch people.

Don's office was part of OLAP, the Oregon Lawyer Assistance Program, which was the social service division of our malpractice insurer. All Oregon lawyers paid malpractice insurance to the same company, a quasi-public monopoly that made sure that every attorney in the state was insured. In order to reduce payouts OLAP sponsored programs that fixed the underlying causes of malpractice. It sponsored Lawyers Helping Lawyers to keep alcoholic lawyers on the wagon and thereby reduce the amount of malpractice that alcoholic lawyers commit. It sponsored programs for over-stressed lawyers, for workaholics, for procrastinators, for career changers, and for the adult children of people who had crappy parents. If you had a problem, OLAP had a support group for you.

The OLAP programs were the bureaucratic enemies of Bonnie Kutala and her pals at the Office of Morals and Ethics. The counselors at OLAP were paid by our insurance premiums. The harpies at Bonnie's office were paid by our yearly bar dues, and that made all the difference. At the Office of Morals and Ethics, where Bonnie worked, the problems of the Bar were the fault of a few bad apples who needed to be identified and expelled from the profession. At OLAP the problems of the Bar were caused by good lawyers suffering from overwork, anxiety, and stress.

Don Yerke had worked around the OLAP programs forever. He had thirty years sober and was the first AA contact for a whole lot of Oregon's alcoholic lawyers. He was the first one in the State to have marked on his Bar application that he was an alcoholic. The fight over his admission made him famous in local AA circles, so famous that he could quit practicing law, set himself up with the OLAP and spend all his time handing out advice to other alcoholic lawyers. This result was a good one. Don, although a great sponsor and AA member, had never been much good at practicing law, staying married, controlling his obesity, or anything else. He was at his best giving advice about sobriety, and the world was better off when he stuck to that.

I poked my head into his office. "Don, how are you?"

He looked up, "Still suckin' air."

"Yeah, me too. But they are throwing me out of that apartment you got me. No reason. Can you help?"

He rolled sideways in his chair and stared at the wall to my right. "Probably not. You can find a new place on your own. Tell me about the Avians."

I sat down in one of the client chairs. Don was wearing a Portland Trailblazers sweat shirt and hadn't shaved in several days. His desk was covered with paper, his office as unkempt as his person.

"I told you on the phone what happened."

"Tell me again," he said. So I told him about my aborted attempt to be inducted into the Avians, once again skipping the stuff about Daisy, the Bergan Twill Trust, and the burglary.

"So it was Ed Ralston who pulled you into that shit?"

"Spiritual Ed, yeah," I said.

"Spiritual, my ass."

"What do you know about the Avians, Don?"

"It's an AA offshoot. Here in Oregon it's the Avians. Other places it has different names. They aren't connected in any organized way, but they all push the same crap. Bill Wilson or Dr. Bob or some combination of the AA founders had secret writings or a secret plan or something by which, if you kissed the right asses, you could not only get sober, but get rich, or whatever you wanted. I never got sucked into it, but as I understand the system you get invited, you join up, then the existing members make sure you get a little grease in the career department. Once you've got yours you are expected to repay by helping out other members. They give you some mumbo jumbo to make it all part of God's plan that you get rich and on special occasions you get to wear silly clothes. I got an invite in the late seventies from a lawyer here in town. I turned it down, and as I understand it they never make the offer twice. But if you hang in AA circles you still hear stuff. I've known about Ed Ralston for years. I know a couple of others and suspect a few more.

"The thing is, Leo, you got no business in crap like that. Assholes like the Avians have been around since the very beginning of AA. When Bill and his crowd first had some success and the article in *Life* came out, a lot of people decided they could make some money off of it. A lot of people did make money off of it and a lot of people still do make money. I'm one of them. The treatment centers make money off of it. The speakers you see at the big meetings make a living telling their stories. There's hardly a sober person in AA who after a couple years doesn't envision himself throwing off the old job and spending the rest of his life helping others get sober. But some people had a different idea. They wanted more than just helping other people get sober and getting a crappy coun-

selor's salary for their efforts. They wanted to use the
principles of the program and the existing fellowship
to advance other goals, mostly the goal of increasing
the size of their bank accounts.

"AA was nationwide by the fifties and then new
books started showing up. They were always privately
printed. Sometimes they would claim to be the secret
writings of the founders. Sometimes they had no author at all. But it was always the same thing. If the
Twelve Steps could overcome alcoholism they could
also help you conquer poverty, or poor social standing, or sexual unattractiveness, or anything else. All
you needed was to learn the secret stuff that the rest
of AA doesn't want you to know.

"Mostly these are guys who simply don't understand the program. Half of them can't even manage to
stay sober, much less get rich. AA was meant to help
the alcoholic get back into the regular world as a useful member of his family and community. These guys,
the Avians and those like them, want to make you better than everybody else."

"So what's so wrong with that?" I asked. "The Elks
do it. The Mason's do it. I'm not so well off that I can't
wear a dress and learn a secret handshake in order to
increase the number of good paying clients coming to
my door."

"If that's the way you feel, join the Elks or the Ma-
sons. You have a problem with alcohol. You do know
that by now, don't you? You need to deal with that
problem in AA. The Avian's have their economic fu-
tures riding on what happens at Avian House. Paying
their mortgages and affording their Audi's depends on
everyone playing by their rules. With money on the
line everything changes. That is what they learned in

AA when they went to Rockefeller and asked for the money to turn the program into a nationwide chain of treatment centers. He said no. He saw what the founders couldn't see themselves, that the money would tear apart the idea of one alcoholic helping another. Look what happens in the meetings. Someone goes out and screws up. He or she drinks. When it is over, they come back and the group welcomes them back into the fold. When there is money involved that doesn't happen. When you screw up with the Avians, they are going to screw with you."

"I already did and they already have," I told him.

"What do you mean?"

I gave him a very short and misleading version of how I may have looked at certain records they wanted to keep private, that I had screwed up so they knew it was me, and that a corporation created by the Avians owned my apartment. I told him about the bargain on the Explorer and how it had been stolen.

"Leo," he said, "you fucked up. You should have known better, and I can't undo what you did."

"How about a line on another apartment?"

"I'll ask around," he said.

"So what do I do?"

"Go to meetings," he said. "Don't drink in between."

"Okay. Anything else?"

"Watch your back."

I got back to the office about four o'clock in the afternoon. Peggi had her feet up on the desk while she read the new bar journal. When I was through the door she put her feet back on the floor in a way that gave me a brief but clear look at the black underwear she was wearing beneath her pantyhose. I had the sense it was intentional. "What's up?" I asked.

"Things haven't been good," she said.

"What happened?"

"Mr. Martson and Mrs. Albers both called. They are getting someone else to do their probates." They were my two newest clients.

"Did they say why?"

"No reason. They both just decided to go with someone else. And that's not all."

"What else?"

"Churley Dowd called. Daisy is missing."

"Missing like how?"

"Missing like he doesn't know where she is. He thought she might have contacted us."

"How long has she been gone?"

"A week."

"Leo, tell me the truth," Peggi asked, "Did you ever tell her about the settlement?"

"I didn't get around to it. See if you can help Churley find her."

"Leo," she continued, "are you okay?"

"I'm fine. You're fine. Everybody is fine." I went into my office and checked my bank accounts. I shouldn't have bought the furniture.

Chapter 14

I spread the pages of the Bergan Twill Charitable Trust across my desk and went over it again. The trust had two purposes. The first was to provide an income for Daisy's father, Elmo. The second was to support the work of Alcoholics Anonymous. The trustee, the person in charge of carrying out both purposes, was John Murdock, but there was no evidence that Murdock's had ever benefited from the trust. Murdock's survived, just barely, on the one large donation each year and the spare change its members contributed when they passed the basket. It was possible that the trust was never funded. More than one old geezer has hired a lawyer to write a trust and never got around to putting any money into it. In the case of Bergan Twill's trust, however, the monthly payments to Elmo had been as regular as clockwork. Someone was paying attention. Someone was writing checks every month and if they were paying out they were also bringing in.

"Peggi," I said, "get me whatever you can on a guy named John Murdock. He started an AA group here in town sometime in the fifties. He's dead now. That's all I know."

She swiveled her office chair to face me. She had on a new navy business suit and a white blouse sheer enough that it barely qualified as office attire. The slit on the side of her skirt seemed to go higher with each new outfit.

"That's not a lot to go on."

"It's all I got. I'll make some calls and try to get you some more."

The phone rang. She answered and held the mouthpiece against her shoulder. "It's David Twill."

I took the call in my office. "David, how are you?"

"Not so good, Mr. Larson. Your client tried to kill me last night." I had no response. After a moment of silence, he asked, "Are you there?"

"Yes, I'm here," I said. "I don't know what to say. Are you sure it was Daisy?"

"Who else tries to kill me?"

"I mean . . . what happened?"

"Ask your client. Let her tell you."

"I will," I said. "Listen, I have never had anything to do with any violence against you or anybody else. I don't even know where Daisy is. When I find her I will ask, but right now, tell me what happened."

"I was going into my house last night when someone shot at me. Two shots. Both of them missed, but I dropped down like I'd been hit. The shots came from a car parked in front of my house. She shot, she started the car, and she drove away."

"You weren't hit?"

"No, I wasn't hit, but it wasn't because she wasn't trying. As far as she or anybody else could tell I dropped dead right there on the steps."

"What kind of car was it?"

"Something small and fairly new. A Toyota or Nissan, or something American with a similar look."

"What time was it?"

"Just before midnight. I'd been out with friends."

"I'm sorry," I said. "I want you to understand that I had nothing to do with it."

"Your client did, though. Thus, the firm has decided to withdraw its offer. We feel that your position has been substantially weakened by the fact that your client will soon be in custody."

"You've reported this to the police?"

"Immediately. They are looking for Daisy as we speak."

I finished the conversation with a couple more apologies on Daisy's behalf, and hung up the phone. Peggi was standing in the doorway to my office.

"Someone to see you, Leo." She had a grin on her face.

"Who?"

"Daisy Twill."

Peggi brought Daisy in and the two of them took seats in front of me. Daisy was wearing a black leather jacket and matching pants. She pulled off the wet jacket. Her large breasts were tightly packed into a black bra that showed around the edges of her red Harley Davidson tank top. Her tattooed skin was dry and her face windburned.

"Where have you been? People have been looking for you."

"Up on the mountain," she said. The answer was casual, as if it was of no consequence that she had been missing for a week.

"What mountain?" I asked.

"Mount Hood. Sometimes I just have to go. To get away. So I camp for a while up on the mountain."

"In the middle of winter?"

"This is Oregon. It is only wet. I have a tent."

"Where on the mountain?"

"Here and there. Wherever I can lay down a sleeping bag. I took Dana's Harley, a bag, and a little food."

"Who's Dana?"

"The manager at Coney Bennett. She runs things when I have to go."

"Do you go there often?"

"Now and then." She was annoyed at the questions. "When I need to go, I go."

"What about Churley? He has been calling here looking for you."

"I left him and the kids a note. It was on the kitchen table. He says he didn't find it, but I sure as hell left one. Dana at work knew. It was easy enough to call there and ask. But it don't really matter now. How's it going with David?"

I sighed. Had Peggi not been sitting in the room I might have invented a lie. I left out my invitation to join the Avians and my burglary of Avian House but gave her the rest of the story reasonably unvarnished.

"You turned down twenty-five grand from David's law firm and the cops are looking to charge me with attempted murder? Is that about it?" She said it as if it were happening to someone else.

"Those two things did happen," I objected, "but they aren't closely connected. You aren't being accused of murder *because* I turned down the money."

"Isn't it just David saying 'fuck you.' I was up on the mountain. I couldn't have been shooting at him, and I don't believe anybody was shooting at him. They tried to buy you off. You said no and now they're trying to frame me. I wouldn't expect anything different." Shifting the facts to her own liking, she managed to make me a hero. "Why did you turn down the money?"

"I didn't turn it down," I told her. "I needed your permission to accept the offer and I couldn't find an appropriate time to talk to you about it. Besides, with what I'd learned about the trust, I didn't want to give away our chances at a million for twenty-five thousand."

"Fuck the twenty-five," she said. "What do we do next?"

I had no idea what to do next. As far as I could tell we were screwed. She was being chased by police. I had lost my car, was being evicted from my home, and might soon have a hard time paying my secretary. The probate case I had filed on Daisy's behalf would probably be dismissed. "I need to file something in court about the trust."

"Do it," she ordered. "Don't let the bastards win."

I managed a meek, "Okay."

"I'm going back up the hill. You said David wasn't hit, right?"

"He was not injured."

"Too bad. The cops won't be interested for long. I will be just outside of Brightwood on the Zigzag River. Forest Service road number thirty-four. About a mile off the highway there is a big log vacation cabin with a rust colored metal roof. The owner never uses it. I camp just behind it on the river. But don't come up there. I'll talk to Dana and Churley about it this afternoon. If you need me," she turned to Peggi, "talk to one of them."

"Wait a minute," I protested. "You can't hide from the police."

She gave me a blank stare. "It won't be the first time."

"Did it ever work?"

"Most of the time it did. They look for a while and then move on to looking for someone else."

"Daisy, I don't think that is going to happen this

time. Your brother works for a firm with a lot of pull. If they want the cops to keep looking, the cops will keep looking. I advise you to stand and face them."

"I'm supposed to just turn myself in and let David have at me? And what do I say when they ask me where I was last night. Then I say, 'Oh, I was all alone in a tent on the Zigzag' and they will let me go. Leo, me and Churley probably know more about cops and criminals and how that system works than you ever did."

I admitted to her that criminal procedure was not my specialty. "If you didn't shoot him, hiding makes it look like you did."

She leaned aggressively forward in her chair. "What do you mean 'if.' I told you I didn't shoot him. If I had shot at him he would be hit now. He would be dead or in the hospital. The fact that the shooter missed proves it wasn't me. Besides, I said I didn't do it and you, as my lawyer, are supposed to believe it."

"I may not do criminal law, but even in my practice people lie to me."

"I am not lying." She took a deep breath and sat back in her chair. Peggi reached over and touched her on the hand. "Sometimes I get the blues, Leo. I just can't face things any more and then I go up the hill. I've got medicine to take. It is supposed to iron out the highs and lows, but it doesn't always work. These days I can feel it coming and I go to the hills. It's just me, the tent, the bike, a little food, and the forest. I stay as long as I need to. I wouldn't shoot at anybody when I am down, Leo. That's the God's honest truth. Now the other times, I might shoot somebody, but not when I'm down."

"Does anybody see you? Is there anyone who might

be able to testify that you were up there?"

"No. The spot I have now is out of the way. Like I said, the people who own the cabin never use it. It is my own private vacation cabin with the drawback that I can't go in."

"How about food?"

"I go to the store in Brightwood if I need something. I went in there a couple of days ago for bread and tuna fish."

"The store clerk might have seen you."

"I suppose, if she remembers."

"Daisy, nobody ever forgets seeing you."

She glanced at her tattooed arms. "I guess not."

"Maybe she could be your alibi."

"Leo, I am not turning myself in. It's not my way." We were silent. I had no arguments against 'it's not my way.' Daisy broke an awkward silence. "Leo, if this trust exists am I rich?"

"Daisy," I said, "I don't know. You may be very rich. On the other hand, maybe we should have taken the twenty-five grand and called it a day."

"Fuck David's twenty-five grand," she said.

"It wasn't really his. It was offered by his boss, Dan Evanson, the top dog in the firm of Evanson Tribe, which is the top dog in the world of expensive Portland law firms."

"Fuck Dan Evanson," she said. Peggi frowned.

"Actually," I said, "I think Dan Evanson may be intent on fucking me, or maybe us, and we don't want to take that lightly. It is possible that if I made nice he might find a way to pull the police off the shooting, and he might renew the offer of the twenty-five thousand. That is a fair amount of money." After having said it I couldn't believe what a mealy mouthed suggestion it was. I consoled myself with the fact that, although cowardly, it was good legal advice.

"Are you afraid of these people?" she asked.

"I'm not afraid of them," I lied. "I just want to know you are sure before you turn down money that could feed your kids."

"I can take care of my own fuckin' kids, thank you, without any help from David or his law firm. If you want out of this case, Leo, just say so. I hired you to find out what my dad left me, or now what my grandfather left me, and you can have the job as long as you want it. But if you don't believe in yourself any more, then let me know and I'll get someone else."

I said nothing.

"And I haven't paid anything yet," she said. She reached down to her leather jacket giving me the scenic tour of her cleavage and took out a plain office envelope. She put it on the table.

"That's your retainer. That's what you guys call money up front, isn't it. It's five thousand dollars. If you need more you just say so."

Peggy grinned. I slid the envelope into my desk drawer. "Thank you, Daisy," I said. "I appreciate your confidence. If I need you, I will send someone up the mountain."

She rose, turned, and gave me a thumbs up as she left. "I believe in you, Leo," she said.

Peggi, in a freckled imitation of the tattooed Daisy, did the same, and silently mouthed the words, "I believe in you too."

The two of them closed the door to my office and I could hear the muffled sounds of female conspiracy in the other room. Daisy and Peggi were happy together.

After the conversation with Daisy, I couldn't take

the offer from Evanson even if it were renewed. I couldn't turn her over to the cops. I couldn't even fire her for nonpayment. There was nothing to do but plow forward.

Bad cases are like bad marriages. They begin with excitement, hope, and a future filled with promise. But then life, other people, and hardship raise their ugly heads. The things we believed in that first star-struck meeting turn out not to be true. Neither the client nor I are quite what we represented ourselves to be. The romance slips away, and we are stuck with making the case and the relationship work. What had been a dream becomes a business transaction. For a while we still control the case. Then one day, the tide turns. Rather than pushing the case through the courts we find that the case is pushing us through our lives. We no longer direct it, but simply try to contain it. It starts to go home with us at the end of the day. It is the reason we lose the plot lines at the movies. It is the reason we can't read novels. The case that began as a dream becomes the reason we lay awake at three in the morning unable to dream at all. In the end, it controls you. And then you will do anything to get out of it. Settle it, try it, sign the papers. Divide the property. Pay up. Get away. Forget it and rest.

In the bad old days when I got to the bad part of a case, I would freeze. I would procrastinate, leave phone calls unanswered, hide, and drink. Without alcohol to fall back upon, I forced myself to do something. Do anything. Don't think about the results. If the road is in front of you, follow it.

When the outer office was quiet again I went outside and said, "Peggi, get me in touch with Miley Bainbridge. If he'll come here, have him do it, or I'll meet him. And while you're at it I want any court records of any type on John Murdock, Murdock's, Bergan Twill, or the Bergan Twill Charitable Trust. Anything in any court."

I left about four o'clock and drove down to Murdock's for the five thirty meeting. Spiritual Ed was there. We didn't make eye contact as I took a seat in the back. It wasn't a good night for me. In days past I felt connected to people at Murdock's. I could forget my own woes and be thankful that I wasn't living on the streets or in some walk-up Section Eight apartment. But that night other people's troubles were incapable of making me forget my own.

Biker Bill droned on about his new way of life, but the word was out that Bill had been getting through his days with the help of triple pain patches. Little Annie had, in a frenzy of amateur counseling, convinced two of the newer women to reveal their sexual histories and had then proceeded to leak the juiciest details to other members of the group, making the two newcomers the object of leering male attention. Some days I could take scenes like that as humans being human, but other times all I could see at Murdock's was the craziness. There had come a time at the end of my drinking, during the really bad times, when I could drink without getting drunk. If you are addicted to alcohol the door to hell opens on the day you realize that you can't quit and can't get drunk either. AA meetings gave me relief like the relief that a drunk feels when he takes that first drink of the day. For a little while, everything is okay. But AA wasn't working for me any more, not even at Murdock's.

Thirty minutes into the meeting Daisy came in waving to the people she knew. She gave me the same thumbs up she had given me earlier in the day in my office. I nodded back at her while watching Ed. He picked up a Big Book and pretended to read, but he was clearly more interested in Daisy's arrival than anything in the book. The chairman called upon me. I wanted to tell them what I truly thought about them all, but I passed instead.

The meeting was about forty-five minutes old when Spiritual Ed got up and left. I gave him a chance to clear the doorway and followed. When I got outside he was walking toward the end of the block talking on his cell phone. I returned to the meeting and sat next to Daisy. She put her hand on mine and smiled at me.

"I think you better go," I whispered to her.

"I'm safe here. These are our people."

"Not all of them. I could be really wrong on this one, but better safe than sorry. You got to get out of here. And go out the back way." She got up as if headed to the bathroom but never returned. I went back out on the front step. Spiritual Ed was returning from his walk.

"Hi," I said.

"Hello, Leo." He stood in front of me, both of us looking directly into each other's eyes. He finally spoke. "You made a big mistake, Leo. A really big mistake."

"It won't be the first or the last, Ed."

He intentionally bumped me as he passed and whispered, "Really big."

I stayed on the front step watching the clouds gather for another storm. Five minutes later the police arrived. Two of Portland's finest double parked in front of Murdock's and got out of the squad car. The first one to the door was an older man with a beer belly.

He was followed by a dykish looking female officer. I met them at the door.

"You can't go in there," I said.

"Why not?" asked the male cop.

"It's a private club and you don't have a search warrant." I was inventing law as I went along. I had no idea whether Murdock's was a private club or whether the cops needed a search warrant to go into one.

"What are you, a lawyer?" the man asked.

"Yes," I handed him my card. "I'm their lawyer." The male cop read the card. The female's name tag identified her as Officer Ames. She just stared at me.

"That is an AA meeting," the male said. "Anybody can go to an AA meeting."

"Anybody can go to church too. That doesn't mean you can walk into a church and arrest people. Several federal courts have held that Alcoholics Anonymous has the same rights and protections as any recognized religious organization."

"I can arrest people in churches," the cop said. I'd been making it up. I read something in the newspaper about churches offering sanctuary from arrest. "Get out of the God damned way," he said, and pushed me aside. The two of them went in. At the sight of the uniforms the meeting fell silent and all eyes went to the two officers. I followed the officers in and stood behind them. Once it became clear that none of the attendees were going to speak the male cop said, "I am looking for Daisy Twill. Has anyone seen Daisy Twill?" No one made a sound. He raised his voice as if everyone were deaf. "I am looking for Daisy Twill. Has Daisy Twill been here?" Again, no response. The male cop looked at his partner and she shrugged her shoulders.

Little Leslie stood up. She looked directly at the officers and said, "I'm Daisy Twill."

Waitress Margie took the cue. She stood and said, "I'm Daisy Twill."

Big Barney, in his work boots and grease stained coveralls stood and said in his deep male voice, "I'm Daisy Twill," and the rest of the room followed suit until everyone was loudly claiming to be Daisy Twill, all except Spiritual Ed who stayed in his seat with his eyes fixed on the Big Book in his lap.

"Shut the fuck up," the cop bellowed. The crowd went silent. "I've seen fucking *Spartacus* too you assholes. We are investigating a crime here and we have a job to do. You tell Daisy Twill that things will go a lot easier for her if she turns herself in."

Someone coughed the word "bullshit" into his hand.

The cop shook his head and said "You tell her what I said. My name is Officer Aaron Mobley of East Precinct. She can call me any time." The two officers backed out the door and I followed.

"You know where she is, don't you lawyer?" the cop said.

"I have nothing to say."

"Well, fuck you then. There may come a time when you need a guy like me, and maybe when you call there will be no one there to answer. You just remember that lawyer Leopold Larson."

"Officer Mobley," I said. "It has been a pleasure."

"Fuck you, lawyer."

When I reached my apartment my heart was racing. I was not the type who could calmly piss off people with loaded weapons. I cooked up some eggs

to settle myself and tried to figure out the consequences of what had happened. The cops had been
right. She should turn herself in. The demonstration
of loyalty at Murdock's was only going to make things
worse for her.

I washed the dishes and flopped on the new couch.
I felt bad that I had never really appreciated the
apartment. The new furniture was out of place in the
old Victorian, and when I had my vision of new furniture I had forgotten to imagine comfortable furniture. I was being kicked out. Soon I would have to
pack up my unread novels and set up again somewhere new. Now that I was being forced out I decided
I liked the place.

I went to the bay window and watched Haven Appliance close for the night. Down the street the upstairs light shown once again from the second floor of
Avian House. Reminded of my initiation, I picked up
my volume two of *A Program for Life* and began
reading again from the start. I couldn't keep my mind
on it. That's the problem with the secrets of the universe. They're boring. I found a Steven King novel in a
drawer and read it instead until I fell asleep.

In the mail the next day I received from Evanson
Tribe a motion to dismiss my request to have Daisy
appointed the representative of her father's estate.
The motion was signed by a Nathan Cole, attorney for
David Twill. I'd never heard of him, but a quick check
at the firm web site filled in what I needed to know.
He was a senior associate in his late thirties specializ-
ing in probate and trust litigation. He would be
hungry for a partnership. He would be smart and
mean.

The motion to dismiss was supported by affidavits

that laid out in detail Daisy's difficult relationship with the law during her formative years and included unsubstantiated but serious allegations that she recently tried to kill her brother. The motion was the classic Evanson Tribe product. The paper was high quality, the words were spelled right, and the arguments were unassailable. Nathan Cole had gone to a lot of work to prove that Daisy should not control the estate of a man who died with no money. The case had reached the point where it was no longer about substance. It was about winning—about destroying the other side. The motion was a message to me that whatever I wanted, Evanson would deny me. If I said white, they would say black. Some cases are about the law. Some are about the facts. In some, neither matter. It is about who has the power.

Peggi's voice came through the speakerphone. "Leo, Bonnie Kutala on the line for you."

"Yo, Bonnie," I said.

"Yo yourself, Leo. I am holding in my hand a signed complaint from David Twill of Evanson Tribe about your behavior in the Twill estate and a copy of a motion to dismiss a case that you told me was settled and dismissed."

"Hey, Bonnie, I really meant to call you about that. The settlement we had sort of, uh, fell apart."

"I'm sorry to hear that. In view of what I have before me I have no choice but to open a formal investigation of your behavior."

"For what?" I protested. "A frivolous filing? You need something better than that."

"How about obstruction of justice, Leo? How about aiding and abetting a fugitive? Even lawyers can go to jail, Leo. I am taking this complaint seriously, and if I take it seriously, you should too. As far as the Bar is concerned you are on a very short leash."

"Okay, okay. What do you want me to do?"

"I want you to quit practicing law. But you don't seem receptive to that idea. I'll tell you what. Convince your client to turn herself in to the authorities, and I will see what I can do."

"Between me and you, Bonnie, I tried. It was no go."

"Try again," she said. "Try harder."

Chapter 15

Peggi stood in the door to my office. "What is *cy pres*?"

"It's Latin for a legal way to change the purpose of a charitable trust," I said. I was proud of myself. I hadn't heard the words since law school.

"The court docket in December of 1964 shows a filing under the name of the Bergan Twill Trust with the notation *cy pres*, but the court file is missing. It isn't in the archives. It isn't on micro-film."

"How could it be missing?"

"It's government. Half the files down there go missing sooner or later."

"What information could you find?"

"Not much. Whatever relief they were asking for was granted, and the lawyer was Edward Bohum."

"Who was the judge on the case?"

"A guy named Linden Brown. He's been dead for twenty years."

"How about John Murdock?"

"Nothing. No criminal record in the local area. In 1957 he got one mention in the newspaper for refusing to admit or deny that he had anything to do with starting an AA program for late-stage alcoholics in downtown Portland."

"Anonymity at the level of press, radio and film."

"What?"

"It is an AA rule. The anonymity thing. We are not supposed to talk about our AA membership at the level of press, radio, and film. Outsiders think the anonymity is to protect the identity of the members. That's not it. The anonymity is to protect the organization by preventing every crazy ex-drunk who has a few days of sobriety from declaring himself the unofficial spokesman for AA. That's why you never see the celebrities on Oprah saying they got nicked for drunk driving and joined AA. They always say they joined a support group, or a twelve-step program. We can't admit to membership on TV or in the newspapers."

Peggi sat down at the desk in front of me.

"So tell me, do you actually do all that stuff? The Twelve Steps I mean. A lot of folks in my park go to the meetings. Some of them do okay. Some don't. Do you do the part where you write down all your sins and confess them to another person?"

"The fourth and fifth steps. It's not really about sins so much. But, yeah I do it. More accurately, I've done it."

"Who do you tell that stuff to?"

"I use a preacher. Preachers can't be called by Kutala to testify against me. Most AA members use other members."

"Do you have to confess stuff you just think about, or only stuff you have done? If I had to confess about thoughts, it might get spicy." She blushed and pulled her jacket closed over her breasts.

"In that case," I said, "feel free to confess to me any time."

"I wouldn't want to scare you." She was flirting. It came to mind that she would look very attractive bent over my desk with her panties around her ankles. Our mutual titillation session was interrupted by the phone. She left my office to answer it, and I am convinced that she gave her butt an extra little wiggle on the way out.

The call was from Don Yerke. "Don," I said, "have you found me a place to live yet." Because I was being evicted from the apartment that he had found for me, I remained convinced that he should find me a new one.

"Not yet," he said.

"Listen. The reason I called you was that I need to know about early AA here in Portland. Who in town has been around long enough to have known John Murdock?"

"I knew John Murdock," Don said. "I went to his funeral."

"I don't mean later. I mean someone who knew him when Murdock's was just getting started."

"By the way, it is not called Murdock's," Don said. "AA groups are not named after individuals. It is the Will to Believe group."

"Twenty or more people have told me that," I said, "but nobody has called it anything except Murdock's since the day it opened."

"Can you get away this afternoon?" he asked.

"For you, sure."

"I will pick you up from your office at three o'clock."

Shortly before three I took coffee out to the reception area of my office and put my feet on the tiny magazine table. Peggi was proofreading my response to a motion to dismiss filed by Evanson Tribe. I was going to lose that battle, but I wanted to give them a taste of my written work in the process. I knew law too, and I wanted them to know I knew it. I eyed Peggi's legs and waited for Don.

At three o'clock Yerke arrived in all his obese glory

and said, "Let's go." He had long ago found belts use-less against his expanding paunch and wore wide red suspenders to hold up his cotton pants. He wedged himself behind the wheel of a small Ford sedan and I took the passenger seat.

"Where are we going?" I asked.

"To an old folks home. Where do you think old AA members live?"

"In AA meetings," I said, "lecturing the rest of us about what we are doing wrong."

"No. That's my job."

I expected some run down depressing nursing home operated by Romanians. Instead, Don navig-ated the little Toyota through the cold winter streets of Portland to the back side of Everland Village. When Peggi and I had gone to see Anita we had parked at the main entrance and gone in through the central dining room. Don used a rear entrance to the complex and parked in a lot connected to a four story building separate from the others. He pulled himself out of the tiny car and lumbered toward the entrance. I fol-lowed.

The interior of the building was well furnished and bright but the attention to expensive detail could not cover the odor of disinfectant and death. Everland offered the full range of end-of-life accommodations, including full nursing and hospice care. Anita Bain-bridge lived in assisted living. We were in a place were the residents needed more than an assist.

Don led me to a large hospital style elevator and up to the second floor. The doors to the residents' rooms were open and the halls were cluttered with medical equipment. The room Don took me to was larger than the average nursing home rooms, but contained the same basic furnishings—a hospital bed, chair, table, and wall mounted television.

"Leo," Don said, "I would like you to meet my sponsor, Amond Garris." Before me in a wheel chair sat a small elderly man. He was dressed in pajamas and a bathrobe.

"I am pleased to meet you Mr. Garris," I said.

"Amond," he corrected, "please."

"Amond, then. How are you today?"

"I am dying," he said, "just like I was yesterday."

Don said, "Leo wants to know about early AA here in Portland. He is a lawyer. He is working on a case, but he is also one of us." Don turned to me. "Amond has been sober and a member of AA for fifty seven years." Turning back to Amond he asked, "How old are you now?"

I could tell from his expression that Amond got that question a lot and was tired of it. "I am ninety-one years old, Don."

I sat on the bed. Don squeezed himself into the single guest chair and it creaked under his weight.

"Amond," I asked, "Were you around the city in the early days of Portland AA?"

"I was born here. I drank here. I got sober here. I met Bill Wilson and Lois in Los Angeles in 1961."

"How did you manage to stay sober for fifty seven years?" It was a stupid question.

"Don't drink, don't die." I had noticed in my practice that people have a tendency to treat very old people like children. I had been doing that to Amond and he knew it. Young people would object to that kind of condescension. Old people have seen enough of boorish human behavior to forgive it.

"What do you know about John Murdock?"

"Johnny Murdock?" Amond said. "He was a nasty little Scotsman. He first showed up at the Couch and Burnside group. Those were heady days for AA. Bill and Lois were still going around the country. Groups were starting everywhere. One of the first was a place in old town that held meetings every night of the week. In those days most of the people coming to AA were hard core living-on-the-street alcoholics. There were many then who thought that AA could only help the people who had lost everything; that it didn't have anything to offer unless you had been reduced to sleeping in doorways. But alcoholics who hadn't lost everything were also looking for a solution and started showing up at the meetings. As the Old Town meetings started to adapt to the fact that not every alcoholic had slept in doorways, Johnny Murdock became angrier and angrier. He claimed the meetings were getting soft, and that they weren't any longer based on the Big Book. He hated all the "Hi Bob" stuff. He hated sponsorship, which he claimed had no authority in the Book. So eventually he bought himself a coffee maker and started a meeting more to his own liking."

"The place that is today called 'Murdock's?'"

"He would roll over in his grave if he knew that his name has become the name for the place. He was a book thumper. To put a person's name on a meeting violated everything he believed in."

"What was he like?"

"He was mean. He lived on Social Security in a transient hotel and he chaired two meetings a day, every day of the week, until just before he died. He did AA his way, and for a certain kind of alcoholic, it worked. People too far gone to get sober at other places sometimes went to Murdock's and got it. The group was never my cup of tea, but other meetings fizzled out and died while Murdock's never changed and never died."

"Did you ever hear of Elmo Twill, The Duke of Morrison Street, Bergan Twill, or the Bergan Twill Trust?"

The old man shifted himself in his chair and looked directly into my eyes as if deciding whether he should continue or not. He looked at Don and by some unspoken message, Don indicated to him that it was okay to continue.

"Like I said, those were heady days. The article in *Life Magazine* had come out, and AA itself did not know where it would go. The promise of AA was attracting more than just alcoholics. One of the people it attracted was Bergan Twill. Bergan wasn't an alcoholic, but his kid was. From his first taste of alcohol as a teen, Elmo was off and running. It tore Bergan apart. Dad had worked his way up from nothing to the owner of a prominent and profitable bakery. He wanted to pass it on to his son, but his son was a drunk. And then AA came to town. Somehow, Bergan Twill hooked up with John Murdock. Nobody is quite sure how that happened, but I think it is simply geography. Murdock had moved his group to within a few blocks of the bakery owned by Bergan. Together they got the son Elmo to go to Murdock's and the son got sober there."

"Elmo got sober?" I asked.

"For a while, anyway. Elmo turned out to be an AA prodigy. He picked up the language very quickly, and could talk AA like nobody's business. The problem was that he couldn't stay sober. He would get sober

down at Murdock's, where John managed to limit his
grandiosity, but as soon as he had a few weeks under
his belt he would be off to other meetings to entertain,
educate, and amaze. He was damn good at carrying
the message. I saw tough cynical men brought to tears
by his talk. Dozens of people credited him with their
sobriety. God blessed him with the ability to carry the
message but denied him the ability to live it or even to
stay sober himself."

"What did his father think of all this?"

"Bergan was thrilled. Elmo was sober off and on,
which was better than he had ever done before. The
kid was also earning respect. The respect he was earning was among recovering alcoholics, but in Bergan's
mind that was still an improvement. The father gave
all credit for Elmo's success to John Murdock. Bergan, because of the success of the bakery, had gotten
to know a few of the movers and shakers around Portland. For a while he took some pleasure in dragging
Johnny Murdock around to fancy restaurants and
presenting him to his well-heeled business associates
as the answer to the alcohol problem. Johnny liked
the attention. John had gotten sober, but never made
it up the economic ladder. When they were done with
the fancy dinners, Bergan went to his nice home.
Murdock went home to a hotel room with the bathroom down the hall. Bergan stuck by John to the end,
but as far as I know, was never able to introduce him
into higher class company or convince anyone that
John was anything more than a destitute alcoholic
who had managed to become a destitute sober person."

"So what happened?"

"Nothing. Bergan quit dragging John around to

restaurants, but remained convinced that John held the secret to sobriety. Elmo's inability to stay sober eventually became well known enough that his eloquence couldn't make up for it. Then there was the car accident. His kid and wife were killed. I don't think he ever came back to Murdock's after that. Later he remarried and became the Duke of Morrison Street."

"Did you ever hear anything about a trust established by Bergan Twill?"

The old man furrowed a brow, trying to remember. "I don't know anything about a trust."

"Do you know how Elmo supported himself in his years as the Duke?"

"No. I never really thought about it. People leave AA all the time. They go back or go forward or go somewhere. I don't keep track of them. I do know that he had a sister named Anita. She lives here at Everland in one of the other wings. She was in this building for a while, but they moved her back. She is a delightful woman. Very pleasant."

"Let me try some names on you."

"Okay."

"Daisy Twill."

"Nothing," he said.

"David Twill."

"No. Nothing."

"John Edward Bohum."

"I know him. He's a judge now. Got appointed very late in life. He used to practice law in the same office with Bergan Twill's lawyer, Dan Evanson. I knew people who used to go to him. He worked hard, but as far as anybody could tell, he never made that much money at it. At an age when other lawyers are retiring, he takes a judgeship."

"How about Dan Evanson?"

"He was Bergan's lawyer for years. Dan was completely different from Bohum. Dan was a comer. They said back then that Bohum was the better lawyer, but Dan knew how to get clients. The bakery was probably Dan Evanson's first big client, but it would be far from his last. Whenever a new business arrived in town, or a small business suddenly became a big business, Dan managed to be there. He had his fingers in AA back then, but it was only because Bergan Twill was interested. AA was the new thing, and if Bergan was sold on it, then Dan was sold on it too."

"How about the Avians?"

The old man smiled. "The Avians?" he said. "I haven't heard that name in years. I hoped they had disappeared. The way AA shook out meant the folks wanting to make a buck on it had to go elsewhere. And they did. Or, should I say, they still do. Nowadays advanced AA is AA plus psychology, or social service, or therapy. Back then there was another kind of advanced AA. You would go to meetings and if you stayed sober a while and seemed to have some other talent you would be invited to join a secret brotherhood and allowed to wear goofy clothes. The attraction was the promise that you could use AA principles to get rich. The Avians were Portland's version of that story. I got invited sometime in the sixties and turned it down."

"Do you know if any of the people we've talked about were associated with the Avians?"

"I don't think so. That is, I don't know," he said. "I doubt Bohum would have been involved. Evanson is hard to say. He was a money-making kind of guy but I don't remember him being associated with the Avi-ans. They keep to themselves. Once you turn down an invite, you are on the blacklist forever. They don't ask twice and they don't gossip. So you can see they were not about to keep me apprised of their doings."

Our conversation came to an end. Don and Amond talked about people I didn't know for half an hour or so. Then Don drove me back to my office.

"So Don," I asked, as we drove back, "You've been a member of the bar forever. What do you know about Bohum?"

"Not much, Leo. Like Amond said, he got his judgeship late in life, but I never heard anything bad about him. He served as a probate judge from the start and the lawyers who practice before him think he does a good job."

"What about Evanson?"

"He's a legend. He built the biggest firm in Port-land out of nothing. Like Amond said, he may be a better rain maker than lawyer, but I don't know a single senior partner in any major firm that actually practices law any more. Their job is to serve on boards, attend events, shake hands, and bring in the business that keeps all those junior partners and asso-ciates billing away the hours. Good lawyers are a dime a dozen. A good rain maker is one in a million."

"Don't I know," I said. "Spiritual Ed knew Elmo Twill. He never mentioned to me that Elmo was once a member of Murdock's."

"Ed Ralston is dumb, dishonest, and cowardly. He pushes annuities for a living, cheating old people out of their life savings."

"I take it the two of you don't get along."

"We get along fine. Whatever he is today, he is a

better man sober than he would be drinking.
However, I don't use him as my financial advisor."

"Have you found me a place to live yet?"

"Finding you an apartment is not my job?"

"What is your job, Don?"

"My job is to keep guys like you sober on the theory that you get in a lot less trouble sober than you do
drunk. Which leads me to my little talk. Are you going
to meetings?"

"Yeah."

"Where?"

"Murdock's, of course."

"Not drinking between meetings?"

"No."

"Not going to Hal's and brooding?"

"I'm not welcome in Hal's. How did you know
about that, anyway?"

"I know everything."

"How is the practice going?"

"I can pay Peggi and buy gas. What I want is to
boost the income a little, move out of Masoogian's
place, and have a little higher class practice. Oh yeah,
and I want to win all my cases."

"You don't get what you want."

"I know," I said, "trust in God and I will get what I
need."

"You don't get what you need, either."

"So how does it work?"

"You don't get what you want. You don't get what
you need. You get what you get. Go to meetings and
don't drink."

"The meetings aren't working for me any more,
Don."

"What do you mean?"

"It used to be that I could go to a meeting and relax. I felt at home. Now when I go I get pissed off. The people there get under my skin, and I want to go home and be alone in the apartment that I am being kicked out of."

"Do you talk about that in the meetings?"

"I don't talk in meetings."

"You need to start. I have been here before with you and you went out and drank. And when you drink, Leo, your life goes to shit faster than anyone's."

"So keep going, right?"

"Right."

I went to Murdock's that night and sat in the back. Nothing I heard resonated with me. I was not like the people there. I reviewed the facts of the Twill case and watched the clock. Hardhead Steve, the chair called upon me to speak. I thought about what Don had said. I thought about telling them they were all full of shit. Instead I passed.

Don Yerke was right. You get what you get.

Chapter 16

Don Yerke never did find me an apartment. It was Peggi who came through. An old geezer who lived down the road from her died. Peggi put me in touch with the relatives and as soon as they had the old man's belongings cleaned out, I became the newest resident of Heartland Estates. Peggi lived at one end of Lonely Street and I lived in a baby blue trailer house at the other end. Packing my belongings didn't take as long as I expected. The warehousemen from Haven Appliance let me take boxes from their cardboard pile, and carload by carload I moved my stuff to Baby Blue. I moved the bed and the new couch with the help of Pepe, a Mexican with a van. Peggi, who was responsible for getting me the little mispainted Honda, was now responsible for my housing as well. By her association with me she had come up in the world from traffic flagger to paralegal. At the same time I had descended the socio-economic scale from a classic Victorian bachelor pad in the warehouse district to a used double wide off auto row. What really pissed me off was that the trailer was actually more comfortable than my apartment. Unlike the Victorian, the manufactured home was tight, draft-free, and warm.

The old couple across the street brought me a broccoli and cheese casserole to welcome me to the neighborhood. I went to Home Depot and bought a webbed aluminum lawn chair. On the Sunday afternoon before my eviction date I sat it in the carport of my new trailer home, did the Sunday crossword without Hal's silent help, and waved at my elderly neighbors. My Victorian apartment across from Haven Appliance had style. My new baby blue mobile home, with carport and aluminum storage shed attached, had community. It was a community of the elderly, the handicapped, and the chronically unemployed, but it was community nevertheless. In an odd and depressing way, I liked it.

The following Monday I got another packet of legal papers from Evanson Tribe. The lawyer for Evanson had added to his motion to dismiss the probate a request that the court fine me personally for filing a case in bad faith. I returned the legal favor by filing a new case asking the court to interpret and enforce the terms of the Bergan Twill Charitable Trust. In the petition I alleged that Daisy was a beneficiary of the Trust, that John Murdock, deceased, was the trustee, and that Avian House, Food for Life Inc., and other unknown parties were either successor trustees or beneficiaries. Evanson filed a response on behalf of Food for Life Inc., asking that the second case be consolidated with the probate case and that both of them be dismissed. In support of the motion they alleged that there was no such trust and that my claims were desperate fabrications to prevent the probate proceeding from being dismissed. They also renewed the request that I be fined. I filed a motion to allow me to take the sworn testimony of David Twill and Dan Evanson. They opposed the depositions and sought more fines. For the next few weeks Nathan Cole and I played a game of histrionics and hyperbole in court documents that had numbers down the sides. He failed to accuse me of burglary but he accused me of almost every other misdeed a lawyer could commit and there were ample hints in the pleadings that if I did not back off the police would come knocking at my door.

Copies of all the pleadings sent to the court ended up on the desk of Bonnie Kutala. She made occasional calls to remind me that if I did not cease and desist from whatever I was doing I would be disbarred. I responded to her calls by saying whatever I could to piss her off and trying to get her to go out with me. While no one associated with the Twill case seemed happy with me, the elderly couple across the road at Heartland Estates came over a couple of times a week and seemed genuinely pleased that a lawyer lived across from them.

Judge Bohum was uncharacteristically grumpy about the case. He was normally gregarious and willing to drag lawyers into chambers for a bit of arm twisting. In the Twill case, however, he was staying quiet. The lawyer from Evanson repeatedly demanded a hearing on whatever motion was pending. The judge denied every request for a hearing and ruled upon written submissions. The rulings always went against me. Nathan Cole and I did not talk to each other directly. There was no reason for us not to talk. People sometimes just decide not to talk to each other. Lawyers do it a lot. Our communication consisted solely of terse transmittal letters and legal arguments.

"Miley Bainbridge has agreed to see you," Peggi said. She was standing in the doorway of my office wearing a dark red jacket and seemed to have grown taller.

"How did you get him?" I asked.

"I called up and asked him to meet you," she said.

"Very clever. When?"

"Tomorrow. You are buying him lunch at the Ringside."

"Can I afford to buy him lunch at the Ringside?" The Ringside was at the upper end of my food budget.

"Use Daisy's money. Wear the gray suit." She looked hot in red.

Shortly before noon the next day I slid the shiny butt of my gray suit across the leather seats in the bar at the Ringside and ordered a soda water. The Ringside was an upscale steak place attached to one of Portland's public golf courses. The bar was one of those leather-and-mahogany hard liquor bars where businessmen in shirts and ties drink single malt whiskeys and watch the golfers tee off on the back nine. The Ringside was the kind of place that gave drinking a good name and the kind of place in which I never drank. I drank at Hal's. I drank at the windowless taverns with the pool tables and little sausages in a gallon jar, but I didn't drink in places like the Ringside.

I spotted Miley Bainbridge because he came on time and looked like he was looking for someone. Bainbridge was closer to my age than Daisy or David Twill. He wore a yellow sweatshirt and sweat pants, both bearing the duck logo of the University of Oregon, my undergraduate alma mater. He was going bald but made up for it with blond moustache and goatee. The man was attentive to his surroundings, looking at the bar and the other patrons with the curiosity of someone who had never been there before. He recognized me by Peggi's description, introduced himself, and slid onto the seat across from me. When the waitress came, we both ordered burgers and soft drinks.

"I am afraid I am underdressed," he said, nodding toward the line of suit-and-tie businessmen drinking their lunches at the bar. "I teach high school English. Teachers used to hope that by dressing in clothes that command respect they would influence teenagers to dress in a manner that respected education. Unfortunately, the teenagers won that battle and influenced the teachers to dress like slobs. It is only when I get away from school that I realize it."

"Your dress is fine, especially the Duck shirt. I was a Duck myself." He smiled, but didn't answer.

"I understand you are Daisy's lawyer."

"I am," I said. I gave him my card.

"I don't envy you that job. She is quite a handful."

"She is," I agreed. "Today, however, I am trying to find out as much as I can about her father and her grandfather."

"I knew her father of course. Everybody knew Elmo. I don't know if I can help you much regarding our grandfather. I was eight or nine when he died. I remember him but they are all kid memories. You can talk to my mother. She can tell you whatever you want to know about him."

"I have talked to her already. She is delightful."

"Mother lives in a bit of a fantasy world—in a past that never really was—but in certain respects it is a better world than the one we have."

Our food came. We turned our attention to the burgers and ate in silence. Then Miley continued.

"I was about eleven when my cousin Andrew and his mother were killed in the car accident. Andrew was three years older than I was, and I looked up to him. Then, both he and his mother were gone. It was traumatic for everyone: my mother, my grandfather, the whole family. After that I didn't have much contact with Uncle Elmo. There was no reason to see him. He remarried, but his second wife, Lena, never became part of the family. Elmo had always had trouble with alcohol and after the accident he took to drinking again. I didn't know about the drinking at the time because my parents kept it all hush-hush. I didn't have much contact with Elmo or his second set of kids until the eighties."

"Did you have brothers and sisters?"

"I'm an only child. Dad worked for the gas company. He started out installing gas lines and by virtue of showing up for work and not getting fired, he was promoted to paper pushing. He retired a low level vice president. My mother was a homemaker and sometimes volunteered at Cleveland High School where I teach now. I was a straight B student in high school, went off to college, and returned to the neighborhood to teach English in the high school that I graduated from."

"Do you like it? The teaching, I mean."

"I like it. I work a hundred and ninety days a year. I get a Christmas vacation, a spring break, and summers off. I have a good union and a great retirement account. Best of all, ninety percent of the people I have to deal with every day, students that is, are dumber than I am. It makes me feel smart."

"That's got to be nice."

"It is, but you have to stay in the school to keep up the illusion. That's why I don't go to places like this very often. A thorough knowledge of *Huckleberry Finn* and *To Kill a Mockingbird* doesn't get you very far in adult society."

"Are you cynical?"

"Not really. In my heart I buy the 'children are our future stuff' but I don't like to lay it on too thick."

"How did you end up with David Twill in your home?"

"I was back from college and used local connections in the union to land the teaching job. I got married, bought a house, and figured I would get to know my extended family. Uncle Elmo had two children, my cousins, who I knew nothing about, so I made an effort to find out who they were. I tried inviting Elmo and the kids over to the house. Elmo would accept and then cancel at the last minute. But he was usually willing to send the kids.

"Daisy and David were the saddest children I had ever seen. She was the mother of the house, fiercely independent and loyal to both her little brother and her absent father. David was like a deer in headlights all the time. Daisy would put him in the middle of the living room while she went to help my wife with something and he would just stand there staring, as if he were lost in the forest. My own children were toddlers and they adored their older cousins just because they were older. Daisy tended to them like she tended to David, but David never really seemed to notice them. He would come over carrying an armful of his books and sit in our den and read. I would take all of them, David, Daisy, and my own kids, on outings. We went to the zoo, or museums—places like that. David would go along, but would never really engage with the world.

"It became clear to me that they had nothing at home. Daisy was raising David and doing it on whatever she could beg or steal from their father. Elmo kept the water running and the electricity on but that was about it. I had them over to the house once a week or so for a couple of years. Daisy pretended it didn't matter to her, but we became a lifeline to normal living. Eventually Daisy discovered boys, David wasn't cute any more, and the system broke down. One summer day Daisy was out with friends and I had David over to the house alone. Evening came and he refused to go home. He begged to stay with us, and said if we sent him home he would run away. We managed to get hold of Elmo and asked if David could stay a few days. The few days turned into forever."

"How did Daisy take it?"

"It drove her mad. I don't know when she started with drugs, but it wasn't long after the move that she was a regular outside our windows in the middle of the night screaming and swearing for David to come home. We would call the police and they would either catch her or they wouldn't. She ran away from home soon after David left, lived on the streets, and the streets were probably no worse for her than the empty house. I tried to get her help, but I'd been teaching long enough to know that there was not much I could do. Kids will run their course. In the end, adults don't have much to do with it."

"What course did David run?"

"In a sense, David was the perfect kid, at least a lot more perfect than any of my natural ones. He was a straight 'A' student. He did his chores around the house, he was polite, he did what was expected, but he never really lost that 'deer in the headlights' way about him. He lived in our family without ever connecting to it. He did what good kids did and reaped the rewards, but he never gave me the sense that he had internalized it. I think he was so scared of having to go back home that he would have done anything anybody told him to do in order to avoid it. He remained a bookish kid. I come from an outdoorsy family. My mother and father taught me to hunt, fish, and camp. I taught the same to my children. David did those things with us but never took to it, and I doubt he has been out of the city since he left my house. He lived in the home of a school teacher, so he went to school and did well at it. If he had lived in the home of a meth cooker, he would have cooked meth and been good at it."

"How did he become a lawyer?"

"One time when he was with his father he went to a law firm downtown and came back wanting to be a lawyer. Unlike most kids he never changed his mind. I asked him about it several times, and he couldn't really tell me why. He talked about the building and the way the lawyers dressed. He wanted to live like they lived. He set his mind on working in a downtown firm and accomplished it. I think his father may have helped him with that. I never knew him to talk to Elmo, but they communicated somehow. As an undergrad he worked summers in the firm started by his grandfather's lawyer, and I am pretty sure it was Elmo who got him the job. After he graduated he got a full scholarship to law school from some foundation I never heard of. I think that Elmo had something to do with that too, but David never talked to me about it. Between getting his four year degree and going to law school he got his own apartment and that was pretty much the end of our relationship. We get nice Christmas cards every year, but he doesn't visit. I spent a decade with him and I don't really know who he is."

"How smart is he, really?"

"He's intelligent. There is no doubt about it. He is well read, book smart, and a survivor. But in the big picture he is really only a notch or two above the rest of us. He did great at a state college and graduated near the top of his class at an average law school. He is local talent, he is not national talent."

"Capable of being a big fish in a small pond."

"Like most of us. The trick is in finding the right pond."

We talked about other things for a while and watched the golfers teeing off in the drizzle outside. After a bit Miley made his excuses and left. I watched him walk out and could see the genes of Bergan Twill in him. Daisy was big and muscular. David was big and soft, but both of them wore their bodies like uncomfortable clothes. Miley was not like that. He was comfortable in his skin.

I went back to the office to find Officer Mobley and his dyke sidekick parked in the lot of the Villanova Building. The police car was positioned for a quick exit and blocked most but not all of the entrance to the parking lot. The two of them got a good look at me as I squeezed the rumpled Civic by them to my parking place.

"Nice ride," Mobley said, sneering as I walked from my car to the building.

"It has one great quality," I said, "it's paid for."

"So where is Daisy Twill, Larson?"

"I'm her lawyer, Mobley, not her mother."

"Well, she don't have much of a lawyer then." He got out of the car.

"Mobley," I said, "why don't you make a disability claim and stay home watching Oprah like the rest of the force?"

"It ain't about me, Larson. Ms. Twill, your client, fired a gun at a citizen and we intend to bring her to justice. If we need to disturb some alkie lawyer to do that, we will."

I held up my hands in a gesture of surrender. "Listen, Officer Mobley, I am just doing my job. If I were to tell you where she is, there is an enforcement officer over at the Oregon State Bar who will have me disbarred and take a lot of pleasure in it. If I get disbarred, I have no other skills and will have to turn to crime. In the mean time, Daisy Twill is no threat to anyone. By keeping her whereabouts secret I am actually advancing the goals of law enforcement."

"I think you have already turned to a life of crime," he said.

"And how's that?"

"How did you get a copy of the Twill Trust?" I thought back to the night at Avian house, the trip across the roof of Haven Appliance and the sprained ankle. There was enough there for both Bonnie Kutala and Officer Mobley.

"And does the police academy have a course on the Uniform Trust Code as well as the Criminal Code?" I asked.

Mobley glanced over his shoulder at Ames. She was attending to paperwork in the squad car. He lowered his voice. "I didn't say I understood trusts," he answered, "but I do understand burglary. Sometimes people steal jewelry and stereos. Sometimes they steal copies of trusts."

I fell back on my old ways. When cornered, make things up. "And sometimes a person doesn't need to commit crimes to get copies of trusts because someone with legal access to the trust wants it to be public."

It worked. Mobley was not absolutely sure I was lying and walked away from the conversation. "If you change your mind, Larson, call me." He got back in the police car.

The office was empty. Peggi was gone, the lights were out and the answering machine was on.

I had work to do in the office but couldn't do it. I put my feet up. I turned on the radio and turned it off again. After half an hour or so, I locked up the office and got back into the Civic. My first stop was Coney Bennett. I parked just down the street in a spot that allowed me to see in the windows. People were lined up outside waiting for food. Inside, Churley and the punk woman were making hot dogs and fries. Churley's Harley was parked outside. I left Coney Bennett and drove up Highway 26 toward Mount Hood.

On clear days a person can see Mt. Hood from Portland. This wasn't one of those days. The clouds were close to the ground and a light rain hung in the air. I needed the car heater.

A few miles out of Portland the forest crowds in around Highway 26 creating a cold green tunnel to the mountain. Thick soft moss covers the rocks and tree limbs. Forest ferns, the scraggly sick versions of their domesticated cousins, fight for life in the darkness beneath the pines. The floor of this forest is mushy with rotting foliage. Wild rhododendrons fill in the few spaces that get sunlight, but for the most part the darkness and the acidic poison of rotting pine needles prevent anything except moss from growing in the darkness.

Small desperate businesses have punched holes in

the trees, their owners eking out a living off campers and skiers traveling from the city to the recreation areas higher up. The people who live on the slopes and earn a living from these businesses both despise and depend upon city dwellers like me who stop briefly at the bait shops and pizza parlors on our way somewhere else.

Where the gift shops, coffee stands, and last chance hamburger shops end, the national forest begins. This is where I was headed. The bottom part of Mount Hood National Forest is a honeycomb of dirt roads and cabins. These recreational structures sit on government land with hundred-year leases. They are second homes for Portland's elite. The mountain residents, with their junk yard lots and clapboard houses, hate the flatlanders who own these cabins the most of all. It is hate for the rich, for people who own a home they don't need, who treat a house as a toy. The forest cabin that Daisy had described was one of these.

I took the turnoff to Brightwood, a small town consisting of a tavern and a convenience store, and turned onto forest road thirty-seven. The dirt service road wound for several miles through the somber green forest. The homes were cabins only in the loosest sense of the word. With electricity, phones, microwaves, and multiple bedrooms, all of them were nicer than my trailer in town, and all of them were deserted until spring.

About a mile in I spotted the cabin with the red roof that Daisy had described. I pulled into the circular driveway. The cabin was built with artificial logs, huge round dowels stained brown and mechanically weathered. It stood two stories high and had a small satellite dish on the red metal roof. I could hear the rush of the Zigzag River. I got out of the car, walked around the cabin and down hill toward the sound of the river.

At the back of the cabin a broad redwood deck extended on stilts over the sharp drop to the Zigzag. At the bottom of the drop-off there was a small meadow tucked in a turn of the river. Daisy's camp was at the edge of the meadow. The camp consisted of a medium-sized dome tent, a camp stool, and a small fire pit. Daisy herself sat about twenty yards away in rain gear staring at the rushing river. I picked my way through the forest toward her pushing wet pine boughs out of my face as I went. I thought that the sound of the river would cover my approach, but as soon as I emerged into the meadow she turned to look.

"You live here?" I asked when we got close enough to hear each other over the sound of rushing water.

"I do," she said. "Would you like some coffee?"

"You have coffee?"

"Sure, from this morning. It will just take a moment to heat it up." She led me back to the tent and started a one-burner propane stove. In a few minutes I had a hot cup of coffee. The rain had started to fall harder. "Come inside," she said.

We crawled into the tent. The inside was immaculate. A sleeping bag sat rolled up in one corner. Several items of winter clothes lay folded against the tent wall. She had a Coleman cooler and a metal box for dry foods. I took a seat between the two food containers and cupped the coffee in my hands. On top of the cooler lay a thirty-eight caliber revolver.

"What are you doing here?" she asked.

"The police were asking about you this morning.

They hang around my office. I wanted to see how you are doing."

She waved her hand at her surroundings. "This is how I'm doing."

"I had lunch with Miley Bainbridge today."

"How is Miley?"

"He seems fine. What do you think of him?"

"He's okay. I used to hate him for taking David away from me, but I hated everybody then. I don't see it that way any more."

"Did you hate David too?"

"Sure. He left us and went to live with Miley. I hated Davie for leaving and Miley for taking him."

"He says that you harassed them at his house."

"I did. It was years ago."

"Tell me again that you didn't try to shoot David."

"Leo, I didn't try to shoot David." Daisy was calmer and more relaxed than I had ever seen her.

"What's that?" I nodded toward the pistol.

"It's a thirty eight caliber Smith and Wesson revolver, and it's loaded."

"What's it for?"

"Protection. For my protection out here, and not for shooting my brother."

"Okay," I said, "I just wanted to hear you say it."

"How is the case going?"

"Not so good. Bohum is holding or denying everything we file. The probate I filed will be dismissed. It might be dismissed because of your criminal background. It might be dismissed because there are no assets to probate. The trust case I filed—the one where I ask the court to enforce the Bergan Twill Trust—may be dismissed because I can't prove there is a trust."

"I thought you had a copy," she said.

"I have part of a copy. And I can't really explain how I got it."

"How did you get it?"

"Daisy, I stole it. I burglarized a place called Avian House and I stole it."

She laughed out loud. "Way to go, Leo. When was this?" I proceeded to tell her about the Avians, Spiritual Ed, and the burglary.

"I take it things would not go good for you if they can prove you broke in there."

"I will get disbarred. They won't bother with criminal charges. I won't go to jail but I will never be able to practice law again, and that is the only thing I know how to do."

"If you told them, could I win my case?"

"I don't know. The law is always a crapshoot, but unless I tell them something, I will lose."

"Lose it then."

"You're okay with that?"

"It's just money. I make good money at Coney Bennett. I don't want you to risk your law practice to get me money."

"Daisy," I said, "how did you come to own Coney Bennett?"

"I bought it. The guy who owned it before me wanted to sell and I made him an offer. Churley and I make monthly payments. How did you think I got it?"

"I didn't think anything," I lied. "I just wanted to know. About your case, I don't know that I can lose it."

"What do you mean?"

"I don't know if I can keep quiet and lose the case."

"Even if it costs you your law office?"

"Even then."

We were silent for a while. We sipped our coffees and listened to the sound of the river.

"Why didn't you join the Avians?" she asked.

"I was going to . . ." I couldn't finish the sentence.

"But, you broke into their headquarters instead."

"Yeah."

"How long have you been sober now, Leo?"

"Three years."

"Do you do the program. I mean do you do the steps and all that stuff."

"I try to," I said.

"Me too."

Daisy stayed at the river and I drove back to town. The rain pounded on the car roof as I drove back down Highway 26 to Portland.

Chapter 17

I got back late to Baby Blue and stayed up much of the night thinking about Daisy giving me permission to lose the case. That was a new one for me. I'd had clients before who had demanded assurance of victory, and all it did was make me tentative. Permission to lose was an invite to do anything. I slept in late the next morning. When I finally got to the office Peggi was hard at work.

"The court called," she said. "Judge Bohum wants a prehearing conference in Twill tomorrow afternoon."

"How can we have a prehearing conference when there is no hearing scheduled?"

"I'm just passing the message. You're the lawyer."

"Smart ass." I went into my office, closed the door and called Olga at probate court.

"Olga," I snapped into the phone, "How can you set me for prehearing conference on one day's notice when there is no hearing scheduled."

"I didn't do it," she protested. "Judge Bohum's orders."

"What are we supposed to do at this conference?"

"I don't know," she told me, "you're the lawyer."

When I arrived at Bohum's court the next day, Olga said that Nathan Cole from the Everson firm was already in chambers. She escorted me in and motioned toward the empty chair next to Cole. Bohum was not at his desk.

Nathan Cole had cut his legal teeth in New York.

Lawyers from New York, most of California, and probably a lot of other parts of the country practiced law differently. In Oregon, we clung to the idea that lawyers all belong to one big club. Big firms differed from small firms. Small firms differed from no firm, but there was camaraderie across the spectrum that allowed hearing dates to be set with a phone call and cases to be settled with a handshake. We managed cases with the belief that a good relationship with other lawyers was ultimately in our client's best interest and that no individual case was worth destroying those relationships. Part of the rule was that you never made another lawyer look bad in front of his client.

Nathan Cole came from a different culture in which amiable relations with opposing counsel was considered both a sign of weakness and a failure to zealously advance the goals of the client. Reducing the cost of litigation, one of the consequences of courtesy, was pointless if your client had unlimited funds, and many of the clients of Evanson were nationally known companies with bottomless bank accounts. For these clients, reducing the cost of litigation was little more than bestowing a benefit on the enemy. Similarly, maintaining amiable relations with other attorneys and allowing them to look good in front of their own clients did nothing to advance the interests of a client whose corporate policy was to crush all opposition. Lawyers like Nathan Cole were kept on staff at the large Oregon firms to do interstate litigation with other lawyers like himself, usually outside of Oregon. There was no reason, other than simple meanness, to assign him to me.

But assign him they did, and he did the kind of lawyering that he was paid to do. Not only did his filings with Judge Bohum's office address the legal arguments in Daisy's case, they also addressed Daisy's and my personal shortcomings in excruciating detail. Cole claimed that I had filed the probate case in bad faith in order to continue Daisy's harassment of David. The trust case, he asserted, was part of the same plan. Unless I could produce a signed trust, a trustee, and some evidence that my client was entitled to something, the whole thing should be dismissed and I should be sanctioned by the court, the Oregon State Bar, or both.

That day in Bohum's office was the first time that I had seen Nathan Cole in person. He was a short dark haired man about thirty-five years old. His well tailored gray suit emphasized his athleticism. When I came in he was paging through his file and jabbing at the margins of his papers with his pen. He was doing it to avoid looking at me. This was war. To make eye contact would be to personalize the enemy.

I took the seat next to him and browsed my own file for no particular reason. After a few minutes Bohum came in and laid the Twill files on his desk.

"Good afternoon, gentlemen," he said. He kept his eyes on the papers in front of him. "Have the two of you made a good faith attempt to settle this matter?"

"There is nothing to settle, your honor," Cole said. "Mr. Larson has no case."

"Judge," I said, "Mr. Cole's firm had a settlement offer on the table but withdrew it before I could get client approval."

Bohum looked up with a glimmer of optimism in his eyes. "Is that true, Mr. Cole?"

"That was before Daisy Twill attempted to kill my client."

"Daisy did not attempt to kill anyone," I objected.

"Then why is she in hiding?" Cole demanded.

"Gentlemen, gentlemen, enough," Bohum broke in. "Mr. Cole, is there any chance that your client will renew the offer?"

"Judge," I said, "Mr. Cole's client is a junior associate in the Evanson firm. He will do whatever Dan Evanson tells him to do. It was Evanson who made the offer and Evanson who withdrew the offer."

"That is not true," Cole said. "David Twill is my client and he is a full participant in this case. He made the previous offer and subsequently withdrew it."

"The question is, gentlemen," Bohum said, "will the offer be renewed? It certainly would make things easier for everyone if we could find a middle ground."

"If the offer is renewed," I said, "it will be rejected." It seemed like the right thing to say.

Bohum looked up from his file directly at me. "Are you sure, Mr. Larson? The pleadings here suggest that you have certain proof problems if we go to trial."

"Every case has its problems," I said. "This is no exception. However, I have a client who I believe has been denied her rightful inheritance, maybe for years, by people who acted together and knew exactly what they were doing."

"I've read the file, Mr. Larson," Bohum said. "I did not ask for argument."

"It is possible," Cole began, "that my firm could put up a small amount, a nuisance value, to avoid the cost of having to try the matter. I do not have client authority to do it at the moment, but I could see what could be done."

Bohum looked to me. I stared back at him and said, "My client will reject any offer that does not fully provide her what she is due."

The look of hope disappeared from Bohum's face. "And what is she due, Mr. Larson?"

"In order to determine that, your honor, I really need to take certain depositions. I want to question Dan Evanson and some other people associated with an organization called Avian House. These people have been—"

"Stop, Mr. Larson," Bohum said. "Your request to take these depositions has been denied in prior proceedings."

"But your honor," I protested, "I am asking normal discovery. I take depositions like this all the time. I am entitled to do it by law."

Bohum put his hands on the court file in front of him and stared at his fingers. Cole grinned. "Mr. Larson, I am the judge here. I determine the law in this case. You may appeal if you disagree with my rulings, but— "

"Your honor, you yourself have allowed me to take depositions in other cases. Why is this different? It seems like you are afraid of Evanson."

"That's enough, Mr. Larson," Bohum said.

"I am sorry your honor, but there is this organization called the Avians, and they have been—"

"Once again, Leo, I have read the file, I know your arguments and I have made my rulings." He opened the file and began lifting the pages aimlessly. He looked at Cole and said, "We will try this case two weeks from today. I encourage you to use the time to settle the matter."

"Your honor," I said, "I cannot go to trial in two weeks. Preparation will take at least sixty days and considering that you haven't let me do any discovery, no depositions, no document production, I may need more than that."

"In fourteen days, Mr. Larson. Can you be ready, Mr. Cole?"

"Yes, your honor," he said.

"That will be all, gentlemen."

"Please, your honor, I would like to make a couple of requests about—"

"That is all, Mr. Larson. We go to trial on your claims two weeks from today."

Cole slammed his file shut, gave me a fuck-you grin and marched out the door. Judge Bohum disappeared through the door behind his desk into Olga's area.

I went back to the office, picking up a couple tacos from Pedro's along the way. Peggi had already gone home when I arrived. I answered some phone calls, looked at the mail, and headed to Murdock's for the five thirty meeting.

Blue cigarette smoke hung in the middle of the room. I took my usual spot in the back. Spiritual Ed was in the chairman's seat. He didn't look at me and I didn't look at him.

Ed opened the meeting in the usual manner—the Serenity Prayer, How it Works, and a reading of the traditions. After the preliminaries, Ed read from the Big Book for a few moments and then looked up to choose the first person to speak.

"Leopold Larson," he boomed, using my last name in a very un-AA way.

"I would prefer to listen tonight," I responded.

"It seems to me," Ed said, "you prefer to listen every night. Don't you think it is about time for you to speak?"

"I would prefer to listen, Ed," I said.

"Are you a member of this group or not?" he demanded.

"It doesn't matter what I am," I said. "I just prefer to listen."

"Listen to me, Mr. Leopold Larson," Ed began, but Hardhead Steve interrupted him.

"Ed," Steve said, "nobody is required to speak in a meeting of this group. A person can sit there 'till hell freezes over and it is none of your business." A murmur in the crowd suggested that Hardhead Steve's position on this matter had popular support.

"Okay Steve," Ed said, "then you share."

Steve was fine with that. He leaned his tall cowboy body forward in his chair and began, "My name is Steve. I am a member of Alcoholics Anonymous and this group. I am here because when I take a drink I cannot stop drinking and when I am drinking I do bad things . . . " He continued in the same strain for fifteen minutes and by the end of the speech the dispute between Ed and I had been forgotten by everyone but the two of us.

Ed was leaning against the passenger door when I arrived at my car after the meeting. He had parked his Mercedes behind my Honda and had been stewing enough about what he was going to say that his face was already red.

"Larson," he said, "you are a walking dead man."

"Ed, get off of my car."

He glanced back at the Honda. "This piece of crap?"

"It's my piece of crap, Ed. So get off it. Get in your Mercedes and leave me alone."

"I am not going to leave you alone, Larson. And

there are a lot of other people in this town who are not going to leave you alone. I am talking about some powerful people. We are going to pull your law license for starters. But this time there will be no other jobs for you to go to. It is time for you to get out of Portland."

"I'm not going anywhere, Ed."

"Oh yes you are. I don't want to see you at Murdock's again."

"Why is that?"

"You don't belong there. You aren't one of them. You sit in the back listening, day after day, year after year, but you can't bring yourself to be part of anything, not even Murdock's. So leave them alone."

"I at least like them. You despise them."

"I have a good reason for being there."

"Those reasons have nothing to do with getting and staying sober, do they?"

"Whatever my reasons, I can go there, join in, speak when asked to, and say that I am one of them. You can't form the words. Leo, you are defective. You cannot belong to anything, and men alone wither and die. We offered you a chance at a life of abundance in which you would be part of something bigger than yourself, something that would make you respected in your profession. You wanted it. I could see that, but there was something deep inside you that would not let you accept."

"The Avians are corrupt," I said.

"Everything is corrupt. Politicians take bribes. Priests molest little boys. But people don't forsake their country or leave their churches because of it."

"Ed. What do you want from me?"

"For now, leave Murdock's."

"Why?"

"Things will not go as bad for you if you leave. That's why."

"A threat?"

"Damn right it's a threat. There are people in this city who are not afraid to get physical if you refuse to cooperate."

"Now it's broken kneecaps?"

"Screw the kneecaps, Leo, I am talking about people who will put you in the ground."

"I'm staying in Portland," I told him. "I'm staying at Murdock's too. I like the place and there are people there who like me."

"They will like someone else when you are gone. Leo, I feel sorry for you. You are a man with wasted talent. You are going to die alone. The only thing you can control now is how soon."

"Ed," I said, putting my face close enough to his to smell his breath, "get off the car." He stepped aside. I walked around and got in, and as I drove away I watched him in the rear view mirror until he was too small to see.

That night I ate chicken and rice with teriyaki sauce from a bottle in the living room of Baby Blue. After eating, I turned on my television, but I couldn't pay attention. The conversations with Judge Bohum and Spiritual Ed replayed themselves in my head. I had two weeks until trial. My client was up on the mountains and wanted by the police. I had no witnesses to call. I had no proof of the trust. I had no case.

I went in early the next morning. Bonnie Kutala called about nine to tell me she had been advised of the trial date and that my only chance of avoiding disciplinary proceedings was to dismiss the case. I asked her to out to dinner.

After talking to Bonnie I took the Honda downtown to do some research at the Multnomah County Law Library. In the old days the law library on the fourth floor of the court house was a busy place. Lawyers went there to do use the law books and make phone calls to the office from the free phones. Law books were eventually replaced by the Internet and the library phones were replaced by cell phones. This meant that on most days the library was empty except for a couple of grumpy female employees who had worked there since Kennedy was shot and a citizen or two who, out of personal obsession, had decided to tackle the legal system on his or her own. I needed to look at the law of other states, some appellate briefs, and a couple of law review articles. I went there to do legal research the old fashioned way.

I worked a couple of hours reading trust cases from other states to see if there had been any reported cases that might help, but I found nothing useful. I then took my yellow pads to the basement where they kept law reviews. Law reviews are the quarterly magazines produced by law schools in which students cut their teeth at legal writing and people who want to be law professors publish the articles that lead to tenure. These periodicals seldom have anything useful for the practicing lawyer, but when there is no legal authority in the statutes and nothing in the cases, you go where you can. The law review area was a poorly lit and poorly cleaned section of the library where two people cannot pass in an aisle without risking sexual contact. At one end of a long wooden reading table someone had left a coffee cup, a couple of legal pads, and some open books. I pulled the law review articles I needed and took a seat across and down from the absent researcher.

After about twenty minutes the person who left the coffee cup returned and sat in the chair by his papers. It was David Twill.

David ran his thick soft fingers over the legal pad in front of him and then looked at me with the hard eyes I remembered from our conversation in his office. "Good morning, Mr. Larson, or is it afternoon already?"

I glanced at the clock on the wall. "Still morning."

"How are you doing on my sister's case?" he continued.

"David, you are an adverse party represented by an attorney. I am not permitted to talk to you."

He leaned back in his chair and smiled.

"We—by 'we' I mean attorneys—have, I believe, more ethical rules and regulations than any other profession. We have comments and Bar opinions interpreting those rules and court cases we can read applying the rules to specific situations. Yet we are considered by the general public to be on an ethical par with drug dealers and used car salesmen. Do you find that ironic?"

"I suppose," I said. "Most days I just try to get along."

"Ah, just trying to get along. It is a noble goal; one I ascribe to myself. Rest assured I will not report you to Ms. Kutala if you speak to me in this dusty basement . . . How do you like my attorney?"

"Mr. Cole? A real charmer."

"In the lunch room at the firm they call him, the Rat."

"Appropriate."

"I agree. Dan says we in the firm are family. Some families have a black sheep. We have a rat."

"So why send him after me? If I could prevail in your sister's case it could mean a lot of money for you."

"You did make me think about that. But you won't prevail, Mr. Larson. You will probably end up disbarred. And for all I know it will be a tragedy. An injustice. One of many that passes through the legal system each day. If there is money coming to Daisy and me, I would like it. Who wouldn't? But in some cases the price of winning is too high. This, I fear, is one of them."

"What is that supposed to mean?"

David's eyes softened. "We had a business client a while back who got tangled up with the child protective services people. He had a good business, a big house, and after a divorce, had custody of his seven-year-old boy. He lived by a river and one of the rules of the house was that the child not go down by the river. But the kid went down to play by the river anyway. Dad found out and spanked him with a belt. The belt left bruises, and on the child's next visitation the ex-wife reported him to child protective services. They took the boy into state custody. They demanded that the father admit to all manner of wrongdoing, get counseling, take parenting classes, and waive his right to a hearing. He admitted his wrongdoing, agreed to counseling and the parenting classes, but refused to waive his right to the hearing. The social workers who had taken the child told him that forcing the agency to a hearing was evidence of a bad attitude and things would not go well for him if he did. He brought the

problem to us, and we sent in Rat, or Rat's predecessor, or somebody like Rat.

"At the hearing the guy confessed, apologized and
promised not to do it again. The judge gave him a
firm talking to and ordered his child returned. When
the hearing was over the agency representatives disappeared in a rage. They no longer cared about the
counseling or the parenting classes and returned the
child without a word. It wasn't about the child any
more; it was about his having taken the power to decide away from them. It is the thing an organization
cannot forgive. The agency has been hanging at the
edge of the man's life ever since. He walks on egg-
shells around his son and has been yanked into court
four different times over nothing. He wins every time,
and yet they continue. What he didn't realize when he
went to that first hearing with the Rat was that the
cost of winning was too high."

"You let the bastards get away with it?"

"Yeah, you do. An agency, a business, a law firm is
not like a person; an organization can never be wrong.
It can suffer setbacks such as when the judge ruled
against the agency in our client's child welfare case.
Setbacks can be caused by a bad judge, or a bad lawyer, or even a bad employee. The organization itself,
however, can never err, and when it fails it does so
only because someone inside failed it. The child services agency may well have fired some poor social
worker because of that case."

"The scapegoat?" I said.

"Yes. The scapegoat is an interesting beast. They
say that in days past villages transferred their sins to
the goat and pushed the animal out of the village. The
goat enjoyed its freedom for a few days, but when for-

age became scarce it returned home. The return of sin was unacceptable to the villagers so a change was made. Thereafter, the priest took the scapegoat outside the village and killed it."

"Villages are tough places," I said. "Does any of this relate to your sister's case?"

"Not really, Leo," he said. "I am just trying to show you why you got the Rat."

"So you can't afford to get your inheritance?"

"That is my village up there in the sky. I grew up without family. My father was absent. Daisy tried but had her own battles. Miley did his best to help but he couldn't change the fact that I had no family of my own and we both knew it. One day when I was about fifteen my father took me with him to the firm. We took the elevators up, and there in the waiting room I was above everything. The people who worked there were clean and polite. We went to see a lawyer. I don't know who it was, but he shook my father's hand and called him 'sir.' I could tell, however, that he looked down on my father and that when we left the people there would ridicule him. It seemed to me that if I could be part of something like that, if I could work in a place like that, then I would have a family that would always keep me safe. I told my father I wanted to be a lawyer, and that I wanted to work there. He took me back and we talked to Dan Evanson. Dan talked to me about what it took to come and work for Evanson Tribe and I followed his directions. When I graduated from law school, I went back and they hired me. That is my village and my family."

"If your family is there, what are you doing here in the crappy basement of a public law library? There can't be anything here that you don't already have at your firm."

"Joining Evanson did exactly for me what I wanted. It is safe there. We are above the clouds and above the battle. It is the family I never had, but it is not a happy family. I doubt that any families are happy, but I am sure ours is not. I come here to escape."

"Why are you telling me all this?" I asked.

"Because you are here and you don't matter."

"I don't matter?"

"You are a ghost. You are a dead man. That is all a man alone can be. Who better to bare my heart to than a ghost."

"This is the second time in two days that someone has said I am a dead man. The last one was threatening to have me killed."

"Whoever he is, he is an idiot. There is no reason to kill you."

"Tell me David, has anyone over at Evanson ever said anything about the Avians?" He stiffened, and his eyes turned hard and black again.

"Not a thing," he said. "I never heard of them until I read your briefs."

"How about from your father?"

"Not there either. And don't think because of this conversation that I will help you on the case. I will be sitting by the Rat when you lose. I will feel sad for you, but I won't help you."

"What about Daisy?"

"What about Daisy? She will go on. She always has. She will probably try to kill me again. Maybe someday she will succeed."

"I don't think she did it."

"We know each other. She did it." He began gathering his things into a black leather briefcase. "I spend too much time here," he said, "I must return to the village."

"Be careful up there," I said.

"I will." He started up the stairs and stopped half way to the top. He leaned over the open railing and said, "I think we will talk again."

I spent the remainder of the afternoon reading law review articles. Nothing in any of them helped. About three o'clock I left the library and went back to the office to check phone messages. Peggi was there taking things out of her desk and putting them in a cardboard box.

"What are you doing?" I asked.

"I have to talk to you, Leo." She steered me into my office. I sat. She sat. "I have taken a new job, Leo. I am sorry, but I have to leave." The message was not all that unexpected. I knew that she could take her experience and peddle it for more than I was paying her.

"Where are you going?" I asked.

"They've offered me a position at Evanson Tribe. I'm going to work for Dan Evanson."

Chapter 18

I didn't know which was worse, how angry I was at Peggi or how sorry I felt for myself. On the angry at Peggi side was the pure ungratefulness of it all. I knew that someday she would peddle her freckled ass at a firm with better furniture and health benefits, but going to work for Dan Evanson in the middle of the Twill case was throwing it in my face. Before me she had been working as a flagger at road construction. The very least she owed me was not going to work for Evanson. The legal assistants at Evanson Tribe had college degrees. The only reason that Evanson would hire her was to hurt me, and she knew it.

And on the sorry for myself side, the loss of Peggi was the worst of all the losses I'd suffered due to the Avians. I had liked the apartment across from Haven Appliance, but I felt more at home in the office. Most of what made the office comfortable was Peggi. She was the first human being I talked to every morning. She typed my letters, made my coffee, and told me how to dress.

That night I turned out the lights in the living room at Baby Blue and stared out the window, just like I used to do at the apartment. From the webbed lawn chair I bought for the carport, I could see the blue light from the television showing through the closed curtains of the old couple's home across the road. The only cars to pass were other residents of the park going to their homes farther down Lonely Street. Peggi lived down there. I wondered what she was doing. I thought about her getting ready for bed. I thought about her naked.

The apartment was gone. The green Ford Explorer was gone. My bank accounts needed replenishment. If they paid Peggi even a little more than the starting wage for a paralegal at Evanson Tribe, she would be making more than I did. I was fifty years old, been in and out of law for twenty years, and had nothing to show for it but a rented trailer house, a borrowed Honda Civic, and an income less than my disloyal freckled assistant.

In time of trouble, a person should have friends to turn to, but I had none. I used to have them. When I'd been married there had been friends, or at the very least, the relatives of my ex-wives, but in dividing the property during each divorce my exes had gotten the friends. I got the power tools, the golf clubs, and the bowling ball. In my drinking days I had friends in bars. I always had friends in the bars. They were waiting for me still at Hal's. Well maybe not Hal's, but there were a thousand other Hal's. Every one of them had friends. From my trailer I could walk to the Wetlands or the Lariat, both shit-hole bars a quarter mile or so from Baby Blue. Both bars had friends of mine I didn't know yet just waiting for me to arrive.

A person could slip in and take a seat at the bar. The drinks would be cold and the music loud. What happened there stayed there. The patrons all understood each other. No one ever has to be alone when there are places like the Lariat and the Wetlands. After a couple drinks the barkeeps would call you by name. And there are women there, women who will take you home with them and feed you. And take you to bed.

I didn't go to the Lariat or the Wetland or any place else that evening, but I felt closer to drinking again than I had in years. In the morning things were clearer. I did have friends. Don Yerke was there. All the folks at Murdock's were there. Peggi had left my business, not my life. She was an employee and she owed me nothing more than an employee owes her boss. She had children and family of her own. She had to go where she could do best for them, and if that was Dan Evanson's office, it was no reflection on the time we had spent together. I told myself these things but didn't believe them.

The next day at the office all the personal items were gone from Peggi's desk. I flipped on her computer, then went in my office and turned on my own. The answering machine had a couple of leads on new cases. I needed new work and returned the phone calls. In the morning mail came a notice from the court that the trial was now eleven days away. I read the notice and wanted to drink.

I sat at my desk and tried to make sense of what evidence I could present. I had a copy of the trust, or most of it, everything except the signature page. I had the fact that Elmo Twill had received an income throughout his life without ever holding a job. I had the property records for Food for Life Inc, the company that owned the land under Haven Appliance, my old apartment, and every other building in the immediate area. The problem was, and Nathan Cole knew it, that I could not authenticate the trust. In order to have it considered by the court, I needed someone to testify to where the document came from and who had signed it. The only witness to its source was me and the facts surrounding how I got it would put me in jail.

I thumbed aimlessly through the Twill file looking for something that would help. All I found were Bohum's letter rulings denying my request to depose Dan Evanson, quashing my subpoena of the officers of Food for Life Inc., and denying every other motion I made which might have produced the evidence I needed. I didn't have a single witness that I could bring to court. Murdock had been dead for years. Hal, Spiritual Ed, and the Avians were not going to say anything that would help me. Elmo was dead and his daughter would be arrested the moment she came into town.

I called over to Coney Bennett and talked to Churley. Daisy was still up on the mountain. That evening I went to Murdock's to drown my sorrows in AA.

I got there late. Electric Mike looked up from the chairman's seat when I entered, and the other attendees turned their heads with him. No one made eye contact. Something was different in the room. Normally when I arrived, I received a ripple of welcoming looks or gestures. The group had a quiet language of its own that was greater than the sum of its member's individual actions. I was used to a welcome. This day I got suspicion.

Electric Dave droned on from the chair and the room filled with cigarette smoke. I forgot about the cold welcome and let myself sink into the ritual of the meeting. The message did what I had come there for. Daisy's case was not the only case, and from a God's eye view, was not that important. Despite my woes, I still had a better life than most of the people at Murdock's. For a while I relaxed.

Electric Dave did not call on me. Even though I always passed when called upon, I had been around enough that most of the chairpersons would call on me some time during the meeting. Murdock's had no established rules about who the chairperson should call on, but unofficial group norms led most chairpersons to follow a pattern. Old timers spoke first to set the tone for the meeting. After three or four old timers, the chair picked new people, not because they have anything intelligent to say about getting and staying sober, but as a way of recognizing them and welcoming them into the group. Next came the door openers. These are the people with from three to ten years of sobriety who open the doors and make the coffee. Although I didn't open any doors I was usually called on among them. It was a courtesy that recognized my membership even if I always passed.

After the meeting, I went to Little Leslie to find out what was going on. Leslie was incapable of keeping a secret.

"What's wrong here?" I asked.

"Nothing," she said. She was lying.

I used my stern lawyer voice. "Leslie."

She blurted out her response. "Ed says you turned Daisy over to the cops."

"I'm Daisy's lawyer, Leslie. I didn't turn her in to the cops."

"So she's not in jail?"

"No. She is not in jail."

"Spiritual Ed is saying—"

"Spiritual Ed is an asshole, Leslie." She looked hurt.

I should have talked to Hardhead Steve or Electric Dave about Ed and Daisy but instead I left. Don Yerke used to tell me that if you want the whole world to know something, say it in an AA meeting. Don was being cynical but there was a certain amount of truth to it. Ed's claim would have spread quickly. Leslie, however, would pass on my denial and even if she didn't I would be forgiven. The people at Murdock's forgave everyone. It was AA. They had to.

The next day I put an ad on the Multnomah County Bar Association web site seeking a new legal assistant and applications started to click through on the fax machine. I put them in a stack on the desk where Peggi used to sit. I couldn't read them. Although my caseload was dropping, I didn't have the energy to canvass churches and retirement homes for clients. Doing the reception and secretarial duties on my own, I waited. I thought Peggi might not work out at Evanson Tribe. One of the phone calls might be her calling for her old job back.

On Wednesday I signed for the certified letter from Bonnie Kutala informing me that the Board of Bar Governors had opened a formal investigation into my actions in the Twill case. The letter requested that I appear at Bar headquarters with my files and answer questions under oath.

"Bonnie," I said into the phone, "what are you doing now? Are you mad because I haven't asked you out lately?"

"Leo, I plan to have you disbarred this time."

"Oh Bonnie, everything was going so well between us. How can you turn on me like this?"

"This is serious, Leo."

"So what's the charge this time?"

"Frivolous filing, to start. Obstruction of justice. Aiding and abetting. Do you need more?"

"Is this still about Twill?'

"It is about Twill, Leo."

"The case is before Bohum next week. I hope you will attend."

"I have no interest in being a spectator to your courtroom performances."

"If you really want to disbar me you will be there," I said.

"I don't want to disbar you. I want to protect your clients."

"I'm being framed, Bonnie."

"Why don't you come down to my office. We will put you under oath and you can tell me all about it."

"I would, but I am a little tied up for the next decade or two. My evenings, however, are free if you wanted to catch dinner and a movie."

"Expect a subpoena then."

"I take it that's a 'no' on the dinner."

"You take it correctly."

A long spring rain started the next day. I sat in my office over the weekend with the Twill file in front of me and water streaming down my office window. I stared at the file, made notes, tore up the notes and threw them away, then stared at the file some more. I couldn't work. I couldn't call anybody and I couldn't ask for help. Three times I looked up Don Yerke's number and didn't call him. I wrote down Peggi's number and didn't call her either. I didn't call Daisy or Churley.

I saw Mobley and Ames fairly often. They cruised the parking lot of my building or sat out on Eight-second Avenue waiting for Daisy to show up.

There is a saying in AA: "Do the next right thing." We don't really know what the next right thing is but it is a reminder to do something, something that isn't clearly stupid. But sometimes a person can only wait for life to unfold.

The hours passed, and then the days. The Twill hearing came closer. The afternoon of the day before the hearing I called Bonnie Kutala and got the message machine. I reminded her of the hearing time. I went to Murdock's that night. The usual suspects were there, and after the meeting I told the people there that I wanted them all in court the next day. I lied and said it was for Daisy. I didn't get much resistance. Most of them didn't have anything else to do.

On the morning of the hearing it was still raining. I put on my black suit, put the Twill file under my arm, and headed for Bohum's court. The courthouse was quiet for a Friday morning. As I rode up the elevator, I thought of Daisy sitting on the banks of the Zigzag. I wondered whether Churley had found her; whether she knew that the hearing was happening this morning. She would be watching the river as I walked into Bohum's court to be crushed by Nathan Cole.

Officers Mobley and Ames were sitting on the bench outside Bohum's courtroom. "Where's your client?" Mobley demanded. I looked behind me as if she had been following.

"She was right here a minute ago, Mobley. You just stay where you are. She will be along in a minute. If she doesn't show, wait longer."

"What are you going to do in there?"

"I'm going to take down Avian House," I said. Our stares met for just a moment and despite his best cop acting, his eyes told me that he understood what I was talking about.

"More likely, the judge will take you down, Larson."

"Then I will take down Avian House in the next case . . . or the one after that. One way or another it is all over. The Avians will be out in the open and all of you will be exposed as the pieces of shit that you really are." The attack made Ames raise her eyes from her lap and look first at me and then at Mobley.

"Fuck off, Larson," Mobley said. I went into the courtroom.

Bohum's ornate courtroom was as I remembered it. My Florsheims clicked on the marble floors as I walked down the center aisle to the wooden bar that separates the spectators from the lawyers. Nathan Cole was already there. He and David Twill sat together at the right hand counsel table. Cole refused to make eye contact with me. David was less disciplined. He looked up at me and lifted his fingers from the table in an uncomfortable acknowledgment that we knew each other.

Mobley and Ames followed me into the courtroom. I turned to survey the seats behind me. My own invitees, Little Leslie, Hardhead Steve, Electric Mike and Copper John, were half way back on the right. When our eyes met the four of them grinned in unison and waved energetically.

In the very back sat one observer I had hoped for and one that was completely unexpected. The hoped for one was Bonnie Kutala. Our eyes did not meet because her attentions were being monopolized by my landlord, Torkum Masoogian. I left counsel table and walked back to the two of them.

"Hello Bonnie," I said. She nodded uncomfortably. "Torkum, what the hell are you doing here?"

"I have a client," he grinned, "whose name must

remain confidential, who is interested in train wrecks. I'm getting paid by the hour to sit next to the lovely Ms. Kutala here and watch you go down in flames." Bonnie grimaced and shifted in her chair. She was wearing the same gray uniform she had worn in our previous encounters. I winked at her.

She looked at the two of us. "You two deserve each other."

Olga from probate entered the courtroom from the door that led to chambers. She motioned for the two lawyers to approach the long clerks table that sat directly beneath the elevated judicial bench.

Olga whispered, "Judge Bohum would like to see counsel in chambers."

She led us into chambers and took a seat at a small desk in the back of the room that allowed her to witness the proceedings yet be out of view. Cole and I took the chairs in front of the judge's desk, still not making eye contact with each other. Judge Bohum was leaning over the file. After an awkward moment he looked up at me.

"How many witnesses do you have, Leo?" he asked.

"None, your honor."

"None?"

"Is your client, Ms. Twill, with you?"

"She is not, your honor. Mr. Cole's firm has trumped up a criminal charge against her that makes her unable to attend. There are police in the courtroom—"

Nathan Cole leaped to the attack, "I strenuously object, your honor. No one in my firm is responsible for the criminal activity of Mr. Larson's client. The fact is she tried to kill David Twill, her brother, and an associate at our firm."

"Daisy did not try to kill her brother."

"Then she should turn herself in to the police. If she is innocent she has nothing to fear." The veins in his neck were throbbing already and the trial hadn't even started. He perched on the edge of his chair like a cat poised to pounce.

"Gentlemen, gentlemen," the judge said, "let's return to the matter at hand. Current allegations aside, I have examined the criminal record of Ms. Twill and have determined that because of her past convictions she is not qualified to serve as a personal representative of an estate under Oregon law. I am prepared to grant Mr. Cole's motion to dismiss the probate petition."

Cole leaned back in his chair and loosened his iron grip on the arm rest. "Thank you, you honor." Bohum paid no attention to him.

"The trust case presents a different matter. Mr. Larson alleges the existence of a trust to which his client is a beneficiary. He has filed with this court what appear to be photocopies of a part of a trust document suggesting the existence of such a trust—"

"Unsigned, unproven copies, your honor. They are hardly sufficient—" Bohum put up his hand to stop Cole from going on.

"Now is the time," Bohum continued, "for you, Mr. Larson, to prove with admissible evidence the allegations in your pleadings."

"Yes sir," I said. Both men looked at me.

"Yet you have no witnesses?" Bohum continued.

"None," I said.

"If it please the court," Cole broke in, "I move that the matter be dismissed with prejudice right now and that Mr. Larson be sanctioned by the court for a bad faith filing. He cannot authenticate this trust. He doesn't have a signed copy, much less a witness to prove that it was ever executed or funded. He has been wasting court time since the very beginning in this matter, and it should stop now."

The judge looked at Cole and then at me. "Mr. Cole has a point."

"I ask only that I be allowed to present my case in my own way."

"I do not see, Mr. Larson, how it is that I have to let you attempt to do something that cannot be done. If you have no witness to testify that the trust exists, how can you prevail?"

"There are many ways to prevail, sir. No matter what you think of my case or my behavior in this matter, I am entitled to have this proceeding heard on the record and entitled to appeal any adverse decision."

"There is no point, your honor," Cole objected, "and as for appeal, how can he appeal a case in which he has no admissible evidence."

"He is entitled, however, to have my rulings on the record."

"You can make written rulings, your honor," Cole said, "and he can make written objections if he has any."

"No. He is entitled to be heard in open court. I will meet you there in ten minutes." Cole and I returned to counsel table to wait. A few more people from Murdock's had arrived and taken seats in the audience. Cole whispered to David loud enough for me to hear, "It's over. We are going to make a record and then go home."

Judge Bohum emerged from the door to chambers and took his seat on the bench. The court reporter fussed with the paper in her machine, and then indicated by hand signs that she was ready.

Bohum began, "Now is the time set for hearing in two matters, the Estate of Twill, and the petition for instructions in the matter of the Bergan Twill Charitable Trust. Counsel and I have met in chambers, and all parties have reported ready.

"As I told you in chambers counsel, I have examined the criminal history of the petitioner, Daisy Twill, in the Twill probate case. I find that due to various criminal convictions she is not qualified to serve as personal representative of the estate of Elmo Twill and find that the respondent, David Twill's motion to dismiss is well taken. I hereby grant the motion."

Back in the audience, Electric Dave gave a disapproving hiss as if he were at a sporting event. Everyone in the room looked his way. I turned and frowned at him theatrically. He said, "Jeez, I'm sorry already."

Bohum continued, "Now for the matter of the Bergan Twill Trust. Are counsel ready?"

"Ready for the petitioner," I said.

"Ready for the respondent," Cole said.

Bohum shifted into automatic judge mode, doing what he had done a thousand times before. "Opening statement, Mr. Larson."

"Yes sir." I stood behind counsel table and closed the file in front of me. I shut my eyes and let my mind go blank. I never prepared speeches. I prepared cases and let the speeches happen. But this time nothing came. I waited for the words to arrive.

"Mr. Larson," the judge warned, "you must either make an opening statement or waive it. You cannot simply stand there."

"My name is Leo Larson," I said, "I am an alcohol-

ic. I am a member of Alcoholics Anonymous and a
member of the local group known as Murdock's. I had
my last drink at the Jack London Hotel. At that time I
was unemployed, unemployable, sick, and suicidal. I
had been kicked out of my home, my marriage, my
job, and my profession. The police found me passed
out on the sidewalk that night a few blocks from the
hotel. They took me to Hooper Detox on the east side
of Portland where I was hosed down, housed, and
fed."

Cole rose from his table, "I object, your honor. This
has nothing to do with the case. We do not have to
listen to this."

Back in the audience, Electric Dave lost control
again and leaped to his feet. "Shut the fuck up, punk,"
Dave yelled. Cole's head swung around in anger. The
two stared each other down and Cole was the first to
look away. Physically, Dave was no match for the athletic Cole, but Dave was crazy and between physical
ability and crazy, crazy wins.

Bohum hit the bench with his gavel. "Sit down
both of you."

I continued, "I ended up at Murdock's by accident
or by God's plan, but at Murdock's I am learning to
live again from the ground up, not from teachers or
preachers, not from social workers or counselors, but
from drunks like me who have passed out on sidewalks, gone to detox centers, and survived.

"Murdock's is named after a man named John
Murdock who started the AA group in an old storefront on the east side. It is still there. The front window is broken and the roof leaks because the group
pays its rent from the loose change in the pockets of
its members. One of the reasons that Murdock's is so

poor is because AA prevents a group from accepting large donations. Another reason the group is so poor is because money was stolen from it four decades ago and used to create Mr. Cole's law firm, a bar, a used car dealership, and to make you, John Bohum, a judge."

Nathan Cole leaped to his feet. "Objection! I most strenuously object." The judge leaned back in his leather chair and closed his eyes.

"It began in 1955," I said, "when a prominent baker named Bergan Twill was despondent over the alcoholism of his son, Elmo."

"I demand a ruling on my objection," Cole shouted.

Bohum opened his eyes looking tired. "Mr. Larson appears to want to end his association with the legal profession today, Mr. Cole. I think that we ought to allow him to do so."

"The only one who was ever able to stop Elmo Twill from drinking," I continued, "was a man named John Murdock. Murdock and AA had done what no one else had been able to do. The father visited Murdock's, studied Alcoholics Anonymous, and eventually decided to contribute the greatest part of his wealth to the battle against alcoholism. With the help of an up-and-coming lawyer named Dan Evanson, he put a significant amount of cash and the real property beneath his bakery into trust for the benefit of Murdock's, AA, and the rehabilitation of alcoholics. At the time, it seemed the only way to save his son. But Bergan Twill's designs were not purely altruistic. His son, Elmo, had a beautiful wife and a new child. The trust also provided an income for Elmo so that he could care for his family. Evanson took the trust and the money to John Murdock and asked him to serve as trustee. John Murdock wouldn't do it. AA would be in debt to no man, no matter how noble the sentiments.

"Dan Evanson should have returned the money, or rewritten the trust for a changed charitable purpose, maybe one that helped alcoholics in another way. But he did not. He lied to Bergan Twill, telling him that it would work as planned. Instead of using the money to help the alcoholic, Dan Evanson used it as an investment fund to make his clients financially successful. And as we know, when a client is financially successful the law firm goes along for the ride.

"The first people to benefit from the Twill Trust were the people that Evanson had to keep quiet. These were people in AA who knew Bergan Twill, who knew that he wanted to help alcoholics, and knew the money was being used for other purposes. Most but not all of these people were members of AA. One of them was Bergan's son, Elmo, who was entitled to an income from trust assets. From this alliance of lawyers, dissatisfied AA members, and the alcoholic son of a baker, a group called the Avians was born.

"Avian House, the home of the Avians, now sits on the property next to the bakery owned by Bergan Twill. Dan Evanson turned charity and altruism on its head so for the members of Avian House, greed is virtue, and a man's worth is measured by the size of his bank account.

"Up until Bergan Twill's death, the disposition of the trust money had to be kept secret. After his death and with Elmo on their side, the Avians became emboldened. In 1968, Bergan was dead, Elmo's wife and child were dead, and Elmo was drinking again. The conspirators came out into the open. They went to court on an action for *cy pres*. This little noticed lawsuit had a judge change the terms of the trust to name Avian House, rather than AA, as the beneficiary of the trust and permitted the transfer of the real property to Food for Life Inc. The file on that case is missing from the archives, but at the time a good lawyer wouldn't have had too difficult a time convincing a judge that Avian House was a suitable successor to AA. He would simply point out to the court that Avian House was made up mostly of AA members and used the same philosophy. The lawyer who made this argument as a favor for an old office mate then waited for his reward. That lawyer was John Bohum. Eventually the reward came, for when the most powerful firm in town wants a certain person appointed judge, it can be made to happen.

"Elmo never sobered up, but he did remarry and fathered two more children. One sits over there next to Mr. Cole. The other, my client, is being hounded by the police as the Evanson firm continues to hide what it has done, and the judge sitting on this case has known for years that it is all true. The trust originally stated that if AA could not or would not accept the money, the income was to be paid to Bergan's son Elmo for life with the remainder, the real money, to his children. The court order allowing Avian House to take control of the assets was obtained by a fraud on the court. David and Daisy Twill are Elmo's children and the rightful beneficiaries of the trust.

"While Murdock's struggles with a leaking roof and unpaid bills, the person who helped Dan Evanson steal money from street drunks and addicts sits in judgment of my client. Murdock's, by its tradition, cannot fight back but I as one alcoholic can stand here and tell the truth. And if telling the truth ends my legal career, I will accept that result knowing that I got up this morning, put on my suit, and did the right thing."

I sat. The courtroom was silent. Finally, Nathan Cole stood up at counsel's desk. "Once again, I object."

"Objection sustained," Bohum said.

"Do you have any evidence to present, Mr. Larson?"

"No, your honor."

Bohum looked at Cole. "Based upon lack of evidence, I am granting Mr. Cole's motion to dismiss the matter of the Bergan Twill Charitable Trust. Mr. Cole, will you please submit the order." Judge Bohum rose and left the courtroom.

Cole came over to me. "What was all that crap?"

I looked at him. "Sometimes the truth just needs to be said."

I left Cole standing there and went to catch Leslie and Dave in the hall. "You guys know what to do now?" They gave me thumbs up.

Chapter 19

Bonnie caught up with me in the hallway outside of Bohum's court. "Leo, was any of that true?"

"I might have gotten something wrong here or there in the heat of the moment, but for the most part it is. Maybe the only way to truly get to the bottom of it would be an investigation by the Office of Morals and Ethics."

"I am supposed to prove the case that you couldn't?"

"Yes. I'm just one guy in a crappy two-room office. You have the power of the Bar and you won't have Bohum ruling on your motions."

"I don't know, Leo. It won't change the fact that you brought a case to court with no evidence."

"You are hopeless, Kutala," I said. We walked the rest of the way to the elevator in silence.

In the elevator she said, "You used me. You lured me here to force my office to investigate Bohum."

"It was your job to be here," I told her, "to protect the public. By the way, did Masoogian say why he was here?"

"Something about a special assignment for an old divorce client."

"Nothing more than that?"

"Not that I recall. I didn't listen to it all. He's a most unpleasant man."

We parted in front of the courthouse and I drove back to the east side for a taco lunch at Pedro's. Nathan Cole and the lawyers at Evanson would be back at

Big Pink writing the order of dismissal. Everything was beyond my control.

I left Pedro's with a burrito to eat later at the office. I would be there late into the evening. At three o'clock in the afternoon the proposed order of dismissal came to me by fax. It was a two sentence order dismissing both the probate and the trust case. There was no mention of sanctions against me. The cover letter indicated that the original would be hand delivered to the court in seventy-two hours, giving me three days to object.

At six o'clock that evening I got a call from Copper John. "It's all coming down right now," he said, "They are taking boxes and files out of the building."

"Where are you?"

"Leslie and I are right across the street. Electric Dave is down a block. Hardhead is digging in the cardboard dumpster at the appliance place."

"Have they seen you?"

"Sure they've seen us, but not seen us. We are being homeless. No one sees homeless people."

"How about Spiritual Ed."

"He's in there. He's upstairs and very excited. We can see him through the window."

"Don't let him see you. He could recognize any of you."

"We won't, Leo."

"Where are they putting the files?"

"In the back of a red van. Do you want the license number?"

"Yes. Write it down and keep it."

"Churley is going to follow it when it leaves."

"Churley?"

"We called him. Was that wrong?"

"John, that's fine. I just didn't expect that."

I waited a couple of hours, ate the burrito, and went home. Rather than parking in my carport I drove to the end of the lane. Peggi's big white doublewide was dark and her car was gone. I made a u-turn and went home.

The trailer was warm. I thought about the morning in Bohum's court and wondered what he was doing now. I picked up my volume two of *A Program for Life* and thumbed through it again.

Just after nine o'clock Copper John called again. The boxes were being unloaded at Big Pink.

"Who's there?" I asked.

"All of us. Me, Leslie, Hardhead, Churley and a couple of his buddies. Do you want us to go in?"

"No, that's good enough, John. Those are watched elevators. None of you will be able to get in after hours. Just have Churley find out where the van goes when they are done. The rest of you can go home."

"Oh, and Daisy is here too. Did I say that?"

"Where did you see Daisy?"

"She is on the back of Churley's bike."

"Shit!" I said.

"Is that bad?" Bob asked.

"Never mind. If you talk to her, tell her to call me at home."

"I will, Leo. I'll keep everybody out of the building."

"Yeah, Bob, you do that. And, then all of you go home."

No one else called that night. I went to bed about midnight, but didn't sleep. The worst parts of lawyering were those times when I had to let things happen. Doing things, making plans, and taking charge were all easy compared to letting things take their course.

I bought myself a breakfast sandwich at a little place on Foster Road and opened the office early the next morning hoping that the message machine or email would bring some news. There was nothing. I was fairly sure that all the Avian House records, including the boxes that had held Elmo's stuff, had been locked away on the top floor of Big Pink by David Twill, Nathan Cole, Dan Evanson and a host of assistants and paralegals. Perhaps they had been shredded. More likely, considering who it was, they were being marked, scanned, and catalogued.

The phone was silent the entire morning. Nothing from Evanson, nothing from Bonnie, nothing from Daisy. That afternoon Copper John called with the license number for the van and the fact that after the delivery to Big Pink it had been dropped off at World of Wheels, the car dealer where I bought the green Explorer. I ran the plate through the Oregon Department of Motor Vehicles. The van was in dealer stock.

The afternoon was as quiet as the morning. At sunset I headed to Murdock's for the evening meeting. Leslie, Bob, Steve and the others who had been involved the previous night, surrounded me asking for details and news. I told them I had nothing. It was all in God's hands, I said. At Murdock's that was a sufficient answer for any problem.

In the socializing after the meeting, I asked about Daisy. Everyone confirmed that she was in town and had been with Churley on the night they moved the files from Avian house, but no one had talked to her. After the meeting, I picked up a dog at Coney Bennett. The woman at the drive-up window didn't know me, and neither Daisy nor Churley were working.

I didn't sleep any better the second night than I had the night of the hearing. No one was talking to me. I spent the following day unenthusiastically producing documents for the few remaining cases in my office. I recalled from last time around how difficult it is to work on a case when you are on the verge of disbarment. It saps one's energy. I ate tacos from Pedro's, played minesweeper on the computer, and at one point, went down to Torkum Masoogian's office to pump him for information. He wasn't in.

That evening back at Baby Blue I called Daisy's house once again and got a live voice. It was Churley.

"This is Leo," I said. "Let me talk to Daisy."

"She has gone to meet with her brother."

"David?"

"Yeah, David. The only brother she has. His secretary called saying David wanted to meet with her."

"Where are they meeting?"

"At the place we went the other night, Avian House."

"Avian House?" I said, "Are you sure?"

"That's what Daisy told me on the phone."

"Why there?"

"I don't have the slightest idea, but I don't think he was inclined to have her over to his house, and I don't think he would want to come here. Maybe it was a public place?"

"Avian House is not a public place, Churley. We need to get over there. When are they meeting?"

"She is supposed to meet him there at nine o'clock."

"That's right now."

"I guess it is," he said.

"I'll meet you over there. Drive fast."

"I'm in the bath tub, Leo."

"Well, get out. I will meet you there." I hung up.

I called over to Murdock's to see who I could drum up and then left the house. The Honda was slow to start, and the traffic gods worked against me. Red lights, construction, and traffic idiots made the trip an eternity.

When I arrived at Avian House it looked empty. All the lights were out, even the second floor light that I had watched so often from the apartment. The neighborhood was deserted. I walked up the steps and tried the knob. It was locked. I thought for a moment I heard a noise inside, but when I put my ear to the door there was nothing. I was still on the front landing when Churley pulled his Harley onto the sidewalk in front.

"Where are they?" he yelled as he dismounted.

"I don't know," I said. "The place looks empty."

"Daisy is close by." He pointed down the street. "That's our van. I think the Lexus belongs to her brother."

"How do you know what David drives?"

He frowned. "Don't ask. Did you try the door?"

"It's locked. No lights. No one answered my knock."

Churley walked up the steps and I followed. He knocked again and put his ear to the door.

"She's in there." He turned his back to the door, put both hands on the stout handrail at the edge of the landing and did a hard mule kick next to the door knob. The frame splintered and the door flew open.

"Jesus Christ," I objected, but he was already inside. A light came on and I followed him in. The room reeked the rotten egg smell of natural gas. Daisy and

David were both inside, gagged and bound to chairs with plastic ties and duct tape. Daisy was alert and struggling. David was slumped sideways in his chair, and a large pool of blood was forming beneath him. Churley pulled the duct tape off Daisy's mouth while I struggled to open one of the old double hung windows.

Freed from the tape, Daisy gasped for air. "David is shot. She is going to blow us up."

"How?" Churley demanded as he sawed at Daisy's restraints with his pocket knife.

"I don't know. She had something in her hand, something electronic, to set off the gas." I had pulled a second window as open as it would go. With the door off its hinges and both windows open there was still very little air movement and the gas smell was heavy in the room. Daisy and I freed David while Churley went into the back kitchen to look for the source of the gas.

David had been shot in the knee and had lost a lot of blood. As we cut away at the tape and ties he came to life and began to moan. We got him up from the chair. Daisy and I were large enough to manhandle him toward the door. The one leg hung uselessly, but he had enough consciousness to help a little with the other as we carried him down the stairs toward the street.

We put David on the curb in front and looked back at the building. Churley was still inside. We heard the muffled sound of breaking glass coming from the back of the building. A moment later Churley came sprinting out the door and leaped the front steps to the sidewalk. He collapsed on impact, but like a cat was instantly up again. He was almost to us when the building blew up.

Churley had found the detonator—a box with electric matches attached—had smashed the kitchen window and tossed it out. His plan almost worked. There had been just enough gas close to the window when the detonator went off to ignite. The bottom floor of the building filled with a cloud of flame that poured out the open windows and then softly collapsed upon itself. When the flame was gone we heard the sound of tinkling glass. The remaining bottom floor windows had blown out and a lot of furniture had been singed, but Avian House, with a little clean up, would be fine.

The first cops on the scene were beat cops who just happened to take the call. Right behind themcame Mobley and Ames. Mobley stopped his cop car in front of me.

"Larson," he yelled, "what happened here?"

"Officer Mobley, I would like you to meet my client, Daisy Twill." Daisy looked up at him for a moment and returned to tending her brother. "And her brother David."

"What's a matter with him?" Mobley asked.

"He's been shot in the leg," I said. Mobley glared at Daisy.

"I didn't shoot him, you moron," Daisy said.

"Then who did?"

I pointed down the street. About fifty yards down the block, the Murdock's foursome of Copper John, Electric Dave, Hardhead Steve, and Little Leslie was pulling an angry Anita Bainbridge up the street toward us.

Anita looked as prim and proper as she did in the dining room at Everland Village. As they got closer we could hear Anita yelling at Little Leslie, "Keep your hands off me you stupid cunt."

"Now, now," Leslie said, "we will be there in a minute." Copper John broke from the group with as much of a run as his old body could muster.

"She was easy to find, Leo, and we recognized her right away. She was just sitting there at the Fat Rooster with a cup of coffee and this." He held out a small electronic device. It was a radio-controlled detonator for the electric matches. Leslie, Hardhead and Electric Davie pushed and prodded the angry gray-haired woman up to Mobley.

"There's your shooter, Mobley. She tried to shoot David Twill before, and she succeeded tonight. She killed her brother and she was trying to kill his children."

Anita turned her ire to us. "Fuck you, Larson. And you too cop. My brother was a drunk and a lying piece of shit his whole life."

Mobley turned to the old woman. "Did you shoot this man, ma'am?"

"Fuck you, cop," she said.

"Yes, she shot him," Daisy interrupted, "I was there. And she was going to blow up the building with us in it."

"Is that true, ma'am?"

"Choke on a donut, cop. I am not talking to you."

A fire truck and ambulance arrived, sirens blaring. Daisy helped load David in the ambulance and left with him. Fifteen or twenty fireman stood in and around Avian House talking among themselves. People came out of their houses and apartments to watch the commotion.

Anita kept up a tirade of obscenities toward whoever was around her. Eventually Mobley and Ames handcuffed her and put her in the back of the car. Mobley came over and asked me what had happened. I told him about us breaking in, finding Daisy and David, and the explosion that failed.

"Why did the two of you come down here in the first place?" he asked.

I told him about the call to Churley and the meeting between brother and sister. "You know as well as I do, Mobley, neither David nor Daisy had any reason to pick this place. They were the last two people in the world you folks wanted in there."

"I am not an Avian," Mobley said.

"Maybe not. Maybe you owe somebody a favor and that person is an Avian. I don't really care. Somehow you know enough to know that I am right. Somebody was luring them down there, and I just couldn't believe that it was to offer Daisy a membership."

"How did you know it was Mrs. Bainbridge?"

"I didn't really. It was a guess."

"Why did you guess her?"

"Mobley," I said, "do I owe you some sort of favor whereby I solve your cases for you?"

"You are an officer of the court and if you have information about the commission of a felony— "

"Mobley, fuck off."

"Larson," he said, "you are not out of trouble because of this. Your client probably did not try to kill her brother, but that's all. You had no evidence in Bohum's court and you still don't. That means you lose your license. Your best bet is to tell me what you know and how you came to know it."

"Come over to the office tomorrow. I'll explain what I can."

"Right here will do."

"The office," I said, "tomorrow."

I walked back to Murdock's with the others. We opened the place, made coffee, and sat around the room reliving the evening. Everybody got a chance to tell his or her version of the adventure. Hardhead and Little Leslie had been the first ones to spot Anita Bainbridge. Little Leslie was bubbling. "Your description was perfect, Leo. We started searching the neighborhood, and she was sitting there in the Fat Rooster like a little china doll. She had coffee and used her napkin as a coaster. That electric thing was sitting on the table and Steve and I knew it was her. We waited until the cook went into the kitchen and Steve lifted her out of the booth."

"She may look like a doll, but she sure can swear when she's mad," Hardhead broke in.

Seeing the light on, members who lived close dropped in and with each new arrival the story was told again. About eleven, Daisy and Churley arrived.

"David will be all right," Daisy announced to the room. "They are operating on his knee right now, but they said it was the blood loss that was most dangerous." No one in the room knew who David was but they all showed a polite amount of relief that he would be okay.

After greeting everyone Daisy sat down next to me.

"What happened in there?" I asked.

"She had it all set up," Daisy said. "I got there just before nine. I knocked and someone said to come in so I did. There was David tied to a chair with plastic ties and duct tape. He had already been shot in the leg and was bleeding. She told me if I didn't sit down she would shoot him in the head."

"Why didn't you let her?"

"He's my brother, Leo."

"But you hate him."

"He's my brother. She made me use the plastic ties to strap my arms and legs to the chair, duct taped over top, and put tape on my mouth. David was still conscious then. She said she had turned on the gas. She held up an electronic thing and said it would take about an hour to fill the building with gas and then she would detonate it from outside. She turned out the lights, locked the door, and left us there. Churley said you called him. If it hadn't been for you both, David and I would be dead."

"Left to my own devices, Daisy, I would have stood outside and let the two of you get blown up. Fortunately, your husband recognizes the sounds you make even when muffled by duct tape. He also knows how to knock down locked doors."

"So was it Aunt Anita that shot at David?"

"I think so."

"Why does she want to kill us?"

"She doesn't like you," I said. Daisy didn't smile. "But the real reason is probably the money."

"The money?"

"Your grandfather's trust. If there is no one to receive the money from the trust it goes to his heirs. He left the money to Alcoholics Anonymous and they refused it. The other beneficiary was your father and he is dead. That means that you and David inherit. If she kills you and David the money goes to her."

"Why doesn't it go to my kids?"

"They aren't your biological children, Daisy. They are Churley's."

"We both consider them my children. They consider me their mother."

"But that doesn't count in the law. With you and David gone, Anita was the only heir."

"Can you inherit money by killing the other heirs?"

"Well no," I explained, "Anita can't inherit if she kills the other heirs, but maybe she didn't plan to get caught." Daisy understood. "Or maybe she didn't care all that much whether she got caught or not. The money was for Miley. I think Anita is very ill and can't leave Everland no matter what happens. She was in full nursing over there and now is back in the regular population. It could be because she got better, but it could also be because she will never get better. Killing you and David would leave her son the inheritance she thought he always deserved."

Daisy leaned back in her chair and put her tattooed arms behind her head. "So was Miley in on it too?"

"I don't think so. I doubt Miley had any more clue about what was happening than you did."

Murdock's emptied out about midnight. I went home to the Baby Blue on Lonely Street and went to bed. I left the bedroom window open and listened to the rain until I fell asleep.

Chapter 20

I arrived at the office late the next morning and called Mobley.

"Yeah," he answered.

"Mobley," I said, "how did it go with Anita Bainbridge?"

"She copped to it. She's a tough old broad. I got to give her that. She admitted that she killed her brother, took the shots at David Twill, and was trying to kill Daisy and David last night. She held out for a while, but in the end she wanted to talk. She told everything and was proud of it. No regrets. I don't even think she regretted getting caught. Her only regret was that she didn't succeed."

"So where did she get the detonator?"

"The Internet. Her old man worked for the gas company. She spent years listening to him talk about gas every night. I think it drove her crazy, but over all that time she learned a little about gas. She got these electric matches used for setting off fireworks and hobby rockets, turned off the pilot light on the stove, turned the burners on, and was preparing to blow up the building while she sat in that diner down the street sipping coffee."

"Are you off my client's case now?"

"Hell, Larson, she didn't do this one, but you know as well as I do that she did something else just as bad. I'll just wait until next time."

After talking to Mobley I called Nathan Cole over at Evanson but couldn't get past receptionists and legal assistants. I tried to work on other cases. I went to

Pedro's for a taco. I played solitaire on the computer. I waited.

Just before noon I got a call from Bonnie Kutala. "I have in my office, Leo, a box full of the records of Food for Life Inc., and the Bergan Twill Charitable Trust. They are all originals, sorted, organized and filed."

I smiled. "You better not look at them Bonnie. I believe those records are protected by several different privileges and belong to the firm of Evanson Tribe. Your having them at all could be a serious ethical violation."

"Shut up, Leo. Are you behind this?"

"I am not, Bonnie. I have been too busy saving the life of David Twill, one of the esteemed associates at the Evanson firm."

"The records were shipped to me directly from the Evanson Tribe office. I have not been through them all but they seem to prove everything that you said in court. John Murdock was the first trustee, but after him there are a series of trustees whose names I don't recognize."

"They will all turn out to be clients of, or friends of, Dan Evanson."

"Then in 1968 there is an action for *cy pres* to name Avian House as the charitable beneficiary. Judge Bohum brought the case representing Elmo Twill."

"Daisy's and David's father," I continued for her. "Thereafter, the trust transferred the real property to Food for Life Inc., taking all the stock in return. Food for Life seems to have done just fine renting and managing those properties for the last thirty-five years. Now it all goes to Daisy and David. Assuming we can convince Bohum."

"About Bohum," she said.

"What about Bohum?"

"He resigned from the bench."

"Because of the files?"

"I don't know. I called Olga over at probate to ask if there had been a ruling yet, and she said that Bohum resigned. They haven't seen him since we were there in court."

"So there will be no ruling in the Twill case?"

"Not from Bohum there won't."

"Bonnie," I said, "I would like to report to you a possible ethical violation by a man named Dan Evanson. You may have heard of him—"

"Don't bother, Leo. We will look into it. However, Leo, this does not technically excuse any of your behavior. I admit that it might be difficult for me to pursue the frivolous filing case, but if I have evidence that you broke into Avian house, or that you were responsible for stealing client files from Evanson Tribe, I will prosecute. The acts of other bad people do not excuse what you did."

"Yeah right."

"They don't."

"Let's go do dinner tonight and talk about it?"

"Goodbye Leo. I need to talk to Evanson. You better not be involved."

I clicked on the Wells Fargo Bank button on my computer and checked my bank account. I had six hundred dollars in the office account and fifty-eight dollars in my personal account.

I spent my lunch hour at Murdock's. The activities of the previous night still dominated the pre-meeting conversation. Once the meeting started, however, it was as it had been for decades. Hardhead Steve chaired and I fell into the comfortable pleasure of ritual. In the middle of the meeting he called on me. "My name is Leo," I said, "I am a member of Alcoholics Anonymous and a member of this group." It felt good to say it. I would never again pass when called on at Murdock's.

After the lunch meeting I gulped down a patty melt at the Fat Rooster and went back to the office. Torkum Masoogian waddled through the door. "Hi-ya Larson," he said. "How's it hangin'?"

"It's hanging fine Masoogian. What do you want?"

"I want to thank you. That was a great job you did in court on the Twill case. So good, it landed me the job of defending Anita Bainbridge against several felony charges. I have a pretty good feeling that you will be a witness."

"You represent Anita Bainbridge?"

"Ever since the divorce. You know the whole 'divorce for women' thing. She came to me after her old man retired. She is a ball buster. Came from a rich daddy and no working stiff husband installing gas lines was ever going to measure up. As long as he had the job he could hide from her at work. Then he retired. He put up with her for about three months and was out the door. She came to me and said she wanted the bastard to suffer. By my way of thinking he'd already suffered enough being married to her, but she had money to pay the fee so I gave him a couple extra turns of the knife on the way out."

"Was this about her or about Miley?"

"All about the kid," he said. "She's got cancer. She'll be dead in six months—a year at the latest. It's always been about the kid; him being a teacher and all and dedicating himself to children. Then she sees drunk old Elmo's bastard offspring get all the money."

"Are they bastards?"

"Bainbridge says so. Says Elmo and the second wife never got married, but I haven't looked it up."

"So you were in court the other day representing Anita?"

"Yeah," he said. "Who else could it be? Ever since I did her dirty work in the divorce she calls me to make trouble for whoever she happens to be mad at. And she is mad a lot."

"She presents well."

"She has that cute little old lady act down better than anyone I've ever seen. But don't buy it."

"Did she take the shots at David?"

"I haven't asked her and wouldn't tell you if I knew. Attorney-client privilege, you know. I will tell you she knew how to handle a gun. Old man Bainbridge was a hunter. It was a good way to avoid the old battle axe on weekends. When they were younger, the two of them did it together. The old man taught it to Miley. Miley taught it to his kids as well as to David and Daisy. The whole family knows how to handle guns. Or maybe they are all just crazy. Excellent clients, however, always paying the bill on time."

"Why did she pick Avian House?"

"She hated that place. As far as she was concerned they were the ones who allowed Elmo to piss his life away in bars. She found a master key to the door among Elmo's things. This way she got even with them; she got rid of Daisy and David, and destroyed Elmo's books."

"Elmo's books?"

"The nutcases at Avian House paid him to write

books. Although a drunk, he apparently had a talent for writing. Anita calls them self-help books, although she also adds 'by a man who couldn't even help himself.'"

"*A Program for Life*?"

"Yeah. A bunch of volumes privately published. I looked him up on Amazon, but there was nothing."

"So had she been planning the destruction of Avian house all along?"

"Act of passion. Destroying Avian House was just multitasking. No premeditation."

"I'm not the prosecutor, Torkum."

"Attorney-client privilege then. I really don't know."

"How do you plan on defending her?"

"Who knows? Insanity. Alzheimer's disease. I will probably just bleed her until she can't pay any more and then plead her to some lesser offense. What difference does it make? She's dead in a few months anyway."

"Nice attitude. When you talked to her, did she mention me?"

"Yeah, she thinks you are stupid."

"A lot of people do," I said.

"She called Peggi the 'ugly little gnome.' Speaking of the little freckled slut, where is she?"

"She quit."

"Really Leo? She quit. Come on, what did you try on her? I got me a good smelly finger's worth before she walked out on me."

"I thought you had her doggie style."

"I exaggerated a bit about that. I still think she is a hot little piece."

"It's time for you to go, Torkum."

"Yeah yeah. You always were a pansy. I'll be serving you with a subpoena in Bainbridge's defense."

"You do that, Torkum. But for now, get out." He spun and waddled out to the door.

I went back to Murdock's for the five thirty meeting, driving out of my way to see what was going on at Avian House. It didn't look much worse for wear. Workmen were cleaning up and replacing the windows. A lot of the furniture from inside was sitting on the front landing and the sidewalk in front of the building. One of the items was the glass case containing the blue volumes of *A Program for Life*. I parked down the street and walked back toward the building. The cabinet was open. While the workmen were inside I grabbed a full set of the blue books and took them to my car. I didn't have a good reason for it, but thought it might be my last chance to obtain the complete works of Elmo Twill.

The meeting at Murdock's was comfortable. Daisy and Churley were both there. After the meeting Daisy took a chair next to me.

"What happens now?" she asked.

"I don't know." I told her about Bohum walking off the bench. "It is out of our hands. We just wait for other people to do what they do."

"Will I be getting any money?"

"I think so, but don't count on it soon. These things take time. The trust has been hijacked for three decades. That is a lot to sort out."

"You did a good job, Leo. I was right in hiring you."

"Thanks, Daisy," I said.

Rain was falling as I drove home. I sat in the front room of Baby Blue staring out into the dark. The lights were on at the house of the old couple across the street and I could tell by the blue glow that they were there together watching television again. I was envious. I had no one to sit with me, but I slept well that night.

One of the AA aphorisms is simply to suit up and show up. People who dress for the part they want to play and show up where they are supposed to be are luckier than those who don't. The next morning, I put on the Men's Warehouse jacket, a clean pair of pants and a tie. Down at the office there was mail to read and phone calls to answer.

I pulled the little Honda into the parking lot and saw a light in my office. It would not have been unusual for me to leave a light on, but I didn't think that was the reason.

I came through the door and Peggi was at her desk sitting among the same personal pictures, plants, and knick knacks that she carried with her wherever she went. She had a new haircut that looked expensive. Everybody is beautiful to somebody. Short, freckled Peggi Iverson, the queen of Heartland Estates, was beautiful to me.

"Any appointments this morning," I asked.

"A Mr. Jameson at ten-thirty, Mr. Larson. A new probate client, according to the notes here. That's all I know. As you know, I did not set the appointment." She spun and looked up at me.

"God, I love you," I said.

"As well, you should," she said triumphantly.

She stood. We embraced for the first time in our lives.

"C'mon in. Tell me everything," I said when we finally let go of each other. We went into my office and she told me the tale of her employment at Evanson

Tribe.

Dan Evanson not only brought her in as a legal assistant but as his own personal legal assistant. She had neither the education nor the social skills to fit in among the college educated stable of paralegals at the firm so she did personal favors for him. It was his way of celebrating his victory over me. He was so sure of himself that when it was time to transfer the Avian House files to secure storage he asked Peggi to push the file cart down to the mail room for transfer. She took it to the mail room and forged a request that the documents be shipped to Bonnie Kutala.

"Do they know that you did it?" I asked.

"Sure they do, or they are a lot stupider than they look."

"They will be saying I put you up to it."

"And I can swear that it isn't true."

"Dan Evanson could sue you."

"I live in a trailer park, Leo. Remember the first rule of law you taught me, 'Never sue poor people.' I expect that Dan Evanson knows that too."

"I expect he does. So, are you back with me?"

"Where else would I go, Leo." A great weight was lifted from me. "Now should we get to work and try to make some money?"

"That we should, Ms. Iverson." She got up to return to the outer office. Her cashmere skirt hugged her bottom.

"Peggi, stop," I said. She stopped and turned. "Listen, maybe after work I could take you to dinner or something." She looked serious and sat down.

"Dinner like in a reward for good work, or dinner like in a date?"

I took my heart in my hands. "Dinner like in a

date," I finally said. Her eyes fell.

"A few weeks ago I would have done that, Leo. In fact, hearing that from you would have made my day, or my month, or my year. But something happened over at Evanson. I think I found somebody."

She was letting me down easy. "Can you tell me who?"

"Sure Leo. It's David Twill. I was working for him one day and we just hit it off. He is going to be all right after the gunshot and I think he wants to start his own practice. I won't be going to work for him though. I will work here as long as you want." We were both quiet for a moment. "Besides," she continued, "that stuff about work and romance not mixing is probably pretty good advice." She stood up and headed for the door. She hesitated before leaving, put her index finger on her right buttock and said to me. "Still hot, though. Ain't I."

"Yes Peggi," I said, "very hot." She smiled and disappeared.

We went back to work practicing law.

Bonnie learned about the Iverson connection that afternoon and was on me like white on rice. "You put a spy in a competing law firm and stole client files to obtain an advantage in a pending case. You will be disbarred."

"I didn't do any of it," I told her. "I simply let people act according to their nature. Dan Evanson hired my assistant away because he could and because it would hurt me. He wanted to win the case, keep control of the money, and embarrass me. You know it as well as I do. It is what he has always done and what he will always do. Peggi is loyal. She is loyal to redneck husbands, to her children, and to her job. I just let Evanson and Iverson do what they do."

"I don't like any of this," Bonnie protested.

"Evanson is getting what he deserves, Bonnie. He stole money from Bergan Twill and programs designed to help alcoholics so that he could build a giant law firm and a crackpot fraternity for greedy businessmen. His arrogance brought him down with help from a little freckled girl out of a trailer park. Isn't it time to step away, let fate play itself out, and go out to dinner with me?"

There was silence on the other end. "Bonnie," I finally said, "are you there?"

"I'm here," she said. "I suppose we could do dinner on Friday."

Sorting out the matter of the trust took another year and I billed Daisy like a mad man. It worked out that David and Daisy ended up with a million and a half each. They took five hundred thousand and put it in a real trust to be administered by reputable people for the benefit of the alcoholics and addicts in the Portland area.

The first thing the administrators did was remodel Avian House as the new home for Murdock's. The building had all the best: an up-to-date kitchen, an upstairs library, and plumbing that worked all the time. Hardhead Steve, Electric Dave and the others moved in, and within a few months the place was as smoky, dank, and dirty as the old one.

Daisy and David gave a hundred thousand to Miley Bainbridge.

I took the money I got from Daisy and bought some mutual funds for my old age. I started inviting Bonnie to Baby Blue. Although you wouldn't know it, she had the woman's touch, both in the home and in the bedroom. She still regularly threatened to have me disbarred, often while naked.

Spiritual Ed was never seen again at Murdock's. Hal's place closed, not because of anything having to do with the Avians, but because it was a crappy bar.

Judge Bohum's sudden resignation from the bench caused a few lines in the newspapers, but being that he was in his eighties anyway, there wasn't much hoopla over it. The press never showed any interest in the Twill case. Maybe cases like that happen every day.

Dan Evanson fought with the Office of Morals and Ethics for a couple of years over his handling of the Twill Trust and then gave up his bar membership to spend more time with his family.

Daisy went on with her life as usual, running Coney Bennett and chasing the kids as they grew toward delinquency. Her bother David started a sole practice like mine. He and Peggi dated for a few months and then didn't. I considered making a play for her again, but by that time I was seeing Bonnie pretty regularly and didn't want to risk what I had going.

Anita Bainbridge made bail and died of cancer before going to trial.

I still go to Murdock's every day. Bonnie wants me to dump the place and go to some higher class AA meetings. She wants me to move out of Baby Blue too. I keep telling her I will.

About the Author

Orrin Onken is a probate lawyer who practices in Fairview, Oregon.

15105821R00161

Made in the USA
Charleston, SC
17 October 2012